vérité

vérité

rachel blaufeld

Paperback ISBN: 978-0-9915928-7-6

Edited by
Pam Berehulke
www.bulletproofediting.com

Cover design by
© Sarah Hansen, Okay Creations, LLC
www.okaycreations.com

Image
© Corbis/Inmagine

Formatted by
E.M. Tippetts Book Designs

www.emtippettsbookdesigns.com

For those who believed in me from the beginning—you know who you are. You're my truth.

And for those of you who discovered love in the most unusual places . . . and let it bloom.

author's note

This story took on a life of its own from the very beginning. It wasn't what I was supposed to be writing (*I know, I know*), but I simply couldn't avoid it coming to life in my head. I sat down at my laptop and it poured out of my fingers. One minute it was a dream of mine and the next, a twenty-thousand word document, so I had to move forward with it.

In order to make it all work, I had to exert some artistic license in terms of athletic seasons, as well as dates and times of college events. I also made up a college town and team, so fans could go on cheering for their very own universities and not be hindered by my story.

This whole being-an-author thing for me is mostly about making people think, and this book is about recognizing that the truth isn't always what it seems. After I tossed many stereotypes out the window, Tiberius and Tingly quickly came to life.

I hope you enjoy their story.

prologue

Last August

Although my back was pressed against the door, my entire body surged forward, seeking him. If I'd been in a dream or having an out-of-body experience, I would have seen my long limbs and lean torso straining to get closer to the man in front of me. My heart was beating to the most vibrant pace I'd ever experienced. I felt like I was practically coming out of my skin to get closer to the horny, hot-blooded man caging me against the door.

Mon dieu, he was like a god. His hands were splayed against the wall on either side of my head, and my legs were wrapped around his waist. I was in heaven, and it had only been a few hours since I'd last visited this paradise.

My pelvis rocked back and forth, searching for his erection and my salvation. They were one and the same, the only balm I needed for the yearning that centered between my legs, but burned everywhere else.

I wanted his hand down there, or maybe his mouth. Or both.

vérité

"Pierre." I moaned his name as I moved, trying to connect my sensitive spot with his cock. Desperate, I craved friction like I imagined a habitual smoker longs for a cigarette.

"*S'il vous plaît*," I begged, *please*, then sucked in a breath to indulge in a long inhale of his cologne into my lungs. It was something fancy and French, of course, and another in the long list of reasons why I was head over heels for my Frenchman. *My older Frenchman.*

He shifted his hips away, teasing me, and I whimpered with need, making a noise that unfortunately sounded like a dying guinea pig. I was so desperate for him. He was my world, my universe. I wanted to spend the rest of my life lost among the planets circling his orbit. He was the moon and I was a lowly stalk of wheat bowing to him in the middle of the night, and I didn't care what that said about me. I was that weak and pathetic when it came to him.

I'd never lived a moment until Pierre was buried inside me. We didn't need to profess our love for each other or send each other cute texts. When he claimed me with those slow, languid strokes in and out of me, I knew he was the one to make everything else go away. Far away. He was the man of my dreams, and I wanted him inside me right that second, that very millisecond. I was an extremely demanding girl.

Finally, he ran his hand inside my panties and separated my folds with his slim fingers. He dove in with one finger, then two, and my body bucked into his strong, yet well-manicured hand.

My head fell back against the wall with a soft thud. "Oh, baby, more," I managed to wrench out.

And then he lost control as I'd been hoping and praying he would. When I heard my panties tear and drop to the floor, I moved my hand to his zipper and opened his khakis, firmly grasping what I wanted. He was conveniently commando, hard and ready. I rubbed my hand up and down his length, pumping him. Before I knew it, my hand was pushed away and he was deep inside me, riding me fast and recklessly.

"Faster!" I demanded. "I love it when you're rough." I squeezed his ass, tilting my pelvis to allow him to slide in even deeper.

"Easy, Tigger," he panted, calling me by his nickname for me in that sexy French drawl, but not bothering to slow his pace. He was always in control, even if I thought I held the power.

I was kneading the shit out of his ass with my hands as he ran his tongue over my neck. He nipped and sucked before biting a bit harder, causing my orgasm to build in preparation to barrel through me. I didn't want it to start or end because it always finished the same—with me wanting more.

"*Monsieur*, I'm coming," I semi-yelled or gurgled, I wasn't even sure because I was unraveling, tightening my thighs around his waist like a vice.

"Tigger, *ma chérie*." He growled the sweet words, pumping faster, his release vibrating through my bones. A drop of sweat fell off his brow into my cleavage, and he leaned in to kiss me.

My entire body trembled; I was shaking with release and need all at the same time. I never wanted that feeling to end.

At that moment the door from the hallway into Pierre's office banged open, apparently not locked as securely as we'd thought. The fancy diploma hanging on the wall above my head—the one that read DR. PIERRE DUBOIS—rattled from the impact, nearly falling. It didn't really matter if it had because within a matter of days, the gilded frame was gone. And so was Pierre.

It all ended, and I felt like my life was over.

chapter one

One year later

"Yes, sir. I'm older now. Wiser. Smarter, I promise. I swear I'm ready, Coach Wallace," I said as I nodded, yet I suspect it was more for me than him.

My coach knew what progress I'd made over the last year. My therapist and my guidance counselor had kept him up-to-date without revealing anything personal, but up-to-date, nonetheless.

"I know, hon—" He stopped and caught himself before he automatically called me *honey*. With me and my history, using any term of endearment was an extremely bad judgment call. Even though we both knew he didn't mean anything by it, it was in his best interest to be professional.

With a pained glance at me, he started again, keeping himself on the straight and narrow. "I know, Tingly. I just want to make sure you're ready to handle it all again. School, homework, the practices and upcoming meets." Obviously uncomfortable, he fidgeted with his hands before folding them on the desk in front of him.

Coach Wallace was wearing his dark-green-and-white university tracksuit as I sat across from him wearing jean cutoffs and a dark gray tank top. I hadn't worn my uniform in a year. My teammates told me it still hung in my locker, awaiting my return.

The others didn't get me, but they missed me, or so they said when they texted or called. Mostly it was Nadine who stayed in touch; we'd been recruited together. Like the other girls, she wondered why I couldn't love frat boys and jocks, or why I didn't think beer pong was just *the best*. Or, wait—wasn't skinny-dipping in the university pool even better than beer pong?

Getting in trouble for either of those minor infractions was nothing, nowhere near as severe as what I did. Maybe those girls who seemed so immature and silly were just inherently wiser than me, because banging my French professor in his office and getting caught by the head of the department was pretty damn bad.

Even better was when my professor's fiancée, Patricia, came bouncing into the room a few seconds later, babbling about wedding cake tastings and honeymoon destinations only to find me *in flagrante delicto* with the man she was going to marry. In just a few months, as a matter of fact.

For me, it had been the worst possible scenario. Pierre's semen had dripped down my leg while I stood there trying to cover myself up with a varsity track hoodie. It was the only thing close enough to grab as my underwear lay torn and tattered on the floor at my feet.

So there I was, Tingly Simmons—athlete, foreign language major, professor fucker, and obsessed idiot girl—definitely not a frat rat or beer-pong player extraordinaire. I was only at this school because of my athletic prowess, and I had no explanation for my embarrassing behavior other than I was utterly, totally in lust with Dr. Dubois.

And now, a year later, I was doing everything I could to pick up the pieces of my fucked-up life.

"I'm really good, Coach Wallace," I said with a fake smile plastered on my face. "My shrink signed off on my progress, and my counselor has me signed up for a full course load. And since I took three more credits over the summer, I won't be too far behind. Maybe just a semester." I laid it on thick; it was critical that he accept me back on the team. Being on the track team meant that I could keep my athletic scholarship, plus I needed something to focus on to keep myself out of trouble.

I sat there pulling at one of the frayed strings hanging from the hem of my jean shorts. My long blond hair hid my tanned face as I looked down, which was good because I preferred not to look Coach in the eye. He'd been immediately called to the scene and had been the only eyewitness other than those who'd found us—when I was caught with my hand in the proverbial cookie jar.

Except the cookie jar was a giant hunk of a French professor complete with wavy blond hair, heavy cologne, an aristocratic accent, and false promises.

"Great! That's all I needed to hear." The relief was obvious in the coach's voice. "Practice is still at six a.m. sharp. Be at the track at quarter till, so shoes are tied and drinks are drunk. I still don't wait for anyone. Oh, and Tingly, there's a mandatory nightly study hall for new athletes this year. It starts tonight over in Henderson Hall at seven o'clock. And before you argue, there's not much I can do about it. Since all your trouble started at the end of last summer, before your season got under way and we were lucky to redshirt you last year, you're considered a *new* athlete again this year. I know you're almost caught up credit wise but according to the rules, any student athlete coming off redshirting a season needs to adhere to the academic study session policy. So you're stuck attending study hour with the other newbies." Coach Wallace ran his hand along his forehead, clearly not entirely comfortable speaking about my *trouble* as he explained the rules from the academic handbook.

I nodded, finally lifting my eyes to meet his. "Okay. Thank you," was all I said before I stood to leave.

"And Tingly?"

I stopped in my tracks. "Yeah?"

"Welcome back. I look forward to you competing this season."

I managed another nod and a thank-you before I headed out, avoiding the locker room and anyone else who might want to see how I was doing.

Back in my dorm room, I stepped out of my jean shorts and tank, tossing them on my bed before changing into running shorts and a sports bra. I quickly pulled on socks and laced up my running shoes—extra tight, borderline painful, the way I liked them—and tied up my long hair in a ponytail. Snatching my iPod Shuffle and a water bottle from the counter, I was out the door and pressing START on my pacer watch before any of my roommates noticed me.

I started off fast, and my lungs quickly adjusted to the burn. As my feet hit the pavement, striking first with the ball of my foot, I glanced down at my watch. I was running a steady 7:20 pace, and I decided to keep it there for about five or six miles. Speed and endurance were my only true friends these days. They had kept me company through my darkest hours, and the days and months since Pierre left.

Pickles. Dr Pepper. Poisson. Petunias. Purple. Pimientos. Penelope. The artist formerly known as Prince.

Needing to dismiss Pierre from my mind as soon as he popped in it, I used one of the little coping tricks I learned in therapy. Anytime Pierre and his feathered blond hair and sea-foam green eyes appeared in my rattled excuse for a brain, I was supposed to think of anything else positive that began with the letter *P*. The concept was ridiculous, but it worked.

I played this game for about a mile or so, and then my mind was temporarily free of *him*.

Checking my watch, I kept pushing myself, making a second loop around campus before I headed up to the agriculture department. Clocking cows at ten o'clock and a barn at high noon, I continued barreling forward. As I ran back toward campus, College Avenue came into view, and my mind drifted to the weird contradiction that was my university.

Hafton State University, a Division One school, was situated in the middle of Ohio near the bustling cities of Cleveland, Cincinnati, and Columbus, but surrounded by miles and miles of pristine farmland. Hafton, the school's namesake, was the quintessential small town, ripe with big-city wannabes and earthy granola crunchers.

My friends—or my classmates, to be more accurate—were a strange mix of agriculture majors and business-minded people, nothing like me in their professional or personal pursuits. And none of them slept with their professor, or fell in lust with him. Not one of them was desperate or foolish like me, or had a nervous breakdown when her professor chose his fiancée over her.

Then again, none of my classmates came from a bullshit family and a fake place like me; they weren't needy and craving attention and acceptance like I was. They were more worried about finishing their exams and calling *next* in a game of beer pong because they were "normal" college students.

As for me, I was searching for someone, anyone who would love me as I was, for who I was, no matter what truths were revealed. I just didn't have a clue who that might be or if he even existed.

chapter two

tapped softly and peeked inside my roommate's door. "Hey, Ginny, I'm going to go eat. Want to go?"

She looked up from her book, and I felt like I'd been hit in the gut with a sledgehammer. She was so insanely pretty, all blond and blue-eyed, and she was always happy and content. If she wasn't playing soccer or studying, she was reading. She was the picture of perfection—everything I wasn't. My mom would have adored her if I'd wanted her to be a part of my life after fleeing from California.

"What time is it?" She turned to grab her iPhone, then hit the home button and looked at the display. "Oh, wow, it's five thirty. Sure. Let's go."

My hair was damp and up in a ponytail. I'd jumped in the shower and rinsed off after my run, then threw back on my cutoffs and tank.

As I grabbed a sweatshirt and crammed it into my backpack, Ginny asked, "What're you doing? I thought we're just going to the dining hall."

She'd let her hair down and blond waves framed her lightly freckled face, and the citrus scent of her shampoo that filled the room depressed me, making me feel even more inadequate. I couldn't even play the role of cheerful-smelling coed.

"Yeah, I know. We are. But I gotta go to study hour at seven, mandatory pre-season study session for newbie athletes. I'm considered brand-spanking new these days," I replied before grabbing my keys and walking toward the door.

"Bummer, but it's good you're back, Ting. I know it's hard, but you're gonna be okay," she said as she trailed behind me, her ID and key rattling on the lanyard around her neck.

We'd been roommates our freshman year when we were paired in an athletic housing suite with five other girls. She'd been recruited from Pennsylvania to play soccer, and I'd come from the land of the misfits, otherwise known as Los Angeles. I'd been recruited to run track, but mostly I came to Hafton to get away from my family.

Quiet Ginny was like a breath of fresh air compared to what I was used to back home, and I clung to her like a lifeline my first year. She was the only one of my roommates who stuck by me last year during my troubles, frequently visiting me in my single dorm room apart from the athletes, sometimes grabbing coffee or catching a movie with me. Ginny was a great friend to me while I nursed a shattered heart, an even more splintered brain, and a missing spleen.

Did I mention that after being caught, my spleen burst while sitting in the dean's office? One minute I was sitting there getting royally chewed out, and the next I was bending over in excruciating abdominal pain.

Apparently, my spleen had been failing for a while, but I'd sloughed off the tight cramping as stress related—sneaking around with your professor will do that—or dehydration, but it was mono.

Before I knew what happened with Pierre, I'd been rushed to the hospital by ambulance. Alone.

This all worked in my favor. *Sort of.* At least I had a physical reason for redshirting for a year of track, staying out of competition and extending my eligibility.

When Ginny asked me to join her in an athletic quad for this semester, I accepted right away. We'd moved in during the summer, using our athletic privileges to get into housing early. Other than a small group of students who stayed for summer session, it was quiet and subdued on campus. I didn't really care who the other two girls assigned to the quad were as long as they let me live in peace. Turned out they were two senior women's basketball players who had no clue who I was or what I'd done. It was serendipitous. They did their thing and we did ours. It was a match made in leave-me-alone heaven.

Ginny and I trekked across the lawn to the dining hall for athletes. All of us benefitted from the school being big on football and basketball with a long history of boosters with deep pockets. Not only did we get special housing, but top-of-the-line food too.

The August air was muggy, heavy with the end of summer. We were still hours away from nightfall, yet I couldn't stop the darkness from pouring over my soul. This lawn, that bench, the road to the French building all held such fragile memories.

"Campus is so quiet, it's eerie," Ginny said as we neared the Loft Building.

"I know, I kind of like it. It's peaceful," I replied, trying to hide my guilt over being caught thinking of Pierre.

Pasta e fagioli. Pâtisserie. Prairie dogs. Plums.

"Well, I'm ready to be around people other than the guys from the football team," Ginny said quickly, her voice unusually tight. "Those guys are ignoramuses. If I have to watch them shovel five million calories down their throats one more time, chewing with their mouths open and bragging about the girl they screwed the night before, I'm going to scream." She blinked rapidly, as if holding back tears.

I stopped abruptly and waited for Ginny to notice I wasn't behind her. When she caught on, she whipped around to face me and said, "What?" Her emotions betrayed her innocent tone. Closing the distance between the two of us, she swallowed heavily and sniffed back tears.

"Come on, Ginny, just admit you like Bryce. I see your eyes getting all wet, and I've seen you watching him every time he's around. We don't need to sit near the football team. There are plenty of soccer players and runners and just regular nice guys around campus, you know." I grabbed her hand in mine, squeezing her delicate fingers with affection.

She turned and gave me a hug, and I hate to admit it, but it felt amazing. It was the most physical contact I'd had in a year, and I allowed myself to get lost in her arms until she broke free.

Not letting go of my hand, she leaned her forehead on my shoulder. I relaxed, trying to give her unconditional affection and nonjudgmental listening, or at least what I thought those friendly gestures were like since I'd never experienced them before.

"I know," she said with a sniff. "It's so silly. I was his tutor, not his girlfriend, and he wouldn't want a geeky girl like me anyway."

"Ginny, don't say that. You're magnificent in every way. Any guy, football player or not, would be lucky to steal your heart." I gave her cheek a little pinch, making a soft glow spread across her freckles.

How could I be so confident in my advice yet a train wreck when it came to my own love life? That was the sixty-million-dollar question, one I was afraid would never be answered. But that didn't mean I couldn't help a friend.

As I spoke, I caught sight of a colorfully clad group of men leaving the dining hall. All of them were unusually tall, which made them stand out in comparison to the regular coeds in the area. They were loud and rowdy, pretending to trip one another as they made their way onto the lawn.

Keeping a grip on her hand, I resumed walking toward the dining hall, swinging our arms like schoolgirls. I noticed a few of the tall dudes' attention still lingering on us and our bold display of affection, more than likely dreaming up lesbian fantasies of Ginny and me.

Dinner was uneventful. After having my usual training meal—a salad with the dressing on the side, pasta, grilled chicken, fruit, and a small waffle for dessert—I was out the door to walk across campus for study hour.

The sun had begun its descent, the sky's color transitioning to pink and purple. It was a gorgeous evening. I took a deep breath of the crisp Midwestern air, filling my lungs to the max. Even though I'd fucked up so badly here, I loved this place. Everything was so green here, and the change of seasons, the way everyone smiled, it was so different from LA. Despite everything that went down last year, it was still more welcoming here than home.

When my world had been shattered last year, I didn't even want to go home. I stayed in Ohio and recuperated mentally and physically, taking a correspondence class from my tiny dorm room and bullshit deep-breathing lessons from a psychotherapist.

Coming to a stop outside Henderson Hall, I realized with surprise that I'd walked all the way without thinking of Pierre. It was the first time since "the incident" that I'd crossed campus unencumbered by pitiful lovesick memories of my ridiculous schoolgirl affair.

Just then a tall black guy—huge, actually—passed by me. He pulled the heavy door to Henderson open with one hand and held it as he turned to me and said, "You coming in?" Spoken with a northeastern accent, the three words hung heavy in the air between us.

New York, maybe?

He stood there patiently, grinning as he waited for me to move through the doorway or answer him, and pinned me with his unusual blue eyes, so pale in his handsome face against his deep brown skin. His gaze seared right through me, just like it had earlier, before dinner in the courtyard.

Completely unnerved, I didn't respond. His size was daunting, his large frame loomed over the threshold, and I was struck speechless. Uncertain whether it was his obvious good looks that threw me, or the overtly friendly wide grin on display, I simply stood there for a moment, trying to figure out his angle.

As I took in his long athletic shorts, tight gray athletic hoodie, and the pair of spiky Air Jordan slides on his feet, his left eyebrow cocked up at me like I was the next sideshow. Well, I'd already played that act countless times at home, including but not limited to last year when I was caught with the professor's dick deep inside me. Now I was all about slipping under the radar, getting by silently and with little fuss.

"Hey, you okay?" he asked, his deep voice interrupting my thoughts. "I'm talking to you . . . you coming in? I'm over here holding the door."

His pale blue eyes scanned my brown ones as his smile faded. I imagined him knowing who I was and what I did, perhaps mentally undressing me one piece of clothing at a time, wanting to give the slut a whirl.

Oh God, was my name being passed around—again?

Self-disgust consumed me, spurring me to action. "Um, yeah. I am," I answered, averting my gaze as I shifted my backpack up on my shoulder and stomped through the doorway.

I turned ever so slightly to witness him ducking to fit through the doorframe. It was crazy how insanely tall this guy was. Obviously, he was a basketball player, probably with a huge ego to boot.

I managed to mutter, "Thanks," as I swept past him, and the door clanged shut behind us.

"Bad day?" he called after me.

What was with him being all smiling and friendly? Was he for real, or was he trying to bait me? I couldn't help my self-doubt; skepticism was woven so deeply into my personality, I questioned everyone's motives.

"Bad life," I tossed back without thinking. For some reason, I felt the need to share my feelings with this stranger, and it scared the shit out of me.

So I did what came naturally to me—I ran. As I sprinted toward the elevator, I caught him heading toward the staircase out of the corner of my eye. I got off on my floor feeling relieved until I heard a heavy pair of footsteps coming around the corner.

Shit.

As soon as I yanked open the door to the athletes' study hall, he called out, "Hey again. Looks like you beat me, but you cheated by taking the elevator." He laughed good-naturedly at his own joke, but sobered quickly when he realized I wasn't smiling.

I felt my brow furrow and willed it to smooth, plastering a phony smile on my face. Propping the door open and turning my head around, I saw Mr. Tall and Not-at-All Lanky behind me.

"Yeah, I guess I did." I turned away and walked into the room, making only a half-assed attempt to hold the door for him. Hopefully, he'd take the hint to stay away.

But he didn't.

After checking in with the proctor, I took a seat and pulled out the syllabus for my economics class, trying to ignore the way he folded his long body into the seat next to mine. As athletes, we had an advantage of sometimes receiving the class assignments ahead of time, so we could get an early jump. I needed all the help I could get in macroeconomics, and was determined not to visit the professor during office hours, wanting to ensure I had as little teacher-student contact as possible. I wasn't even sure why I needed the class, but it was a mandatory requirement. Although I was finding it very hard to concentrate on my textbook . . .

My new friend sat next to me, very tall and yet broad. I couldn't stop my gaze from drifting, taking little side glances at him while I pretended to read. The room was warm, and when he tugged off his hood and lifted his sweatshirt over his head, his T-shirt rode up, revealing the standard-issue six-pack for male athletes.

I shook my head, forcing myself to focus on the book in front of me, but my attention wandered again as he pulled out a textbook for freshman English.

God, he's a freshman. Was that what I was reduced to . . . ogling jail bait?

The guy was crazy handsome in an exotic way. His skin was a rich brown, neither dark nor light. In stark contrast, his eyes were the palest shade of blue I'd ever seen. They were two translucent aquamarine orbs that complemented a perfectly formed nose, well-defined eyebrows, and luscious lips. His dark hair was clipped tight, but would probably curl if allowed to grow. And then there were his arms. Every time he moved, his sleeves lifted past his bulging biceps and defined triceps.

There was zero fat on this dude's body. He was a specimen. *For a freshman.* Not to mention, he was probably one of those beer-pong-loving jocks about to turn frat boy.

And I wasn't getting involved with anyone, certainly not with a party boy with looks to kill, and trouble written all over his long, lean frame.

I hadn't realized I'd spent the whole hour studying this kid until the proctor stood and dismissed us. When I tossed my book back into my bag and stood to leave, the object of my obsession unfolded himself from his tiny chair and said, "Hello, officially this time. I'm Tiberius. Guess I'll see you tomorrow night?"

"I guess," I said, and turned to head toward the door.

"You got a name?" he asked from behind me.

Surprised, I turned to face him and hugged my bag closer, like a shield. "I'm sorry, that was rude. Tingly," I said, waving my fingers in the air as if they were asleep and all tingly. It was my go-to gesture when telling someone my name, really more a defense than an explanation. I'd rather make light of something so toxic than reveal the disgust that rolled through my stomach every time I heard someone shout *Ting-lee.*

"Well, I dunno what sport you play, *Ting-lee,* but you could definitely win the weirdest-name-I-ever-heard contest," he said with a chuckle. "This may be the first time I met anyone with a stranger name than me."

Sadness bled through me. God, even this kid couldn't just leave my name be; it did nothing more than remind me of my past. The one before Pierre, the real reason I was such a mess. Except there wasn't enough therapy in the world to get me to relive that shit.

"I know," I whispered as I turned again to leave.

"Tingly," he called out. "Hey, I'm sorry, I didn't mean it. Don't be mad; I thought it was funny. I didn't know it would offend you. You have a nickname?" he yelled after me.

As I walked away, I waved my hand in the air and dismissed his apology. "It's fine," I yelled back, then ran down the stairs and out of the building. The last time someone called me a nickname, it didn't exactly work out so well.

"I think I'll call you Tigger because you're fast like a tiger and sweet like honey. You know, the way Pooh is always eating his honey and Tigger is by his side."

And then I ran all the way back to my dorm mentally reciting words that begin with *P*.

Pamela Anderson à la Bay Watch. *Perfetto. Pumpkin pie. Peppers. Pasta.*

chapter three

A week later I was bent over, leaning on my knees, catching my breath as my lungs clawed for oxygen, when a pair of male running shoes showed up in my limited field of vision.

"Hey, Tingly, welcome back. Hope you're feeling better," Logan Salomon said to me before he leaned in closer than I would have liked. Getting right up in my ear, he whispered, "Maybe you'll give one of us guys your own age a whirl this year," before he slapped my ass and ran off.

Logan and I met at freshman orientation when we were new track recruits searching for another friendly face. He was a piece of shit, even back then. He'd tried desperately to get me drunk that night in a full-on hot pursuit of getting inside my pants. Sadly, he was just like all the other rich, spoiled boys back at home who thought they were entitled to anything and everything.

Well, not me.

I'd spent all of my freshman year turning Logan down. Of course, he fell off my radar last year, enjoying his sophomore year while my soul died. Now that I was back, he was apparently chasing me again, unable to believe I would choose to sleep with a forty-something-year-old professor over him.

While I watched Logan run away, his surfer-boy blond hair flopping all around his head, I nearly barfed up my Gatorade. *What an ass.*

Then I heard a whistle.

My section coach, Stephanie, wasn't a big believer in long breaks. Before I could even get my breath back, she was flipping her long shiny brown ponytail around while blowing her whistle, calling us back out on the track. With every strike of my foot, angry thoughts of Logan faded and my emotion bled away, diluted by endorphins. My heart was empty, not capable of trusting or caring for others, and that was a very, very good thing.

Nadine paced next to me, her lean pale legs struggling to keep in stride with mine as her bushy blond ponytail full of curls bounced in the wind. Her breath came out in short ragged puffs, but she didn't waste her energy trying to talk to me. Although normally peppy, she was a quiet running partner, something I could finally appreciate.

As soon as practice was over, I hightailed it out of there, forgoing a shower in the locker room for an extended run back to my dorm. Running, feeling the burn was my only relief. Only when my thighs were screaming and my feet felt numb did I forget the real pain.

Yet I found myself slowing when I neared the field house. As I made my way past the large basketball arena, I wondered if Tiberius was in there, getting hazed as one of the new guys, or maybe lifting weights. We'd been avoiding each other for the last week. At least, I'd been doing the dodging, and he was finally obliging.

For a few days after our first stilted conversation, he'd call after me when study hour was over. "Tingly?" My name would come out all velvety in his deep, husky voice. Although he somehow knew not to drag out the end of it like he had the first night, I kept blowing him off.

Tossing a hand up in the air and giving him a quick wave, I'd say, "Gotta go. Sorry, got an early morning," even though it was only eight p.m.

I couldn't go *there* with him, but oh, my traitorous body wanted to go all the way.

It had been such a long time since I'd made a new friend or someone asked me if I was okay the way he did the first night. I was hungry for contact. I'd starved myself for so long, I was like an Olympic gymnast on a severely low-calorie diet. Except, it was the no-relationship fast. Forever.

Although Tiberius's curious stare made me itchy at study hall every night, I wasn't willing to surrender to his sticky-sweet charm and concern, no matter how contradictory it was to his physical appearance. Yet I couldn't make my feet move from the outside of the basketball arena. Maybe I thought if I stood there long enough, Tiberius would appear, asking me how my run was or how my day had been so far.

I'd never been inside the building or witnessed a hoops game live. Considering I lived with two female players, I'd have to learn a little. Maybe they were working out too—right now? With Tiberius?

Shoving any more errant thoughts of the basketball player out of my mind, I picked up my pace despite my legs begging for a rest. My quads burned, and my calves raged with my brain to stop. Air was pumping in and out of my lungs as I breathed deeply, maintaining my pace all the way back to my dorm.

Ginny was on the couch when I got home—reading, of course.

My practice was in the morning and hers mid-afternoon, so we ended up watching a mindless rom-com together after I showered before lunch. When she took off for her practice after lunch, I decided to take another quick run.

Unsure of what to do with myself following my second brutal workout, I texted Ginny. Last year, all my hours were filled with therapy and crying. The year before that, it was running and Pierre. And now, this year, they were filled with nothing but psychobabble.

Pillows. Peace signs. Pisa. Pilots. Puppies. Puff Daddy. Pomegranate.

> *Me: Hey, hope practice was great. I'm going to grab coffee and read in the Union before study hour. Catch you later.*

It seemed like a normal collegiate activity to fill my time.

> *Ginny: OK. I'm skipping dinner too. Not in the mood for the football parade. See you later.*

As it turned out, sipping coffee while reading in a comfy overstuffed chair in the Student Union was surprisingly relaxing. Every so often, I would glance up from my book and get caught up in watching the people streaming by. This evening it was mostly students grabbing a few extra credits during the summer session, plus a couple of frantic teaching assistants running around with their arms full of stacks of paper. I didn't even know these people existed on campus while I was busy fucking up, but now found comfort in their ordinariness, and the lingering smell of pizza.

Lost in people-watching, I was startled when the alarm on my phone beeped, reminding me it was time for preschool, or study hour, depending on how one looked at it. I reached for my bag and stood up a little too quickly, surprised when my head swam. Realizing I hadn't eaten since lunch, I pulled a protein bar out of my bag to eat on my way to Henderson.

I'd been setting my alarm so I could at study hour arrive ten minutes early, hoping to avoid running into anyone at the door again. But I couldn't be so lucky today because as soon as I hit the steps to the building, a deep voice called out, "Yo, Tingly!"

My feet stopped, even though my brain told them to keep moving, and my head turned, even though I willed it not to, making my long hair swish all around my face. I bit my tongue, unable to stop the "Hi" that automatically dropped from my mouth.

It only took three long strides for Tiberius to catch up to me, and there he was, apparently freshly showered and wearing another pair of shorts and the same hoodie. The scent of deodorant and some woodsy shampoo wafted from him, making him smell so commonplace, like every other college guy leaving the dorms. Yet on him, it smelled just right. Perfect.

"We meet again," he said.

"Yep," was all I said, trying not to encourage conversation, but secretly willed him to keep talking.

He grabbed the door and swung it open, stepping to the side before tucking his head under his arm. With his hand high above his head, holding the door ajar, he looked back at me and said, "After you."

I slipped past him, doing my best not to brush up against him. *I should run in the other direction.*

"You gonna take the elevator again?" Tiberius asked as the door banged behind us.

"Absolutely. My legs are toast," I replied as I looked anywhere but at him.

"Cool, me too." He followed carefully, slowing his gait to keep in stride with me. "You a runner?"

"Why do you ask?" I bit out, then smacked the elevator call button so hard that it didn't even register my touch.

I stared dumbly at it for a second until Tiberius slid his hand across my arm and pushed his ridiculously long index finger against the button. Of course, as soon as he pressed the damn thing, it turned bright red.

"You said your legs were toast."

"Yeah, I run. For Hafton, and for my sanity." I held back a sigh at the realization that I'd just admitted another truth out loud to this total stranger. The worst part was, it felt good to be honest. I sort of liked it.

While we waited for the ding, he tried to make more small talk. "How was your day? I mean, your life? Better, I hope."

"Oh, you know, it's just dandy," I whipped back, unsure why I was being such a raging bitch all of a sudden. I was an emotional yo-yo when it came to this freshman.

The doors chimed, then slid open. "Hmm. Dandy," he repeated under his breath.

We were only enclosed in the steel box for two floors, but it felt like an eternity. His scent seemed overpowering all of a sudden. Masculine, and definitely not flowery. Or French.

I tried holding my breath, but I couldn't. My lungs ached for a whiff of him.

He was handsome and strong, and his concern for me showed he had a protective side. Protection was something I knew nothing about, other than to stay away. Usually when someone said they wanted to protect you, it really meant they wanted to take something from you.

Just as the car came to a halt and the doors shuddered open, he spoke again. "Sorry, if I bugged you, T. I thought we could be friends or something. I'm new, the young guy on the b-ball team and all that."

I had to take control. I'd said all of ten or twenty words to this guy, and he was ready to be BFFs or friends with benefits; I wasn't sure which. I could feel the expectation or anticipation of something practically radiating from him.

Right outside the elevator, I leaned in close to Tiberius. Trying to ignore his über-masculinity filling my nostrils, I lifted my chin so I could make eye contact with the jolly giant.

"Listen, Tiberius, I appreciate the effort. I get that you're new here and lonely, and all that crap. I was a freshman once, and believe me, I was *lonely*. So lonely that I fell for my professor and fucked his brains out for a whole year, and only stopped when I got caught red-handed doing the deed at the beginning of last year."

His eyes grew wide, and before he could react any further, I forged on.

"I had to sit out a whole season while they examined my head. Luckily, my spleen decided to burst around the same time, and I could redshirt without too much disgrace. Ha! But everyone pretty much knows. I'm only telling you this now because you're new and you don't know me, but let it be a warning. I'm not who you want to be friends with, because I'm not right. And by not right, I mean fucked up in the head all the way down to my soul."

Then I turned and stomped down the hall before he could say a word.

He'd have to find a new damsel in distress.

chapter four

The remainder of the week went pretty much the same as the beginning. Practice, lounging around with Ginny, extra runs, and avoiding contact with Tiberius kept my dance card full.

I'd started eating most of my meals in the Union after spotting Tiberius at lunch in the dining hall on Wednesday. The anonymity of the Union was welcoming. I was nothing but a small speck among a bunch of people I didn't know or have to get to know. It was like an airport, except I didn't have to leave anytime soon and board a flight. So I stayed there. A lot.

As for study hour, I continued to arrive late, always grabbing a seat in the front row, and jumping out of my seat five minutes early. This wasn't my first rodeo, so I knew all I needed was to be there for seventy-five percent of the hour for the proctor to mark me present. Plus, my running times were improving, and Coach Wallace was pleased with my effort. Mostly, the coaches just wanted me to run and didn't want to deal with me, unless they absolutely had to.

For the most part, I was still a social misfit, which was why I couldn't believe where I was and how I was spending my last weekend before classes officially started. Shockingly, I found myself at some football soirée on Friday night. We were in the middle of the woods in a shelter that had been decorated with twinkly lights by the cheerleaders, and music pumped from large speakers on either side of the pavilion.

This was no average college kegger—there was a full bar on one side of the shelter and the obligatory row of kegs on the other. The field was lit by floodlights affixed to the top of several enormous SUVs that belonged to the football players.

It was all Ginny's fault; she had dragged me to the event. Her being here was as equally shocking as my presence, but apparently Bryce asked her to come, and she needed a crutch.

"Please, Ting, pretty please," she'd begged. "I can't go alone. I'm not even sure I'll have anyone to talk to, and you're so calm and cool. I'll need that."

So there I was, the wingman, except I wasn't doing a very good job. I was sitting on the back bumper of a truck, kicking at the dirt with my flip-flops, staring at my ugly runner's feet and sipping on a vodka and tonic with lime while Ginny was tucked in a corner attempting to flirt with Bryce.

"Sinister Kid" by the Black Keys played in the background as the alcohol went straight to my head. I bobbed my head to the music, shutting my eyes and feeling the beat, since there was no one to really talk to here for me. What could I possibly say? *Hi! I'm back, and this year, I'm going to be a normal coed, sleep with you guys, and get drunk any chance I can between winning heats.*

The humid air was thick as it swam around my bare arms and legs. I was in a tight white tank and another pair of ripped jean shorts, my ID and key shoved into the back pocket. Despite wearing almost nothing, I was warm, but that could have been the alcohol too.

I was no stranger to being buzzed; it was how I'd survived high school. Back then, I relied on my parents' well-stocked liquor cabinet to keep me numb, and it never disappointed. But the sensation didn't feel right at that moment. I was over-trained, my body a slave to my workouts. It craved fuel, not alcohol, and the liquid courage only deepened my current melancholy.

The bumper I was leaning against dipped, startling me, and even though my eyes were still closed, I knew who was there. Tiberius's scent overwhelmed my senses, despite the fact that we were outside in a meadow of overgrown grass and surrounded by lush trees.

"Hey, T. Mind if I sit?"

Opening my eyes to slant him a glance, I said, "Looks like you already are. Why are you calling me T?"

He cleared his throat. "Well, it seemed like you really didn't like your name. And then I went and fucked up, made fun of it, so I came up with a nickname. Does 'T' bother you too?" He faced me but I refused to turn my head, staring straight ahead into the dark woods.

"It's not very original," I said with a shrug.

He leaned forward, trying to catch my gaze. "I guess I'm just not creative."

I noticed his long legs stretched out next to mine. They went on for miles; it was surprising he could even get low enough to sit next to me.

"Seems that way," I said, holding on to my bitchiness.

His muscular thighs bulged in his frayed jeans, fascinating me; I could sense the power strumming through his quads. The tight gray T-shirt he was wearing tonight allowed me to make out the sculpted planes of his chest. My hand itched to touch, but I refused to give in to purely physical impulses these days.

"Well, what would you suggest I call you? Other than *not* call you," he said, his voice tight as he slung my shit back at me.

I finally turned to face him, eyeing his beautiful features. "Let's see, my friends call me Ting, but you're not a friend. My professors call me Ms. Simmons to avoid any confusion or misperceptions because, well, you already know, I fucked their colleague. And he called me Tigger. So it doesn't leave a lot of room for anything else."

"Yeah, I can see that. Although, I just changed my mind about T. I think T-Rex would be better, because you sure are a man-eater, *Tingly*." His body tense, he stood up to leave.

Some sugary pop tune by Maroon Five started to play, and inexplicably, my actions caught up with me. I realized I wanted him to stay, to sit back down, to say something sweet and seductive to me in his rich baritone.

Before I could stop myself, I grabbed his hand as he turned and said, "Tiberius?"

"Yeah?" he said, frowning down at me, and I dropped his hand.

"Look, I'm sorry. Really, I am. I know I've been quite the mega-bitch to you, but I've spent the better part of this last year alone, only relying on myself, and I was already a bit of a recluse. I'm not good with people, and I have no idea why you'd want to be my friend. Or why you're even here." I hopped off the tailgate and picked up my empty cup, gripping it tightly enough for the thin plastic to pop in my hand.

We stood facing each other, an unlikely pair. He was so tall, my face was level with his rib cage. Rather than look him in the eye, I stared at his chest, watching the even rise and fall of his lungs.

"Tingly, I don't know too many people here other than the team. I like them, but they're all fast-and-wild partiers, and I'm . . . well, I'm not. I gotta go to parties, socialize, be a part of the whole scene, but that's it for me. Some good tunes, a beer or two, my feet moving to the vibe, for me that's a good time."

As he took a deep breath, I studied the letters on his T-shirt, watching the rise and fall of his chest so I wouldn't get lost in the treacherous sea of his eyes.

"To be honest," he said in a low voice, "I saw you outside the dining hall that first night we met. Then when I realized we had study hour together, I was pumped. I thought you were a freshman, and you took my breath away. Not only were you stunning, but I saw the way you consoled your friend in the courtyard. Don't panic or any shit like that; I'm not some crazy stalker. I just liked the way you looked and acted, that's all. After chatting with you for a quick second, I decided I'd never met someone tough and sweet like you. Yeah, I was turned on, but also interested or something like that. Where I come from, people are either tough or nice, but not both."

"Seems to me that you're both," I interjected, my kind words coming out of left field. I bit my tongue, silencing myself, and continued to listen quietly, finally raising my gaze to meet his.

"I wanted to get to know you, but I was nervous and made a stupid joke about your name." Taking a deep breath, he seemed to gather his courage. "Look, I'm just a dude from the streets with a bad Jersey accent and a pretty good jump shot. I get where you're at . . . you don't want any part of a brother like me. But that's not me. I'm not just some guy who plays ball. I'm a decent person."

Looking up into his pale blue eyes, so amazing with their openness and vulnerability, I felt my protective barrier shift. His warmth chipped away at my outer layer of ice, melting it away as I admitted, "I was just being overly sensitive about my name."

"Either way," he said, "I don't know anything 'bout your past, and quite frankly, I don't care now that you told me. We all got secrets and history, so you're not scaring me off with your sordid shit. But I get you don't want anything to do with the likes of me, all young and ghetto, but I'm twenty and probably seen more than you ever did."

"It's not that," I started to say when Tiberius clapped a big hand on my shoulder and said, "See ya 'round, Rex."

And then he walked away, just left me there standing alone in the field. No games, no second chances, nada.

Is that the way this works? I didn't know, because I'd never really done it before.

"Wait! Tiberius," I called out much louder than I meant to, drawing unwanted attention toward me. Christ, I was making a scene when all I wanted was to fade into the background.

He paused at the tree line and looked back at me with a raised eyebrow. "Yeah?"

"Are you walking back to campus?"

"Yeah," was all he said. Apparently, he wasn't going to make this easy.

"Can I go with you?"

He only nodded, which irritated me. We were having this full-on public display, putting on a damn show for everyone there, and he couldn't even give me words.

"Can you give me one sec to check on my roommate?"

"Hop to it, Rex," he said, then leaned up against a nearby tree to wait for me.

I ran over to Ginny, who was swaying slowly to the music in the circle of Bryce's enormous arms, but she stilled when she noticed me next to them. Whispering in her ear, I asked if she was okay for me to leave her there, and she nodded. When she asked if I had someone to walk me to the dorm, I nodded back and murmured my good-byes.

When I made it back to Tiberius, I simply said, "Ready." We walked in silence away from the clearing, making our way through the tall bushes and trees back to civilization.

"I'm sorry. Honestly, I am," I said to break the ice, both literally and figuratively.

"It's cool," he said with a shrug. "So, you're what? A junior?"

"Well, I should be, but I'm three credits shy. After this semester, I will be, but I've got three more years of eligibility on the team . . . if I want that. I'm ready to get out in the real world, though, do what I want and all that. Just turned the big two-one in June. My parents kept me back from kindergarten until I was six and a half. All part of their perfect-princess campaign," I admitted.

Holding back a branch for me, he offered, "I turn twenty-one in March."

"I guess I'm not that much older," I said, and bumped my shoulder companionably against his arm as we headed toward campus.

When we stepped onto the road outside the Ag complex, I asked, "So, what's your deal, Tiberius? And does everyone call you that mouthful of a name?"

He laughed, and the warmth of it coated my chilled skin, wrapping me in a blanket of Tiberius. It soothed my exposed feelings, now that two or three layers of ice had been melted away.

"Well, Rex, my full name is Tiberius Jones, but my friends call me Ty, so it looks like we do have something in common." He winked.

I tried not to melt, but I was turning into one of *those* girls . . . a jock groupie. I tried to hold back my smile, but felt my grin grow wide for the first time in a long time, since the day Pierre first approached me in an unprofessional way. But this was different. This wasn't about being wanted physically or lusted after by an older man. It was about laughing and camaraderie, something I'd never really experienced with a man or a boy.

Campus came into view. The dorm windows glowed brightly but the lecture halls were dark, and the faux gas lantern streetlights illuminated our way as Tiberius answered my questions.

"I'm from Jersey City, right outside New York City. It was just my mom and me in a one-bedroom apartment, but she did good by me. I went to school, played ball, stayed outta trouble so she could work. Graduated two years ago and went to prep school for a year in West Virginia. They polished up my basketball skills and my math, shit like that. And now I'm here on a full athletic ride, so I guess that makes me one lucky man."

"Wow. That's pretty amazing, if you ask me," I replied. Tiberius was such a good guy with his head on straight, I still didn't understand what the hell he wanted with a tainted slut like me.

He shrugged. "I don't know about amazing. When I got to be a teen, my momma told me, 'Tiberius, be extra-ordinary. I don't mean extraordinary, I mean to go out of your way to always be ordinary in life. No need to drive one of those million-dollar cars or think your shit don't stink.'" He chuckled, shaking his head at the memory. "She knew I was good at ball. Good enough that maybe I'd make a career of it one day, at least get into school for it and make a better life with a degree. She never wanted me to get full of myself because of it, though."

I let his words sink in and float through my brain. "Extra-ordinary sounds nice. Where I come from is the land of extraordinary where everyone's shit stinks like Chanel No. 5."

"There's got to be more than that. You're here doing your own ordinary thing. What about you?" Tiberius studied me as we stopped at the corner, waiting for the light to change. The air was muggy and still, the temperature clearly not the reason why my arms just broke out in goose pimples.

"La La Land born and bred—"

"What did you just say?" he interrupted.

"La La Land. You know, Los Angeles. The land of make-believe and silicone lips."

He stopped walking and drew his brows together as he brought the tip of his finger to my lips. Sparks fizzled between his warm touch and my chapped lips.

"Are these fake?" he asked.

I couldn't help but laugh out a *no*, and it came out all breathy rather than giggly.

He started walking again, his hip brushing my side as he weaved around a large bush, and said, "You were saying? La La Land."

"Well, I was born in the heart of Beverly Hills, brought up with a silver spoon in my mouth. The perfect baby for the perfect couple who had trouble getting knocked up, but could afford the best fertility treatments money could buy. I was a little pink bundle of joy with my future all laid out for me when I was little more than a few chromosomes in a petri dish. Except I liked to run and wear cut-off jean shorts instead of ball gowns. I got here on my own too, and then I almost threw it all away."

That was all I was willing to risk saying. If I really wanted to get rid of Tiberius, I would tell him the whole truth, but some nagging feeling wouldn't let me do it.

We stopped in front of athletic housing now, just standing still, neither of us sure what to do next.

"This is me," I said, cocking my head to the right where my dorm sat lit up for the night.

"Okay. I actually live in the townhouses behind the field house. Men's basketball stays there because we live here year-round."

"Oh, wow, that's crazy. And the girls live in the dorms?" I shuffled my weight from one flip-flop to the other.

"Yeah, I guess." He leaned back against the street light, which I was grateful for. I wasn't staring at his chest now.

"Two of my roommates are women's basketball players. Seniors. Seems a bit unfair that they don't get to be in the townhouses too."

"It's all in who brings in the most bucks, Rex," Tiberius said with a little smirk.

"Yeah, yeah, I know."

Nothing left to say, we stared at each other as silence hung in the humid air between us.

"Good night, Ty. Thanks for walking me back," I said, sticking out my hand to shake his.

His brow furrowed, he squinted at my hand before he leaned forward and kissed me on my cheek. Then he slid his finger gently along my non-fake lips.

"Good night, Rex. It's been extra-ordinary chatting with you," he said, then sprinted off toward the field house.

chapter
five

Although I didn't see Tiberius for the remainder of the weekend, I thought about him more than I cared to admit. What was he playing at, wanting to be friends? Being extra-ordinary? Wasn't that what I was looking for my whole life—ordinary? And why wasn't he busy or hanging with the team?

They didn't officially play until the beginning of November. Yes, I'd looked up the basketball schedule, so I knew he was around. But I didn't know what he was doing. Not a clue.

When I got disgusted with myself, I started a new game. *Trees. Tennis. Très. Truth. Tiberius.*

But the game worked against me. It felt like the secrets of happiness—the truth of it all—were tied up in Tiberius.

Ginny was busy with extended soccer practices and her own personal pursuits, which included Bryce and more Bryce, leaving me to my own devices and thoughts. It was an all-too-familiar place for me after last year when I was left to recuperate in my isolation.

I'd long given up discussing the distant past with my therapist. We dealt with my recent past with Pierre, and that was it. When practices picked up again, I took a mental health break from therapy.

I kicked my feet up on the coffee table, absently running my finger over my scar on Sunday afternoon, swinging back and forth between pondering what Tiberius was doing, and thinking about my recent departure from therapy.

Just then, my new reality dawned on me: I was thinking about Pierre but didn't feel the need to do my stupid *P*-related therapy technique. Which was *P-E-R-F-E-C-T*. So perfect, I made popcorn and watched *The Proposal* on TV, idling away the remainder of my weekend.

When Tiberius missed study hour on Monday, I found myself irrationally concerned. As in crazy concerned enough to run by the field house on Tuesday morning after practice, pounding down the sidewalk as I headed toward the townhouses. I told myself I needed to get a little extra mileage, but the truth was that I was curious and maybe a little worried about my new friend.

My quads were working triple-time as I barreled down the hill, my knees feeling every strike on the pavement as "Bad Romance" by Lady Gaga whined in my ears. Watching the concrete to ensure I didn't trip, my eyes widened as several pair of slides came into view. There were purple and red and gold socks tucked into an equally colorful array of squishy flip-flops right under my nose when I finally came to a halt.

Breathing heavily, I stood up straight, craning my neck to meet the eyes of the five giants staring me down. I was a dwarf compared to all of them, and at five foot eight, that was no easy feat. Because it was impossible to speak until I caught my breath, I stuck my palm up in the air to offer a wave, unable to even say hello.

"Heya, Rex."

I nodded at Tiberius as I tugged at my earbuds and breathed out, "Hey there." The words rushed from my mouth as sweat dripped down my brow, despite the dewy early-morning air. My chest heaved the whole time, and I didn't think it was from the running. At least, not entirely.

As the boys, or men, continued to stare, my appearance finally registered with me. I looked down at my sweat-soaked white tank, realizing the lines of my hot pink sports bra were clearly on display. Beads of sweat dripped from my ponytail onto the royal blue running shorts that revealed rather than covered my legs.

Mentally chastising myself, I was sure they were thinking, *Who is this crazy white chick that Tiberius is talking to?*

"What you doing over here?" Tiberius asked, his Jersey accent heavier than before.

"Um, I was just getting a little more distance for my legs and—"

"You come to see our man, Ty?" the tallest of the bunch asked, interrupting me. Even with a broad smile and his longish hair in braids, his height was more than daunting as he loomed over me.

Another one in a basketball tank and wide-legged Nike sweats that read JUST DO IT down the leg threw his arm around Tiberius, shaking his large frame like an action figure. "Looks like this pretty thing has a crush on you, my man," he taunted Tiberius, slapping him on the back.

"No, nothing like that," I blurted. "I was just curious. I've never been down here before." Like an idiot, I waved my hand around, indicating the townhouse complex.

"Uh-huh," came from the darkest of the bunch. He stood off to the back of the group, his head shaved smooth, and large green Beats by Dr. Dre covering his ears. "You gotta a little case of the jungle fever, honey? Gonna let my bro cure you of it? Then you can go back to bedding some white-as-fuck frat boy."

Ty's eyes went wide. His head swung back and forth as he took in the interaction between his teammate and me, which wasn't really a conversation, but more an undressing of my intentions.

Remorse slid over me like a bad chill. I'd never intended to come between Tiberius and his teammates. And his continued silence made it crystal clear that he didn't want that either.

Digging deep, I found a sliver of courage and said, "Hey, I didn't mean any harm. No jungle whatever here." Throwing my arms up in the air, giving them a big whiff of my armpits, I continued in mock surrender. "It's not like that. So sorry I gave off that vibe. Ty and I have study hall together, and he was telling me about your housing. And, well, I've been here two years and hadn't seen it yet, so I was curious. That's it, gentlemen."

The one standing at the back of the group stepped up, pulling his headphones off as he pointed a long finger at me. "Oh, I know you. You're the track girl who fucked the professor. Lemme get this right, you going from old to young now?"

"Jamel, let her be, bro!" I heard Tiberius say as I slipped my earbuds back in and hightailed it back up the hill I'd come down.

Foolishly, I might add.

After my second full day of classes, I was downing a shot of espresso in the Union as I studied a piece of paper spread in front of me with a line drawn right down the middle. Without a word, someone slid into my booth right next to me. Before I could grab my paper, his knees bumped into the table, causing it to shift, casting my notes all over the place and leaving them in clear view.

Horrified, I slammed my hand down, trying to regain control of my scribbles, but Tiberius had quicker reflexes.

Snatching the paper, he started to read aloud. "Pros. I won't get kicked off the team. I won't get into any more trouble. I'll read my fiction book since I'm all caught up with work. Cons. I have to look at Ty. He'll skip and won't be there, and I'll worry even more. If he's there, I have to explain myself to him. His friends think I like him, and they know what I did."

Finished reading, he shoved the paper under his thigh rather than return it to me, maintaining control. "Hmm, looks to me like the cons are winning. You ditching study hour?" he asked, staring me down.

My cheeks burning, I stared holes into the dark green wooden table in front of me, unable to look him straight in the face. "Considering it."

I reached toward his massive thigh, trying to dislodge my paper. He was wearing shorts, and a shock ran from his skin straight through to my fingers as I tried to lift his thigh.

"I'm ticklish, be careful," he teased, but his eyes gave away his true feelings. They were heated, and I could tell the small touch was way more than insignificant.

He picked up his leg, allowing me to snatch back my list and shove it in my backpack. I was so focused on this task, the paper might as well have contained the key to world peace.

Tiberius slipped his hand under my chin, stilling my awkward movements and bringing my eyes into line with his. His head was cocked to the side, and his expression hesitant. It was then that I noticed he was still in his practice clothes from this morning. He didn't smell all that bad, but he also wasn't freshly showered.

Wondering if his practice had run late, or if maybe something had happened, I asked, "You okay?"

"Me? You asking me if I'm okay?"

Our knees knocked under the table as he turned to face me fully, staring me down harder. It wasn't a mean or harsh stare, but curious, as if he was trying to decide if I was being sincere or not.

Confused, I had absolutely no clue what was going on. "Yeah, why are you still in those clothes? The ones from this morning?" I motioned toward his still-damp Hafton T-shirt.

"I was at practice, and Coach kept us late 'bout some scrimmage coming up. Then I came looking for you," he said, whispering the last part as if it were a closely guarded secret.

"Why?" I whispered back, and I may have leaned in, trying to catch a whiff of him in all his manly glory. *God*, I was definitely turning into one of those groupies who went gaga for male athletes.

His brow furrowed. "Why? Seriously?"

I nodded.

He placed his elbow on the table and leaned close. "Because the team acted like a buncha asses, and I . . . Well, I was an even bigger ass because I didn't stop it, that's why. I've been chasing you around since the first night I held the door open for you, and the second I get around you in a group of brothers, I acted like a high-school fuckup." He stumbled over his words, his accent more pronounced with his heightened emotions.

Stunned, I shook my head. "I just wasn't prepared for all that banter. That's it. And I was so stupid to go running down there in the first place," I said, swirling my finger on my bare leg.

"You can run wherever you want, Rex. Especially to check on

me." He placed his hand over mine, forcing my finger to a halt.

I slid my hand away, although it felt at home in his large mitt. Even my fingernails tingled to get back in his grasp. Placing my hands up on the table to keep them occupied, I said, "I made my bed, Tiberius. I deserve any shit flung at me. From them, or you, or anyone else. I get that. And I told you, I'm not the girl to start up with."

"I think that's up to me whether you're the girl or not," he said pointedly, "and no one deserves having shit flung at them."

The only thing I could do was nod. It was the most validating statement anyone had ever made to me. I realized right there and then that Tiberius was truly the first person to see me as a whole person. Not as my parents' daughter, and not as the girl who fucked her professor, even though I tried desperately to drive that point home.

Tiberius brought his free hand up to my cheek and brushed a loose piece of hair behind my ear. I was so mesmerized by the blond strands of my hair sifting through his hand, I didn't want the ends of my hair to end and break contact with him. With my hair tucked securely behind my ear, the moment ended, and he interrupted my strange fantasy.

"You know what? If you're gonna ditch study hour, we should do it together. Go out and eat, or some shit like that," he said with a wink. "What do you think? Should we blow off studying for one night?"

I laughed. "I can't believe you just asked me that. You're crazy, you know that? I was sitting here making lists and figuring out ways to avoid you, and here you are asking me out to eat."

"You're only looking for an easy way out because I make you feel something, T. I can't believe I got to spell this out, but I like you. You got this spunk that you bury deep inside you, but when you think no one is looking, it shines. I want to know more about you and your funky side."

When I raised an eyebrow at the word *funky*, he said, "Stop doing that, acting like a ho because you think I won't like you. I already told you . . . the past is the past. So, whattaya say? Wanna go eat? You can tell me what you wanna do with the econ class you're always studying for."

"Ha! Well, that econ class has nothing to do with what I want to do, which is to graduate. Which is also why I can't go eat. I have to behave, keep myself in line, and show my face at study hour. There's no room for me to make any mistakes this year. I've only got one more chance with the coach."

"So, what're you waiting for? Let's go to study," he said, and slid out of the booth.

I stood and hiked my backpack high on my shoulder. "Well, I guess I'll be a good girl and go to study hall now. Since we got this out of the way and all."

Tiberius grabbed my shoulder, his grip digging into my bony frame. "We didn't get shit outta the way. I wasn't raised to be crass. We didn't have much, but my momma taught me to be a gentleman. Maybe you don't want me to be like that, but I'm a decent friend and an even better guy. The dudes on my team, I gotta get along and have fun with them, but their job is to haze my ass. And that's what they were doing; they just don't gotta take it out on you. And it's my job to make sure of that."

Dipping my shoulder, I escaped his grasp. "Come on, tough guy, we're gonna be late."

"You don't need to make everything into a joke, Tingly," he said, urging me toward the exit.

Raising my arms up by my ears, I flexed my biceps and said, "But

I'm a tough one."

He let out a little snort. "I'm not buying it, T. You may like to act all tough, but inside that sleek runner's body of yours is a cream puff of a heart. I saw it the very first time I laid eyes on you," he said as we walked through the exit.

It was a good thing he wasn't looking at me because he would have seen the tears pooling in my eyes. I didn't respond or say anything to even acknowledge his sentiment; I couldn't. I sniffed once or twice when we walked outside, pretending to take a few gulps of fresh air, but I was really holding back the flood ready to pour from my eyes.

We walked in silence toward Henderson. Halfway there, I realized Tiberius didn't have his books. Going back over everything he'd said—he'd rushed to get to me, his little sort-of date offer, his need to protect my cream-puff heart—all of it only made me more ashamed for acting like such a bitch.

Pushing my pace up to double-time, I tried to keep up with his huge stride. I was trying to think of something to say to make it up to him, but I hadn't a clue.

He threw open the door, its clang echoing throughout the empty corridor. When it slammed closed behind us, the silence was even more deafening. And that was how we stood while we waited for the elevator, how we sat in our seats in the classroom, and how we left the room and made our way to the lobby. Silent, except for the freshman female tennis players giggling and gossiping behind us as we headed out of the building.

The hallway smelled like bleach, and I wished the janitors had washed my brain with it instead of the floor. I wanted to forget the last two years. Even more, I needed to erase the last hour with Tiberius. My heart was whispering a silent prayer for him to ask me out again, begging with my brain and my mouth to suggest it myself, but my conscience was winning. I remained silent.

As we pushed open the door, a massive cloud broke outside, releasing huge droplets from the sky. "Shit!" I mumbled under my breath. I hung back inside the building, dreading going outside and turning into a living, breathing wet T-shirt contest.

I hadn't realized Tiberius was still inside with me until I caught him whipping off his T-shirt, revealing his very broad chest. He was quite a specimen with smooth skin pulled tight over rippling muscles. A small tattoo sat over his heart. From afar, it looked like a pair of initials and an insignia, but I didn't have time to explore it.

Tiberius stepped in front of me, pulled his shirt over my head, covering my white tank, then grabbed my hand and pulled me out the door. "Let's make a run for it," he yelled over the pouring rain, grabbing my bag and tossing it over his bare shoulder before he dragged me toward the campus bus stop, the last hour forgotten.

My feet slipped on the wet pavement in my flimsy shoes, but Tiberius held my hand tightly, convincing me that nothing bad would ever happen to me—ever. Water dripped in my face and trickled into my eyes, and I kept swiping my free hand over them, clearing the way for them to take in all that was Tiberius. Shirtless.

His muscles moved with grace and ease as we fled toward shelter. Water sluiced down his back, and all I could think about was running my tongue down his traps and up and down his broad shoulders, licking each and every drop, and wishing he would get soaked all over again.

Damn, I need to get control of my hormones, and fast.

"Here!" he yelled again as he pulled me into the shelter at the bus stop. "Guess I don't need a shower now." He turned to me with a smirk, and I noticed he had a tiny dimple when he smiled. God, he was such a contradiction. A muscular wall of an athlete with a hard body and clearly an iron will, yet a soft heart and the grin of a little boy.

"Thanks for the quick thinking and the shirt," I said hesitantly, afraid my lust-filled thoughts would wiggle their way into my words.

"Sure." He closed his eyes and ran his long finger across his eyelids, swiping away raindrops. Then he stuck his finger against his eye and removed a contact. "Fuck."

"You okay?" I asked, wiping my wet hands on the even wetter back of my shorts.

"Yeah, my contacts are killing me, but I got nowhere to put them." He popped the minuscule lens back in his eye, blinking hard as he looked down at me.

"I feel so short every time I'm with you," I blurted.

"Well, you are," he said with another smirk, revealing more dimple.

"Not really. Compared to most girls, I'm a giant. Well, except for my two new roommates who play basketball, but I hardly ever see them. They got their own thing going on with their team. They're tight, I guess." I went to sit on the bench, but thought better of it. My slick legs would only stick to the aluminum. "I'm kind of a loner too," I added, trying to make amends for my hot-cold behavior earlier.

"Really? I hadn't noticed," he joked again.

Just then the bus pulled up and we hopped on, the driver giving Tiberius and his bare chest a dirty look.

We stood for the ride, holding on to the oh-shit straps hanging from the ceiling as the rain slowed outside. At my stop, I started to say good-bye, but felt Ty's hand on my lower back pushing me off the bus in front of him.

"It's wet and starting to get dark. I'm not gonna let you walk alone," he whispered into my ear.

We made it to the front of my building, his hand on my back the whole way. I wanted to keep walking so he didn't have to take it away.

"Wanna come up?" I asked, my heart pounding, my mouth its own boss, only taking demands from my racing heart. I stripped off his enormous T-shirt and handed it back quickly before I clutched it to my chest like a toddler holds on to her security blanket.

The rain had stopped, and tension snaked around our damp bodies as I waited for a reply. Tiberius brushed his knuckles along my cheek and I leaned into them, branding myself with his strength. He didn't bother putting his shirt back on, and I really needed him to cover up.

"You remember, I said we all got demons?"

I nodded, a huge lump of regret lodged in my vocal cords.

"Well, you got yours and I got mine, and they're . . . different. And yeah, I wanna be friends with you, Rex, but like I said, I kinda want more. I know you're hesitating, and if I come upstairs and we make a mistake, then what? Then I don't even got you as a friend anymore." His light eyes stared into mine, the moonlight reflecting in their crystalline depths.

"We're adults, Tiberius. I don't think we need commitments or anything like that," I answered, zipping up my hard shell.

If I could have a one-night stand or an affair with my teacher, of course I could sleep with a younger guy. So, what gives? I certainly wasn't going to admit I wanted more, that I yearned for commitment or for someone to love me unconditionally. But I was charged up, thanks to the man in front of me, and for some odd reason I didn't feel the need to apologize for feeling that way.

"Well, I do." His hand continued to stroke my cheek. "You wave your sins around, blaming having a past or some bullshit like that for not getting close. Well, I got no past like that. I got little experience because if it doesn't mean anything, why bother?"

I stared at him, waiting for him to change his mind as the floodlight in front of the building cast a warm glow around his body.

"First we'll have that dinner like I wanted earlier, then I'll come up." He gave me a small smile, then kissed me on my cheek and walked away without another word.

Little experience? And he wants me?

chapter six

Since I'd lost my hiding spot at the Union and Tiberius knew where to find me, I'd gone back to eating in the dining hall with Ginny for the last week and a half. Of course, this meant listening to her constantly giggle over "Bryce this" and "Bryce that." I had to keep from laughing out loud at what a lovesick puppy she'd become, but she was happy, so I swallowed any negative feelings and smiled at her.

I had to give it to the guy. Bryce had moves, showing up at her practice with flowers and taking her for romantic Italian dinners in town. As for me, I was running at an excruciating pace, punishing myself with every footfall, and sneaking in and out of study hall with ten minutes to spare on both ends.

I wasn't sure if Tiberius was happy with the arrangement or just letting me have my way. We were back to not speaking, and rightfully so. Everything was weird now that he went and called attention to my whorish tendencies. Who the hell was he, some kind of altar boy? *Apparently.*

vérité

The following Friday, while munching on a few carrots, I half heard Bryce approach our table. "You better eat something more than that, Tingly. You're fading away to bones with all that running," he taunted me.

"Yeah, yeah, Bryce. You just worry about yourself and fitting into those tight spandex pants of yours," I shot back, returning his sarcasm in earnest.

He turned to Ginny, saying, "Hey, babe," and leaned in to kiss the top of her head.

Blech.

"What're you girls up to this weekend? Last weekend before classes, you should live it up a little. Or a lot." He squeezed in next to Ginny on the bench. He was as wide as Tiberius was tall.

"Nothing. Running." That was me.

Ginny sat quietly, waiting for an invite to whatever Bryce came over to hype up.

Laying his enormous arms on the table, Bryce said, "Well, good thing, I got something for you to do. Big party over at the Commons Apartments. Saturday, top floor, ten p.m. until the next morning. Gonna be a rager, so come ready to get down."

Fireworks were practically going off in his green eyes at the prospect of a *rager*. God, he reminded me so much of the guys back home, all about booze and babes. And incredibly boring. But Ginny really liked him, so I had to be nice.

"Not sure, but I'll sleep on it," I said, going back to my carrots and eyeing my pasta.

"Come on, Ting, it'll be fun. You can't sit in the dorm all weekend, and you have meets starting soon," Ginny pleaded, both with her words and her eyes.

Looks like I'm going to be a wingman again.

I simultaneously chastised myself for agreeing and consoled myself for having to go as I got dressed for the party on Saturday. I wasn't wearing anything fancy. Jeans instead of shorts, a navy tank, hoop earrings, and my hair down. That was as dressed up as I got unless my mother had anything to do with it.

I was slapping on a little makeup, just lip gloss and mascara, when my phone dinged with a text.

> *Unknown Number: Hey, stranger! You going to the athletes' bash tonight at Commons?*

> *Me: Who is this?*

I don't know why I even replied. I should have just deleted the text and gone about my business, but curiosity killed the cat.

> *Unknown Number: Ty. You should be careful who your basketball roommates give your number to.*

What? I didn't even think they knew my full name, let alone had my number.

> *Me: Well, when I see them, I'll let them know.*

> *Tiberius: So, you going?*

Me: Unfortunately.

Tiberius: Me too. Apparently a requirement of the team. Unofficially, of course.

Me: Well, I'm sure your crew will have fun. I'm going for a bit with my roommate and leaving early.

Tiberius: Maybe you'll need someone to walk you home?

Me: Doubtful.

He didn't respond, but why should he? My schizophrenic emotional display over the last two weeks was enough to make anyone crazy. If he were smart, he'd leave me alone.

I wish I could leave him *alone.*

Unfortunately for me, Tiberius was standing right by the door when Ginny and I walked into the party, our eyes meeting the instant I crossed the threshold. Surveying the scene, I was secretly happy he was there. The room was thumping with the beat radiating from speakers at both ends of the apartment. I caught a peek of his teammate—the bald one, *Jamel?*—behind a makeshift DJ table, big cans on his ears, his head bouncing to the beat, and feet shuffling underneath the table. Rap was blaring, the place reeked of pot and beer, and I felt totally out of my element, even though I'd been at college for two years.

Glancing around, I noticed the dozens of already inebriated willing-and-able girls slurring the lyrics to the song and dancing around the apartment. They belonged here, not me.

I started to walk forward, a little hesitant to move since I wanted nothing more than to turn around and march right out of there. Two adorable little tennis girls hanging near Tiberius drew my attention. They were practically eye-fucking him and drooling over his biceps—literally, because that's where they were eye level with his body. He was paying them no mind, chatting and laughing with one of the other guys from that awful morning. One who had thankfully remained quiet.

Tiberius was clearly not in a hurry to approach me, and I didn't blame him after my text. On the other hand, I was desperate to see him. His large frame and protective nature called to me, drawing me to him, but I resisted.

Knowing I either needed some liquid courage or something to numb the jealous pang forming in my gut, I decided to grab a beer. As I headed toward the kitchen, one of the wide receivers went streaking through the hallway, his bits and pieces flapping in the air for everyone to see. I tried to step out of his way but my reflexes weren't on top of their game, and just as I turned, Mr. Cock-and-Balls collided with me head-on. In all his naked glory, he went falling on top of me, toppling both of us onto the floor. We landed in a crumpled heap, my head in his crotch.

"Oh shit!" he yelled over the music.

Mortified, I pushed up and away from the dick in my face, propping all my weight onto one hand on the floor as I ran the other across my face, trying not to puke as I checked for errant pubic hairs. There was clapping and cheering and lots of "Oh my Gods" punctuated with shrill whistles being repeated all around us, all while the music still raged, vibrating the room with the bass beat.

Mindful of how bad this looked, I held my hand over my face, expecting at any moment for someone to snap a picture. That would make my humiliation complete, and would transform this incident from a horrible memory to something that lived forever on the Internet.

"You okay?" the naked idiot next to me asked just as I felt hands slip under my arms, lifting me away from the fiasco.

Ginny was saying something like, "You okay, Ting? Ting?" but I couldn't fully hear her because there was another voice swimming in my ear.

"Christ, Rex, you okay? I'm gonna take you out of here," came out all breathless from behind me as I was pushed from behind toward the exit.

I wriggled against his grip a little, wanting to walk out on my own, but he wouldn't let up on his hold around my shoulders.

"I'm fine, Tiberius. Let go," I huffed out.

Ignoring me, he just kept walking and threw a peace sign up in the air for our audience as we left the apartment.

"Please, let go. I'm embarrassed enough as it is," I said through clenched teeth.

"Tingly, wait!" Ginny called after me, running up and grabbing me from behind.

"Please, Gin, let go," I said as tears burned my eyes.

She released me and I turned to face her, mentally ordering my eyes to stay dry.

"I'm good." I stood stock-still, worried that any movement might set off the emotions racking through my body.

"Sure? Where are you going? And who's this?" she demanded.

"Hey, I'm Tiberius," he answered for me. "Rex and I got study hour together."

"Rex?" she said, looking up at him with her freckled brow all scrunched up in confusion.

"Yeah, Rex. This one is a real tough one, you know what I mean.

A carnivore. Almost ate me alive a few times," he joked, tilting his head toward me.

As for me, I was as stiff as a statue, afraid to even move a muscle in my jaw.

"Well, I don't know you," she told him sternly, then turned to me. "You okay with going with him, Ting?"

Clearing my throat, I said, "Uh-huh. This is Tiberius, my *freshman* friend from study hour." I don't know why I added that— probably more for myself than anyone else—a healthy reminder of our boundaries. *As if those ever stopped me in the past.*

"That's me, her freshman friend. Come on, Rex." He threw his arm around my shoulders again and guided me toward the elevator, the music becoming fainter with each step.

Uncomfortable silence while waiting outside elevators was becoming a theme of ours. I wasn't going to be the one to break it. I'd thrown myself at him a few nights before, and he'd walked away. He needed it to mean something, and I demanded it mean nothing, although I was starting to suspect that was a lie.

"Are you okay? Did you get hurt?" he finally asked, breaking the ice.

"Just mortified," I answered honestly.

"No one will even remember tomorrow."

The bell dinged. We moved into opposite sides of the car, and the doors slid shut. Tiberius reached out to press the button for the lobby, but instead pulled the stop.

"What are you doing?" I asked, my thoughts wild.

He stepped toward me until his body was flush against mine, my back now melded to the wall, and he kissed me. His lips landed on mine without any further notice. They were soft to the touch but rough in their pursuit. The kiss was bruising and punishing, heavy with weeks' worth of longing. When you're our age, fantasizing for weeks is like wanting something for years.

"You sure you're okay?" he said into my mouth.

I nodded.

"We should have gone to eat instead of this party. How many times are you going to make me ask? How many weeks do I gotta wait?"

"I've never done that stuff before."

"What? Eat?"

A giggle bubbled up in my throat, and his lips came back to mine.

His hardness pressed against my abdomen, and I tried to rub myself up against him like a dog in heat. In response, he pulled his hips back a bit, denying me any further friction. He was sending a silent, but serious message that this was more than a quickie in the elevator.

I opened my mouth to protest and he slipped his tongue inside, curling it with mine, and I realized he was right. When I slowed my hormones and actually let myself be in the moment with Tiberius, my body flooded with unfamiliar feelings. Not just want or desire, but something else. Affection of some sort, and I wanted to feel it deeper, not simply to get off, but to embrace what was happening between us.

Desperately trying to get him back closer, I wriggled while my arms made a futile attempt to pull him close again. But he was too big, too determined to stay in control, and too headstrong. His hands gathered mine and stretched my arms above my head, securing me, then he pressed a gentle closed-mouth kiss to my lips. There was no tongue and no grinding, yet it was the most sensual kiss I'd ever experienced.

His lips broke free from mine before he whispered, "This means something, T. I'm not having a quick fuck in an elevator."

I shook my head. Dazed, I glanced at the aluminum wall across from me, catching my reflection, and saw myself for who I truly was: a disheveled, desperate coed. I continued to shake my head, unsure if I wanted to knock some sense into my brain, rid myself of the nasty image I'd seen, or both.

"Yeah, it does, babe," he whispered, then ran his lips over my cheek and down my neck before his tongue traced a trail over my clavicle. "It does," he repeated and dropped my arms. He released me and walked over toward the wall and pushed the stop button, the elevator jerking to move again.

The second the elevator doors opened enough, I slipped through them and ran, picking up my pace as I barreled through the exit and out to the street. It didn't matter that I was wearing sandals rather than running shoes, I went as fast as I could, ignoring the pieces of gravel that flew up, cutting my feet.

"Tingly, don't run," Tiberius said as he caught up with me, easily keeping pace next to me. Even with my speed and endurance, I was no match for him.

"Let me do what I want," I tossed back at him.

"No."

"Why?" It came out breathless, but I wasn't winded.

He swerved closer and caught me in his arms, stopping my forward motion. As if I weighed nothing, he lifted me and stood me on top of his feet so we were closer to eye level.

"Because two people don't kiss like that and it not mean shit," he spat at me, keeping me in his grip.

A little crowd of onlookers gathered to watch us—the jilted coed and her new beau. Annoyed at their interest, I realized they probably saw mostly our differences, both in race and perceived age, since

vérité

Tiberius was a freshman and me a supposed junior.

But to me, I'd always just be the girl no one wanted. Not her parents, the nice boy next door, or her French professor. Nobody. Certainly not the basketball stud with the body of a god and a heart of gold. Yet I kept acting like all I wanted from him was his dick.

"Let me go. I can't do this," I said, and pulled free and ran.

This time, he didn't chase me.

chapter
seven

My class load turned out to be grueling, but lucky me, study hour changed to being mandatory only twice a week. With a buffet of sessions we could choose from, I took a lucky guess that Tiberius wouldn't attend the early morning one, so I went to it religiously. Willing to sacrifice a shower after practice two mornings a week was a small price to pay to avoid Tiberius and discussing my feelings with him.

Between preparing for an upcoming meet and taking fifteen credits, I was busy enough to avoid most parties and anything other than a quick dinner with Ginny. Truth be told, I was doing well; I had my shit together. I was even back to taking French, but this time with a female professor. This was a good thing since I actually was still a foreign language major. I was fluent in French, Italian, and Latin.

Originally, my choice of major was a great big fuck-you to my parents. Picking a career outside their longtime expectations was my second step in breaking free. The first was when I'd been awarded an athletic scholarship to a school in a place so opposite from home, they'd never wanted to visit.

The real clincher was when I withdrew my entire trust fund left to me by my grandparents, the one they were dying to get their hands on. I moved the funds to a new bank and selected a new financial advisor, changed my cellular number, and packed all my shit without ever looking back. They didn't need the money; they just craved the control. Of course, they got my new number, but rarely used it unless it was to discuss money . . . or control.

I'd barely touched the money since moving it. To cover most of my expenses, I took a small stipend from the interest; the rest was covered by my scholarship, even when I redshirted. So I was in good shape financially, but always looking for something to fill the gap.

Which was why I was standing in front of the bulletin board in the Union, pulling a paper tab for a part-time tutoring job in Italian, when someone came up from behind me. I felt a little tap on my shoulder and turned to find a very large basketball player still wearing his practice jersey. A sheen of sweat covered his brow as his dark eyes assessed me.

I didn't know his name, but this was the one who'd been laughing at the party with Tiberius, the friendly guy with the braids, which were now pulled up in a ponytail.

Squinting up at him, I asked, "Can I help you?"

"Tingly, right?" He kept his eyes trained on me, scanning me from top to bottom and then back up again.

A shiver ran through me. Yeah, he was big and looming, but I didn't care about that. He felt ominous. Ultimately, I was worried about Tiberius, but shoved the feeling away and maintained a tough facade.

"Yeah, I'm Tingly. And you are?"

"Lamar."

"What can I do for you, Lamar?" I crossed my arms over my chest and rocked back and forth like I didn't have a care in the world. Who the fuck was this guy to survey me from head to toe?

"Well, ya don't have to get bitchy. I was looking for you, heard you hang out 'round here."

"Yeah, I do." Still rocking back and forth on my toes as I stared at the patterns in his hair, I put on a tough face.

"Listen, I don't mean to rub you the wrong way, babe. I don't even know what he sees in you. You're all skin and bones and blond hair everywhere. But Tiberius is heading home, and I thought you'd want to know. Should know or some shit like that."

That got my attention, and I stopped rocking. "What? Why? What happened? Did he get hurt?"

"Nah. He's fine. His momma passed. Cancer. So he's gotta go home and deal with the details."

I reached out and touched Lamar's shoulder, my hand sticking to his sweaty skin. "Thanks, Lamar. Maybe I'll give him a ring? Check in," I said without thinking. Why would I start something I couldn't finish?

"Just Mar," he said. "My friends call me Mar." And with that he turned and said, "Catch you 'round, Rex."

"Uh, 'bye, Mar."

I raced back to the privacy of my room and tossed on running clothes without thinking. Moving quickly, I whipped my hair up and smoothed it back tight in a ponytail holder, then rushed out of the dorm and ran to the townhouses. It didn't matter that I didn't know which one he lived in, or that the last time I was there, I bolted away. Tiberius was leaving, and I needed to get to him. Unsure of what I would say or do when I got there, I just left, flying as fast as I could in my trainers, not even bothering with a pacer watch.

Hustling down the hill, I started to slow my roll as the townhouses came into view. The enormity of what I was doing settling on me. I looked around for someone, anyone, a friendly face to ask if they knew Tiberius. Then, as luck would have it—or not—I ran smack into Jamel.

"Look what the cat dragged in—" he drawled before I interrupted him.

"Cut it out. Your buddy Mar came to see me, and I need to get to Tiberius," I said with unjustified authority.

"So, you coming to mess with his head again?" He crossed his arms as he glared down at me. "He don't need that shit."

Taking a second glance at his arms and long limbs as his dark frame towered over me, I swallowed my fear and demanded, "Where is he?"

"'Where is he, Mel?' Say it nicely."

Geez, what was it with these dudes and their nicknames and crazy mannerisms?

"Where is he, Mel?" I repeated. I didn't have time to argue semantics.

"Unit 5B." He cocked his head toward the left, and I picked up speed and ran off.

When I got there, I nearly banged down the door. It flew open after a few seconds of knocking.

"Tingly? What are you doing here?" Tiberius asked as he glanced around outside over my shoulder. "Did someone bring you here? How did you find me?" His eyes were bloodshot and red-rimmed, and he was wearing a wrinkled long-sleeved white T-shirt and low-hanging sweatpants.

"Um, Lamar found me and told me what happened. I'm so sorry,

Tiberius."

I wanted to hug him or something, but I didn't know if my body would be able to stop, or if he would even welcome the affection.

He rested an arm on the doorjamb as he looked down at me sadly. "She was sick. I knew it was a matter a time. But it still doesn't feel real."

"Is there anything I can do?" I hopped from one foot to the other, unsure whether I should ask if I could come inside.

"Nah. I'm going home tomorrow. Coach gave me five days, and my teachers will get all my work for when I get back. I'm good. Thanks for coming," he said, then took a step back as if he was going to end the conversation and shut the door.

"Tiberius?"

"Yep?" He was obviously trying to be strong, but his bravado bled through his one small word.

"I was a bitch to you. That's not really me. At least, I don't think it is." I let my head fall forward as I tugged at the back of my neck, releasing my ponytail to allow my hair to hide my eyes, which were stinging with the threat of tears.

"I know." He let out a sigh and asked, "Want to come in?"

I nodded.

We did a little dance after he closed the door. I wanted to touch him, and he kept leaning forward and then stopping and pulling back. Finally, I reached out my hand and grabbed his, squeezing it.

Tiberius's entire body seemed to relax as he pulled me in close and kissed the top of my head, but it didn't feel corny like when Bryce made that move on Ginny.

He sucked in a deep, shuddering breath. "She would have liked you, my mom."

"How do you know?" I said in a small voice. "We've only known each other a few weeks, half of which I've been avoiding you."

"Come on." He led me toward a small kitchenette where he pulled out a barstool, and I sat with no further instructions needed.

Tiberius leaned on the counter in front of me and braced himself on his forearms. "My momma was a classy lady. She didn't have much, but she gave in spades. Gave me a good life. Clothes, food, heat in the winter, made sure I met decent men in my life since I never met my dad. God, she cried the day I made the high school basketball team, shook the coach's hand, blessing him for taking me under his wing."

I let my hand wander, placing my palm on his forearm, his sleeve doing little to keep the sparks at bay. "She does sound like a wonderful person. And sometimes unconditional love is worth more than riches," I said, knowing all too well how true that was.

He stared at my hand on his sleeve. "Then she got cancer when I was in prep school. It had already spread, and there wasn't much she could do. We didn't have the money for experimental shit, so she just lived her life. Wouldn't let me leave school or think about putting off college."

"Of course not," I said. "I'm sure she was incredibly proud of your accomplishments." I tried to be supportive, unsure about what I should or shouldn't say as I pretended I knew something about someone loving me.

"Momma never finished college herself. She started, but then she had me and her plate was full. She did the best she could." A tear fell and landed on his shirtsleeve, the fabric soaking up the evidence of his pain.

"I wish there was something I could say. I've never dealt with this, all this emotion or pain. I'm sorry," I said lamely, feeling completely out of my element.

"It's okay. Me neither. But now I gotta go home and pack up her stuff. Guess it'll give me some closure or shit."

With that he stood up and walked toward the back hall. I hesitated, not sure whether he wanted me to stay or follow. I did know that I was deathly afraid of making the wrong choice.

Unable to move, I watched him turn a corner, his gorgeous body just a memory. After another minute, he walked back toward the kitchen carrying a picture frame. His posture was stiff and his expression stoic, but his mood was anything but. He was somber, and I found myself missing the normally happy and sweet Tiberius.

"This is—I mean was—my mom," he said, handing me the picture.

I held the edge of the black lacquer frame with a shaky hand, taking in the sight in front of me. There was Tiberius wearing his prep school basketball uniform. The photo must have been recent— he was tall, fully developed, a grown man with a wide smile. He had his arm wrapped around a woman about my height. She was curvy with big boobs and an even bigger smile. Wrapped in Ty's arms and tucked into his armpit, she looked as proud as could be in a royal-blue blouse. A lump formed in my throat as I ran my finger across the glass, circling her curly dark blond hair.

"She's beautiful," I said. "I can see how happy she is here. It must have been something for her, seeing you reach for the stars. You can see she knew she'd done something right in raising you, which I'm sure wasn't easy." My breath lodged deep in my throat, hindered by the foot I'd just stuck all the way in my mouth.

He reached over and took the frame, taking his time staring at the picture. "Nope, it wasn't. Bein' a white woman in the hood wasn't easy, but it was the only place her son was accepted, so she did it. In the end, the whole community respected the hell out of her."

"Do you know where your dad is? I mean, do you think he'd want to know she was gone?"

Tiberius took a step back and I panicked once again, but he just set the picture down. Then he braced his hands on the counter on either side of me, and looked down at my face.

"Tingly, I'm gonna tell you something I don't share much, but I'm feeling sorry for myself today. He would *not* care. My momma was a passing phase for him. Most women were until he went to prison for armed robbery, 'bout the same time I started high school. I only knew 'cause I caught my mom reading 'bout it online."

"Oh," I said, feeling a tear spill over my eyelashes. Crap, I was an emotional basket case over someone else's life. Was I getting my period?

Or is this what truly caring for someone is like?

Ty's accent deepened, the hood revealed in his speech as syllables dropped and vowels ran together. "When I was little, we'd see him 'round, always with a new lady on his arm. Each time would be worse for Momma. Eventually, I'd catch him outta the corner my eye and steer my mom the other way."

His expression fierce, he grasped my arms. "Now you get why I shoulda defended you to the boys? I may not be all white or black, but I'm a fucking man who knows better than to watch a woman get ridiculed. It's no excuse, but I never really fit in anywhere but playing ball, so those guys are my family, for better or worse. They know I got white blood running through my veins. My eyes are as blue as any Swede's. Also means my dad had white blood somewhere deep in him. They shoulda known better than to make those comments about jungle-love bullshit."

A tremor ran through his body. I felt it travel through him to his fingertips that rested on my biceps, and it made my heart bleed for him.

"You're the most wonderful man, Tiberius. A handsome, kind gentleman just like your mom raised you to be," I said, staring him straight in the eye.

"I want to kiss you," he blurted. "Is that wrong of me? I mean, I should be grieving, but I want to kiss you so bad. More than take my next breath."

I didn't answer or wait. I hopped down from the barstool, reached up on my tippy-toes, and brought his mouth down to mine. The kiss wasn't hard like in the elevator; it was soft and tender, full of promise.

When I ran my tongue along the seam where his lips met, he opened and let my tongue in. As he slid his tongue into my mouth, we explored the depths of each other—physically and emotionally— because giving in to this was a statement. On both our parts.

Although I would never settle for Tiberius accepting he was anything less than the magnificent man he was, I was scared I wasn't woman enough for him.

Lost in the heat of the moment, Tiberius ran his hands down my sides, his thumbs grazing my small breasts. My hands were wound around his neck, my thumb tracing the edge of his fade haircut where it met his damp skin. Our kiss seemed to deepen with every second that passed until there was a loud banging on the door.

"Christ! What now?" Tiberius yelled as he broke away from me, then turned away to adjust himself in his sweats. They weren't doing much at hiding what he was packing.

A small thrill ran through me at the thought that I did that. Made him that way.

More banging rattled the door, the pounding increasing in intensity.

Tiberius trudged to the door and threw it open. "What, Mel?" he barked.

"Just checkin' on you," Jamel answered, walking straight into the hallway without being invited. "Your little white bitch came lookin' for you," he said as he turned the corner, and his eyes narrowed as he caught sight of me.

"Cool it, Mel," Tiberius said, a hint of steel running through his vocal cords.

My words were once again trapped in my own throat. I plopped back into the stool and continued to stare wide-eyed at the interaction.

"No one is a white bitch, man. Okay? Rex, I mean Tingly, is a person," he said, shaking his head. "A person like you. No one is walking around calling you names." Tiberius paced the room, his large feet padding heavily on the carpet.

"Well, you said yourself this bitch was running hot and cold. I didn't like it."

Jamel stared daggers at me, his biceps flexing and rippling, his dark eyes laser-focused on me. I tried not to flinch, but wasn't very successful.

"Shit, Jamel! Look what you're doing to her. She's shaking in her seat. Fuck! That's not the way you treat women, my man," Tiberius said as he got right up in Jamel's face.

"I think I'll go," I whispered as I slowly stood and tried to sneak behind Jamel to get to the door.

Once again, I felt like I was right back where I started, getting caught with someone I shouldn't be with. Why did I keep doing that?

"Hey, you," Jamel hollered at me.

"Don't," Tiberius yelled, but then controlled his tone. "Don't go." He caught my arm and pulled me up next to him as equal parts warmth and anger rolled off him.

"Listen, you don't need this right now." I twisted my wrist free from his grasp, but chills racked through me as soon as I left his heat.

"Tingly, don't do this," he called out, but I was already running away.

Toward what, I had no clue.

chapter eight

Sweat poured down my back, soaking my sports bra and my tank, but I continued to push on through the workout. The coaches had set up large pylons around the perimeter of the track, marking every fifty feet. Our first meet was coming up in a few days, so we'd been at it all morning, alternating running as hard as we possibly could every other fifty, and recovering the ones in between.

After the final whistle blew, I darted to the Gatorade cooler for a quick pick-me-up before I ran home.

"You doing okay, Tingly?" Stephanie asked as she sneaked up behind me. I must not have heard her approach over my heavy breathing.

"Yeah, I'm good," I said, the air rushing out with my words. "I'm feeling super good these days. I'm ready."

Concern filled her hazel eyes. "Oh, I know you're in top condition, maybe even a little over-conditioned. I meant you-you."

"Yep! Good as ever," I proclaimed with a plastic smile on my face.

Being from LA, I was good at that.

"Tingly, come on. Coach Wallace and I care about you. He trusts me to take good care of you—"

"Because he's afraid of himself? Scared I'll seduce him?" I cut her off, hurling my words instead of my fists. I wanted to punch her, show her how strong I was. No fucking Frenchman was going to break me, especially after what I'd gone through at home.

"No, honey," she said patiently. "He just thinks that since you and I are both females, we'd connect better." She pushed her hair behind her ear and fiddled with her whistle. "Listen, a few of the girls have mentioned you don't hang out with them much, so after the meet this week, make some plans. Go out with them this weekend. You've been in classes for over a month, it'll be good for you. Try to forget about the serious weight you drag around on your back."

"Stephanie, really?" Shoving my hand on my hip, I wanted to stomp my foot.

"Really. Or maybe go back to therapy?"

"I'll go, I'll go," I spat out, then turned to run toward campus. "Please don't threaten me," I called out over my shoulder.

After shoving both welcome and unwelcome thoughts of Tiberius to the back of my muddled mind, I killed it at the meet. It was just pre-season, but our whole team was at the top of their game, and we were just getting started. Sadly, I was only able to keep my jumbled thoughts at bay for so long, and while cooling down and showering, my head was a mess all over again.

I hadn't heard from him, nor did I expect to. It was hard to imagine Tiberius was going through all his mother's precious memories, clothing, and personal items on his own. I didn't suspect he had anyone to help him, and I wondered what that was like. I'd been raised with nannies and maids and gardeners and pool boys. If something happened to my parents, one of the hired help was more than likely already heftily paid in advance to clean up their shit. That thought alone should probably sadden me, but I didn't want any of my parents' crap.

Nothing from their house held any value to me. Not even them.

But Tiberius was weak with grief and he had to travel across several states—by bus, I assumed—to do alone what someone else should be doing with him. I'd considered texting him, but that didn't feel right, especially with how things ended right before he left. I was causing him more stress, so I figured there was some merit to Stephanie's suggestion to hang with the team.

Reluctantly, I finished showering and slipped on boot-cut jeans, a low-cut tank, and a dark gray off-the-shoulder 80s-style sweatshirt. Not exactly an "in" style, but neutral enough. I never paid attention to style trends, especially among the rich socialite crowd with their Lilly Pulitzer pink flamingos.

I dried my hair, curling the ends with a round brush, and put some effort into my makeup. I was going to a barbecue and bonfire at some off-campus housing, and I wanted to get it right. No need to embarrass my teammates; I'd already done that enough with my actions.

Ginny wasn't going with me. She was fully involved with Bryce, and the little bookworm was barely leaving his bedroom, but she definitely wasn't reading in there.

I grabbed my phone, a tube of lip gloss, my ID, and some emergency cash, and shoved them all in my back pocket before heading out. The team had arranged to meet by the bus stop so we could ride over to College Avenue together. I was the last to arrive and the bus pulled up a minute after me, which was a blessing since it cut down on the small talk required.

We got off the bus at the stop nearest to where the party was being held, and then walked a few blocks back to a housing development nestled against the woods with a pool, tennis courts, and a clubhouse. It was mostly grad students and undergrads with money who rented or owned there. As luck would have it, one of the guys on the tennis team was swimming in cash, and he was hosting this little soirée. Apparently everyone who was anyone was there.

Making our way to get a drink took over thirty minutes since the girls needed to stop every few seconds to kiss someone's cheek and declare, "Oh. Em. Gee. You look amazing!"

Finally, I skirted past the social logjam toward the backyard and grabbed a bottle of beer. The party was pure class, not a keg in sight, and some huge beefy guy was manning the grill. "Howling for You" by the Black Keys played in the background. God, they loved those guys at this school. They were like the resident band, and a party could not be had without their tunes.

Dusk may have just fallen but several girls were dancing barefoot in the grass, at least two sheets to the wind already. As I surveyed the crowd, I wasn't surprised to find several people staring at me, mostly people who'd been in my French section, probably checking my sanity.

My mood soured; I needed liquid courage and a lot of it. I chugged the beer I was holding and looked around for my teammates. One was cuddled up with a football player, another was playing with some guy's hair and whispering in his ear, and a third was doing shots by the unlit fire pit.

After tossing my empty bottle, I plucked another before moving on. The alcohol went right to my head, creating a slight buzz that whirred around my chaotic brain and heart. I chatted with Brian from the men's team, rescued Nadine from the guy she'd been whispering to earlier, and eventually found myself on my fourth beer as the last vestiges of sunlight disappeared and the host went through an elaborate fire-lighting show.

Flames licked all around the pit, casting a glow on the night, and the volume of the music kicked up a few notches. Inhibitions were shed as the crowd started drinking and dancing more, and the tunes switched to rap and hip-hop. Shirts came off and girls raced around the property in bikini tops, which I thought was ridiculous considering it was fall in Ohio, but to each her own.

I wasn't in the mood to dance, but I felt good. I'd been so used to spending time by myself over the last year that I was a little overwhelmed by all the activity and needed a little space, some air, so I walked toward the far end of the yard. At the edge of the property, I made my way into the edge of the woods and leaned against a tree, taking in the twinkling pinpricks set against the night sky.

A noise rustled behind me, startling me, and something slithered up my arm. I must have jumped several feet in the air, barely holding on to my beer.

"Hey there, baby," a guy's voice murmured in the darkness. His breath smelled like weed and stale liquor, and his consonants and vowels slurred together like an accordion sliding closed.

Shutting my eyes, I willed him to go away but said nothing.

"What you up to, out here all alone, baby?" he asked.

"Go away, Logan." Moving from the tree, I prepared to walk away when he shoved me up against the bark, pressing his whole stinky frame against me. "Mmm, you smell good enough to eat," he said, breathing alcohol fumes into my face.

The beer and the PowerBar I ate earlier engaged in a nasty tango in my stomach at the smell. Grossed out, I turned my head, wanting to barf.

When I started to protest, his tongue slammed into my mouth. His erection digging into my thigh, he brought his knee between my legs, spreading them wide so he could grind on me while he waged war with my lips.

I couldn't breathe; my lungs were burning more than during any race. Fire from the pit licked upward to the sky, and I felt the same burn in my legs. They wanted to move, to race, to get the hell out of there, but Logan was strong. Not only was his body wedged against me, but he'd wrestled my hands high above my head.

With no other option, I lifted my foot and brought it down hard on his.

"Shit! You little cunt bitch," he shouted, driving my hands harder and higher above my head.

I did it again, this time with my other leg. I drew my foot up and let it come down as hard as I could on his other foot. Hoping I'd break a bone so he'd be off the team, I quickly brought my original foot up and slammed down again.

"Cunt!" he muttered. "That's right, I'm gonna fuck your sloppy cunt and teach you a lesson."

He drove me so hard into the tree that I was flung to the left, my legs swinging out and back. Flailing, I tried to kick at Logan's shins as his mouth tackled mine. Bile rose up, causing my throat to burn as I desperately tried to use my pelvis to shove him off, but that only acted against me. He rubbed his dirty cock on me every time I moved.

Why wasn't anyone worried about me? Looking for me? Glancing in this direction? With my hands trapped, my legs were my only weapons, and I desperately kicked again.

When I tried to scream for help, Logan trapped my wrists with one hand while he moved the other over my mouth, squeezing my cheeks with his harsh grip and bruising my lips. Just as I closed my eyes, admitting defeat, I felt him gone and gasped for fresh air as his weight disappeared. Too afraid I was imagining it, I kept my eyes glued shut.

"Yo, motherfucker, get the fuck offa her!"

Only then did I open them, and it was like a tornado had landed in front of me.

Logan was on the ground, held down by one big guy while another rained punches on his face. Blood was spurting everywhere as one of my rescuers said, "Mel, it's enough. Leave the scum to whine in peace." They each landed one stiff kick to Logan's gut before stepping away.

I bent forward and this time, I actually did barf. Emptying my stomach of beer and protein bars, I continued to dry heave even when it was empty. Tears dropped unbidden from my eyes, mixing with the awful pile of vomit.

I didn't want to lift my head and face my saviors. Earlier this week, I'd seen them as enemies, but now they were busy rescuing my ass.

Eventually, I had to look up. Jamel kept his distance, standing vigil with one eye on Logan, the other on the party. The other guy—I didn't know this one—inched toward me.

"You all right?" he whispered, his warm breath forming puffy clouds in the chilly air. His deep voice was smooth like velvet, and coated my soul with a layer of honey. "Just nod your head, okay? Are you hurt?"

Chilly waves rippled up and down my spine—shock or fear, probably a combination of both. I was still speechless, wanting more of his soothing voice.

He reached out a hand, and I couldn't help but flinch. "It's okay, I'm just checking on you. Making sure you're not hurt." He ran his hand down my arm and took my hand, encouraging me to stand up next to him. Once I was on my feet, he said, "I'm Trey, another friend of Ty's."

He stood with my hand in his, looking at me, and I nodded. Through blurry eyes, I finally recognized him as the one wearing the Just Do It sweats near the townhouses. He was long and lean, his hair buzzed short around his face, highlighting dark eyes and long lashes. Those lashes were so beautiful and full, I was mesmerized for a moment. And slightly jealous.

"Anything hurt?" he asked.

I shook my head, feeling a little weak. Before I knew it the sky was falling, the ground was closing up, someone was lifting me, and then I was in someone's arms, being carried.

My head spinning, I heard a mumbled, "What the fuck are we supposed to do now, man?"

"I'm gonna take her back with us." That was Trey, his words sprinkled with chocolate and amaretto. I wanted to taste them.

"Bro, we can't be toting a white piece around, carrying her back to our place." That was Mel. As in Jamel, who had insulted me every time I'd seen him.

"Well, I'm not about to leave her. You know Ty likes her. She cares for him, and she just got assaulted. So, she's coming."

Wiggling, I tried to get out of Trey's grasp as he carried me away from the scene, through several backyards. "Can I get down," I barely rasped out.

Finally, he set me down next to an enormous silver SUV and opened the door. "Get in, we'll talk in there," he said. Trey helped me in the backseat and hopped in the driver's side while Jamel walked over to the passenger door.

"Thank you." My words came out gurgled. My throat was dry from gagging, and my head still spun slightly from all the commotion.

Mel slammed the car door and turned to me. "You all right?"

"Yeah." It came out weak, but it was the truth. "He didn't get too far, thanks to you."

"You gonna tell the cops or what?"

I shook my head. "I don't need any more gossip about me here, so no. I'm okay."

"You need a doctor or shit like that?" Jamel was firing off questions while Trey pounded on his phone.

"No." I looked down at my hands twisting in my lap. "Just a shower and my bed."

Trey finally spoke up. "Not gonna go there tonight."

"What the fuck, man?" Jamel protested.

"Just texted with Ty, he says she stays with us. That asshole could come back, she needs to be protected."

"Goddamn it, that fucker. Thank fuck he can ball," Jamel said, slamming the dash with his hand.

"Really, I don't need to," I croaked out, shaking my head.

Trey threw the car into drive and off we went. Pulling into the steep lane down to the townhouses, we stopped in front of a unit past Ty's, parked, and Trey swung my door open. Gently grabbing my arm, he guided me to the house.

"This is Mel's place. He's gonna keep an eye on you, okay? Ty's gonna catch a bus back tomorrow and be here as soon as he can." He squeezed my arm and ran back to the car, leaving me with Jamel.

It was going to be a long night.

Jamel opened the door and said, "After you."

I walked in, taking in the testosterone-fueled chaos inside. Multiple TVs and gaming systems lined the far wall, and the huge couch opposite was every teenage boy's wet dream. There was a Gatorade machine in the kitchen and a giant heap of basketball shoes by the door. High school and prep school jerseys were tacked to the walls, apparently meant to be decor.

"Thanks, but this isn't necessary," I said to Jamel, breaking the awkward silence.

He shrugged. "It's what we do, the team, I mean. Even if I don't agree that you're the lady for Ty, we take care of each other. You wanna shower?" he asked, his usual laser focus directed at me.

Uncomfortable at his suggestion, I glanced around me, unable to get out much more than an unintelligible mumble.

"It's fine," he assured me with a frown. "I'm not gonna look or hurt you. Got a girl and a sister back home, got my hookups here. I'm cool." He walked toward a closet, rubbing his hand across his smooth head, and pulled out a large navy towel.

"Here." He beckoned for me to follow. After leading me toward the bathroom, he opened the door and said, "I'm gonna be out there playing games, so you do what ya need to do."

I nodded and locked the door behind me. After turning the water to its hottest setting, I slowly undressed, all my energy suddenly gone. The adrenaline had worn off, and I was nothing but a loose sack of bones. With my clothes in a pile on the counter, I stepped into the shower and let the scalding water burn my skin, hoping it washed away the pain and stink of the night. Salty tears mixed with the water and the AXE body wash I kept squeezing onto my arms and legs.

Leaning back into the water, I closed my eyes as I washed my hair, trying to determine if I'd led Logan on at all. Did I do anything?

No. The answer was no. I didn't do a thing to make him think I liked him.

He should get into trouble, but being beat half to death would have to do because if I went to the authorities, my name would be dragged through the mud again. Even Jamel thought I was a stupid skank. He'd said as much during our first meeting, and his reactions summed it up this round.

Toweling off, I couldn't stop thinking what Tiberius would think. Would he think I encouraged Logan? Shaking my head, I didn't allow myself to go there. I would get through this like I'd survived everything else.

As soon as the door clicked open and I walked out of the bathroom, Jamel yelled from the main room, "Go to sleep, Tingly. Take my room. I left a T-shirt in there."

His tone brooked no argument, and I didn't want another confrontation. So I did what he said and crawled into Jamel's bed wearing his T-shirt, but thinking of someone else.

chapter nine

"Tingly. Tingly, you up?"

I felt my shoulder being shaken and heard my name on repeat, and then I felt the mattress next to me sink a little. Jumping up with alarm, I hit my head on the headboard.

"Ouch!"

"Oh shit, Rex. You okay?"

I rubbed my eyes and squinted at the blurry form in front of me. "Tiberius? What time is it?" It came out scratchy, my throat still raw from the night before.

Without taking my eyes off the shadow in front of me, I felt around on the nightstand for my phone. When I pressed the HOME button, the screen illuminated, reading ten o'clock in the morning.

Panicked, I grabbed my forehead. "Practice! I slept through practice."

"It's Saturday," he said and reached toward me, hesitating with each inch. Finally, his fingers landed in the loose strands of my hair and smoothed them away from my face.

I took a long inhale before mentally putting the facts together. I was in Jamel's bed after Logan attacked me. It was Saturday because I went out with my teammates the night before. And Tiberius had been in New Jersey, but now he was here. Massaging my temple with his large calloused hand.

Squinting at him, I asked, "How are you here?"

"I came back when I heard." His hand stilled, but didn't move from my hair.

"But how? Why?"

He inched closer. "Is this okay?"

"Yeah." It was just a whisper, but I wasn't afraid of him. Not Tiberius.

"How?" he repeated. "By bus all night. Why? I can't answer that. Just because I'm a good guy. I like you. You got hurt. All of the above."

"I'm fine," I stated matter-of-factly, but then a single tear betrayed me. It slid down my cheek before dropping onto Jamel's black T-shirt.

"I know you're okay," he said softly. "You're tough, I get that. But, shit, if the boys hadn't been keeping an eye on you, I don't know what that ass woulda done."

His blue eyes searched mine, and for a moment, I wondered what he saw inside my brown ones. Did he see fear? Glimpses of my past? Or maybe a glimmer of my future?

"Keeping an eye on me?"

"You're my girl, friend or more, and that means the boys keep an eye out. Though I suspect this time, they were hoping you fucked up. But doesn't matter because when you needed them, they were there."

He slid even closer, his hip flush with my side. Oddly, I didn't mind.

"Well, the part about them hoping I fucked up, that I believe.

Your friend Trey is real nice, but Jamel . . . God, he hates me."

"Nah, he's just bitter. Got a chip on his shoulder. Had nobody his whole life, so he can be an angry brother, but he's got a sister so he knows right and wrong."

It was then I realized the irony of my situation—the girl with the silver spoon in her mouth had been taken in by a group of men who essentially grew up with nothing. Yet they'd given me more than I'd ever been given at home. Even Jamel.

Tiberius leaned down and ran his lips over my cheek, caressing my skin, kissing away the shame of the night before, and I felt myself leaning my face into his mouth. I wanted more, but yet I didn't.

"You scared me, Rex," he whispered when he got to my ear.

"I'm good." That and "I'm okay" seemed to be the only words I could form since last night. "Are you okay?" I asked, finally able to add something else to my repertoire. "I must have screwed everything up."

"Nah, I was done with cleaning everything out. I was just hanging around the old hood, shooting the breeze, talking 'bout my mom."

Taking in his appearance, I noticed his T-shirt was wrinkled and he was wearing the same sweatpants as the day he left. He must have really rushed to get back.

"Thank you," I said.

"Missed you." When I opened my mouth to respond, Tiberius placed two fingers over my lips and muttered, "Shh, don't ruin it. You don't have to be the big, bad Tingly for me. I missed you, and that's it. Don't say it back. Don't give some explanation. And don't run away."

I couldn't respond. Even with bossy Pierre, I would assert myself and stand up to his dictatorship. That was how we got caught. He hadn't wanted to fuck in the office, but I'd insisted, seduced him into it with my words and my tits.

But with Tiberius, I didn't push. I asked politely, "Can I have my clothes? I need to go back home."

"Yeah, I'll take you to the dorm in Trey's car and then bring you back to my place." He placed a kiss on my forehead, and I was certain this was something his mother did to him countless times. I wanted him to do it again.

"I can just stay at my dorm. The girls will be in and out."

"No. Not now. First, the boys and me gotta pay a visit to your friend, make sure he knows the rules."

He stood and walked to the dresser, leaning his tall frame against it as he kicked his feet out in front of him. He ran his hand along his hair, tugging at it. The length had grown out a bit, and the ends were starting to curl.

I wanted to run my fingers over and through his hair, but I didn't. Instead I crawled out of bed and stood up. The hem of Jamel's T-shirt dropped down my legs, almost brushing my kneecaps.

"Don't hurt him, okay? Jamel already got him good."

"But not me," he said, his eyes darkening. "Not me."

"I don't care. It's over."

"Listen—you, me, we just met, I know. But we've been circling 'round each other for weeks. Hot, cold, kissing, me walking you home, you running away. When my momma passed, you came running to me. That means something, a whole lot of something. And I'm telling you, you're my business to protect, and that boy is gonna get a piece of me for hurting you."

He gathered me in his arms and held me tight against his rock-hard chest. "Feel that, Rex? That's my heart beating for you. You can push and shove and run and whatever other stupid shit you want, but I'm coming for you."

I couldn't move, frozen in place, breathing and feeling all that was Tiberius.

"Now, come on," he ordered. "I hate that you're standing there in Jamel's T-shirt after sleeping in his room—before you ever wore mine to sleep or spent the night in my bed. Or we even had dinner."

And just like that, Tiberius snatched my jeans from the night before and tossed them at me, and we were out the door.

chapter ten

I couldn't help but explore Tiberius's condo while the guys were out "talking" with Logan. Nerves made me restless; there was no way in hell I could sit still while I waited.

I'd begged to take a run, but Tiberius and Jamel had looked at me as if I'd meet an early death if I tried to leave the premises, so I was held hostage by only the memory of their evil stare-down. With nothing better to do after they left, I explored the kitchen and wandered down the hallway, touching nothing, just looking, quietly investigating my captors through their belongings.

Turned out, Trey and Tiberius were roommates. I found this out before they left, when Ty borrowed Trey's car to take me home.

"Nice of Trey to loan you the car," I'd said as we pulled away from the townhouses.

"Yeah, he's my roommate," Tiberius had answered. When I furrowed my brow, mentally considering the coincidence of Trey rescuing me, Tiberius cleared it up for me. "That's why Trey was watching you. Because he lives with me and I dig you, and that's his job."

"Why didn't I just stay in your room last night then?" I asked.

"No way Trey was gonna stay under the same roof with you. He didn't want to leave anything up for misinterpretation. No way he'd want it out there that he'd crossed a line with his roommate's girl."

Taking in his profile, I noticed crinkles forming beside Ty's eyes and a smile turning up his lips. His eyes were on the road, but I couldn't help but notice his amusement.

"What?" I said. "What's so funny?"

"Well, no one would believe anything 'bout you and Mel. The whole team knows he's not feeling you," he'd said, putting it all out there.

So here I was. Although I knew it was wrong, curiosity killed the cat and all that, I peeked inside Trey's room as I made my way around the condo. I wanted to know more about the guy who'd been watching me, but I didn't want to cross any lines.

After rolling my eyes at the heap of green-and-white uniforms and practice jerseys in the center of the floor, I laughed at his mess. The bed was unmade, and an enormous pile of junk covered the dresser. The speaker was on and set to some hip-hop station on satellite radio.

When I saw the strip of condoms and a half-empty bottle of whiskey sitting on the nightstand, I understood then how something might been misconstrued by my staying with Trey. From what I gathered in the car ride back from my dorm, he was a junior, a self-professed ladies' man, and a starting guard on the team. Tiberius had gone to the same prep school as Trey—one of the reasons Hafton went back to recruit another player. Tiberius would supposedly be coming off the bench to relieve Trey at shooting guard . . . and hopefully be a starter soon.

I pulled Trey's door closed, then padded down the hall toward Ty's room. It was all together and controlled, just like the man who lived there. The navy bedspread was tucked in on all four corners, and there were no condoms or booze to be seen. Above his bed was a poster from his high school with their logo and his number memorialized in the middle. A team photo held a place of honor on his dresser, and curious, I crept closer to inspect it. A young Tiberius sat in the middle of the front row with a faux thug expression in place of his normal bright smile, and all his teammates were woven around him with the same hard-ass look plastered across their faces. They were a tapestry of colors and heights and widths. Despite all their physical differences, brotherhood and love jumped off the photo.

As I backed out of the room and pulled the bedroom door shut, I heard the front door open and close.

"Tingly?" Tiberius called from the hallway.

I called out, "Here," my response weak from the fear that ripped through my body like the tornado whipped through Kansas in *The Wizard of Oz*. I was afraid to show my face, scared about what may have happened to Logan, and absolutely terrified over what might come next between Tiberius and me.

I'm not in Kansas anymore.

"You good?" Ty's voice was louder as he made his way into the open main space. He turned the corner and walked toward me in the same ratty T-shirt he'd had on earlier. Only now there was a spray of blood across the shoulder.

My heart rate amped up to such a frenetic pace, I felt like I was at the track. "I'm okay. You?" I asked, my eyes not meeting his as I stared at the red spatter.

"All good. I could use a shower. You down with waiting another few minutes?"

As if I had a choice. I'd been kept prisoner there all afternoon, and now I couldn't walk away from the bloodied guy in front of me if I tried.

I nodded. He stepped close and slipped his hand behind my neck, sliding it along the nape under the heavy shawl of my hair.

Bringing my face underneath his nose, he said quietly, "Don't be scared, T. It's all good, okay? Everything's good, and now you're protected and nobody's gonna touch you."

How did he do that? Read my thoughts so clearly when I'd spent the greater part of my life masking them?

Slipping from his grasp, I said, "Go get a shower, I'll wait."

After he nodded and headed back to his room, I sat on the couch, my hands tucked under my thighs, my legs beating up and down to some unknown frantic rhythm. The water came on, the pipes roaring to life. I took a deep, calming breath and let the calming whoosh in the background soothe my frazzled nerves.

My phone beeped, then buzzed in my pocket.

> *Ginny: Hey, you okay? I just got home from last night. You're not here.*

> *Me: Yeah. Stayed out last night after going out with the track team. I came back for a little. With Tiberius now.*

> *Ginny: You sure you're okay? What are you doing later for dinner? You going out?*

> *Me: I don't know. Tiberius is showering, so I'll see when he gets out.*

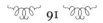

Ginny: Ooh, showering. Sorry to disturb. Wink, wink.

Me: I think I liked you better when your head was tucked in a book. Wink, wink.

Ginny: Ha. Very funny. Text me later.

I bowed my head in silent thanks. Ginny would have told me if she'd heard anything about last night. If rumors were going to spread, the athletic dorms would be the first place they would steamroll through. The last thing I needed was to call attention to myself. Again. Which was why I hoped whatever happened with Logan this afternoon didn't get out either. Even if people knew the truth, they would side with him over me. After all, I was already branded with a scarlet letter.

The water stopped, the pipes clanging for a few seconds until quieting, and then Tiberius walked out with just a towel around his waist. Beads of water slid down his chest, coming to a rest on the edge of the towel, where they were absorbed.

First, I focused on his tattoo, now recognizing the crest as being from his high school. Then my eyes wandered, drinking their fill as they ran the full length of him from his dark nipples to his ankles, stopping to widen at his thick and muscular legs.

"You hungry?" Tiberius asked, interrupting my perusal.

"Um, what?"

"Are you hungry?"

Warmth crept up my cheeks at the suspicion he was referring to the hunger that was probably dancing in my eyes. "Um, you mean for lunch or dinner?"

"Yeah. What did you think I meant?" he asked, smirking.

"Sure. I'm a little hungry."

"Good. I'm going to throw on some clothes and then we can go eat. Want to go to the dorms or somewhere in town?"

"How about the Union?"

"Good idea. One sec and I'll be ready," he yelled as he headed back toward his room.

I wondered where Trey was; could he be finishing up something with Logan? A chill climbed my body like a roller coaster heading toward the top of a steep drop. As soon as my stomach dipped, more thoughts clawed up my spine.

Was this our first date? First I was sequestered inside his apartment, and then Tiberius casually asked if we should go eat as if that was a normal, everyday occurrence. He'd been asking and I'd been refusing to go eat, and now he had me at his mercy.

Luckily, Tiberius was dressed quickly, so I didn't have long with my free-falling thoughts. Otherwise, I may have bolted—with or without permission.

"Let's roll." He held out his hand, then pulled me up from the sofa.

"Let's roll," I said, mocking him as I rolled my eyes.

"What?" He stopped to stare at me, and his smile faded. I wanted it back.

"Nothing, it's just you came back with blood on your shirt after going to explain 'the rules' to Logan, and now you just want to go eat. Don't you think I deserve an explanation?" Afraid to meet his gaze, I stared at the beige carpet as if I thought it was the most fascinating thing I'd ever seen.

Tiberius shook his head. "Come on, that wasn't Logan's blood. I'll explain when we walk."

Before I could argue with him he pulled me out the door, steering us up the path toward campus. Tiberius's even-tempered nature was soothing, and I took deep breaths to summon the patience to let him tell me what happened in his own time. Lucky for me, he didn't make me wait long.

"Look, Rex, I get you care about what happens to Logan because he's part of the team. I would never jeopardize that. I thought you'd know that about me, seeing as how I only got the guys on the team now."

We walked side by side, making it easier to talk since I didn't have to face him. His straightforwardness was refreshing, something I definitely wasn't used to, but I wasn't sure if I could ever take his motives at face value. It was so unlike the world I grew up in, where everything was fake and phony. In LA, posing and posturing took precedence over loyalty and love.

"When I said we were gonna talk, I meant it. The guys and I went to take Logan's pulse on what happened, make sure he's going to take the boys' little beating as a warning and stay away from you. Mostly, I wanted to make sure this didn't blow back on you." Catching my eye, he said pointedly, "It's not gonna."

"So, whose blood was that?" I couldn't help but blurt.

"Mel's."

"What?" I stopped walking and turned to face Tiberius, craning my neck to see his face, and saw nothing but honesty and openness in his eyes. "Mel? Why? He took care of me."

What the hell is wrong with me? I'm defending Jamel?

"It was just a bloody lip, and he deserved it. The lip bleeds a lot, so when I got up in his grill, it went flying everywhere."

Tiberius took my hand and started walking again, his words tumbling faster. "I'm trying hard not to be jealous of him, you in his T-shirt, you defending him. And I'm not telling you this to make you mad, but he doesn't like you, T. He doesn't like anyone except for the team, so he's agreed to accept you. But today he didn't get away with his skinny-white-girl bullshit, and I let him know I'm not gonna hear any more of that. So, that's it. And I may have busted up his lip while letting him know."

He squeezed my hand, making my fingers disappear inside his gigantic paw. How could he be so gentle with me, but act like busting someone's lip was no biggie?

At my dubious expression, he shook his head. "We're guys. We don't use our words all the time, Rex. The team is a family, they're like brothers, so when they act shitty, they get my fist. I don't say, *pretty please don't do that.* That wouldn't settle shit."

"Did I just say what I was thinking out loud? Or did you know what was rambling through my brain?" I stopped again, needing clarification of what just occurred between the two of us.

"I could tell. Hey, it was just my momma and me growing up, I know how to read women. Don't make fun of me!" Laughter vibrated in his chest, the rumble of it traveling down his arm to where our hands were still entwined. Then he became very serious, almost ominous, his eyes turning a dark blue beneath his furrowed brow. "I would never use my fists on a woman, though. Never. You get that, right?"

"Yeah, I know. *Tu fait l'amour aux dames,*" I said with a heavy French accent.

"Say what?" Tiberius shot back in heavy Jersey.

"You make love to the ladies," I translated, and I swear to God, I thought I saw a faint blush creep over Ty's cheeks. "Hey, I was just kidding. I'm a French major, Italian and Spanish minor. Sometimes I can't help it. But I can tell you're gentle, the *make love, not war* kind of guy," I joked back, wanting to move away from this discussion.

And clearly so did Tiberius, because he quickly added, "Come on, I'm hungry, and I'm finally getting to take you to eat."

We talked and joked the entire way to the Union, laughing about different words in French and Spanish, and what few jobs would be available for me as a language major. Tiberius told me he was a business major, and moaned a little over Statistics 200.

When we finally made it to the food line, he made a big deal out of using his student ID to pay for both of our meals, even though we were both on athletic meal plans. "It's our first date," he reminded me, his eyes shiny blue again, their lightness matching his wide smile.

I'd just muttered my thanks and reached up to give him a quick kiss on the cheek when a burst of clapping and whistling broke out. Careful not to drop my salad, I turned slowly to see Trey and Lamar grinning and punching each other in the shoulder like goofballs.

I was surprised to see them both wearing low-slung jeans, Nike T-shirts, and clean basketball shoes—basically what Tiberius was wearing. It was the first time I'd seen all of them without their uniforms or practice clothes on. Well, the night before, I guess Trey had been wearing something else, but I was too frazzled to notice.

They looked good. All of them, especially Tiberius, who finished paying and was ready to sit.

It was impossible not to pass the other guys as we made our way toward a table.

"Hey, Tingly," Trey said.

"T," came with a chin lift from Lamar.

Tiberius gave them a frown. "Cool it."

"Hey." I smiled at the other guys and flashed a dirty look at Tiberius. I had to admit, I was afraid he was going to go all robo-possessive again and start busting up lips.

"What you two up to?" Trey asked, lifting his chin toward us.

"Eating," I answered.

"Cool. We'll sit with ya'll." Lamar mugged at us as if he were joking, but then he grabbed a giant Gatorade and a few slices of pizza and made himself comfortable.

We took up a table large enough for ten people, so the guys could make themselves comfortable with their impossibly long tree-trunk legs spread out in front of them. Then they woofed down more calories than I'd ever imagined was possible.

Tiberius was making his way through a meatball hoagie, a side of fries, and a blue drink when he waved a fry at me. "Want one?" he asked.

"Are you sure you can spare one?"

"Yeah," he said, before adding with a chin nod, "There's more up there."

I grabbed the fry and plunged it into the ketchup before popping it in my mouth. Sadly, a small moan escaped my lungs as I had my way with the salty, greasy, crispy piece of potato.

"You know you wish she'd do that for you," Trey said slyly, taunting Tiberius.

"Here, have another." Tiberius offered up another one and I lunged for it, nearly falling out of my chair.

"What, you starve yourself? That why you're so skinny?" Lamar asked with another chin lift. These guys loved their chin lifts as much as their not-so-gentle ribbing and nicknames.

I shook my head. "Nah. Just a bad habit from growing up. We didn't eat fried food," I said without thinking, then froze. The differences in our two worlds crashed head-on with my lungs inside my chest, stunting my breath. I was worried I'd offended them, but they continued to surprise me, these basketball boys.

"Shit, girl, we got to get you some fried food and put some meat on your bones."

Trying to hold the emotional storm raging inside my heart at bay, I said, "A little fried food is a go, meat on my bones is a no-go. I need to stay lean for my season. That would be like me suggesting we chop a few inches off your height."

That earned me a huge laugh from Trey. "Nah, girl. Our boy Tiberius needs something to hold on to. Little bit's all you need," he teased with a glance at Ty, tormenting his roommate again.

"All right, enough, you two," Tiberius said. "You make a habit of interrupting people's dates?"

This got another big laugh, this time from Lamar. "Is that what this is? Come on, man. You gotta wine and dine her a bit."

Trey clamped a huge paw on Ty's shoulder. "Bro, we gotta talk when you get home. Don't worry, Tingly, I'll set him straight and next time, you'll be eating some damn good food somewhere nice and shit." With a grin, he stood up and smacked Tiberius on the back. "We outta here. Come on, Mar, let's let the kiddies play in the sandbox. Don't forget we got a team meeting in the morning, Ty. Coach'll be making sure we didn't party too hard over the weekend. We all know that's not you, dude, so try to be happy."

Trey and Lamar walked away, chuckling and working their swagger as every head in the room swung their way, following their progress out the door of the Union with interest.

Watching along with them, I realized most of the room probably had had their eyes on the four of us when we were sitting together. Surprisingly, I didn't care, because for the first time in my life I was doing something normal—or as normal as I could.

chapter eleven

"Who's there?" I called through the door.

It was Sunday afternoon, and I wasn't expecting anyone. In fact, I'd had the place to myself and was still sweaty and gross from my mandatory weekend practice and run. I'd been lounging around in my running shorts and tank, studying and watching TV when I heard a knock on the door.

"Ty."

"Ugh, I wasn't expecting you," I said as I unlocked and opened the door.

"Thanks. Great to see you too," he said with an award-winning grin.

Unlike me, Tiberius had showered. Quite recently, considering his hair was a little damp and a few drops of water still clung to his fresh buzz cut. Much like his long frame and powerful arms and legs, his scent overpowered me as he entered my quad's common room. Pheromones floated on the air like dust bunnies.

We'd parted ways the night before after Tiberius walked me back to my place and took his time planting kisses on my neck, cheek, nose, forehead—anywhere but my mouth. To say I was turned on was an understatement. Yeah, I wanted him, but my body craved the comfort and affection it had come to know for the first time with Tiberius. And his friends, even Jamel.

"Sorry I've been AWOL, but Coach had a team meeting and some of the older guys were acting up, so we had to stay for a last-minute practice . . . which was really us running suicides. Wanted to know how your practice was. Any problems?" he asked as he leaned in and backed me into the wall, running his hand over my cheek as his thumb ghosted over my lips.

"None." I shook my head. "Logan apparently copped to a fight at a party and took his one-meet suspension. Which he needs anyway, the guy is beat up."

Tiberius backed up. "I told you that wasn't me."

"I know. I was there and saw Jamel in action," I said as I headed toward my room.

"Were you scared? Of Jamel?" Tiberius asked from behind me.

I shook my head again. "I don't want to talk about it anymore. It's in the rearview."

Opening my door, I caught a whiff of myself. "Ugh, I smell. Shit, you probably think I'm so gross."

"Rex, I'm an athlete. I get the odor; it means you worked hard. Plus, on you it's sexy. I can't stop thinking about you all slick with sweat."

Okay then.

"What are you doing now?" I asked, unsure of where I should sit in my room, unclear of what was expected of me—or him.

"I came to see you. Wanna go for a walk or something?"

"Um, sure. Let me take a quick shower and change."

He was leaning against my dresser, but I needed to get ready. "Do you want to sit in here or out there? While I, uh—"

"Out there," he mumbled while maneuvering his big body past me and out the door into the common room.

"I'll be quick," I yelled after him.

Cleaned up, in jean shorts and a long-sleeved tee with my wet hair loose and combed out down my back, I walked next to Tiberius up the hill toward the Ag building. It was early evening and the sun was starting to set, painting the fields in front of us with a golden hue.

"It's so wild every time I see this, coming from LA," I said as we hiked up the path, neither of us out of breath.

"Yep, I felt the same the first time I saw it, coming from right outside the city. I couldn't believe all that space and open air."

"Made me appreciate small-town living, breathing room. I don't think I ever want to go back," I added.

"Well, I like both. Glad I'm getting to experience all this, but I love the noise of the city. Actually, I sleep better with ambulances and police sirens in the background. That was my favorite part of having to go back home last week. The noise. And the grime."

Tiberius grabbed my hand like he had the day before and slid his fingers between mine. I was shocked with his soft touches and gentle ways of showing affection—in a good way. For a guy who didn't have a dad or live with a positive male influence, he was incredibly considerate and warm to women. At least, to me. Then again, I'd never had soft touches growing up, and I was lapping up each and every one Tiberius doled my way. I definitely wasn't complaining.

Without any words, we stopped at the top of the hill and took in the view. I experienced the same awe at the open cornfields most people did for the Hollywood sign. We continued to stand there, hand in hand, swinging our arms, acting corny until he turned toward me and laid a kiss on my lips.

His arms wrapped around me, drawing me close and pulling me to my tiptoes, pelvis to pelvis, his mouth soft and warm, inviting in a way I didn't know or understand. My tongue stroked his, exploring his mouth and learning how to make him moan, and I swallowed his growls. I didn't know how long we stood there kissing as the air chilled, the sun dropped to the horizon, and time stood still.

Tiberius broke the moment, shifting his body and angling back the way we came. "Come on, let's go get something fried in town."

It wasn't what I was expecting or hoping for, but I agreed with a quick, "Okay."

"Where do you want to go?" he asked as we made our way back down the hill, no longer holding hands, but cloaked in some strange sexual tension.

"You're the fried-food boss, lead the way," I said, trying to lighten the atmosphere. Truth was, my heart was pounding and my nerves tingled; I wanted to get close to Tiberius. But he was putting it off, and it wasn't about control like it had always been with Pierre. Not for Tiberius or me.

With Pierre, he demanded control and I was always vying to break his spell over me, seducing and luring him into my lair. Fuck, I didn't want this moment to be tainted with even a thought of the French prick.

Plush. Poseidon. Pink. Papyrus. Papillon. Pearl Jam.

Following my inner monologue, I took a deep breath and then

released it, letting out my anger with the carbon dioxide.

"You good?" Tiberius asked.

"Yeah, my mind wandered," I admitted. "Sorry."

"S'okay. So, fried food . . . let me think. You like the diner? They make wicked fried chicken patties and pie."

"Never been."

The streetlight at the corner of College Avenue came into view as he stopped and faced me, his expression incredulous. "Come on! You're kidding." His blue eyes pinned mine as if trying to catch me in a lie.

"Nope. Never been. It's not really a fave with the track team."

"Let's go. What are we waiting for?" he said, dragging me across the intersection.

Minutes later we were seated in a booth, his legs stretched out in front of him, crowding mine as he flipped open his menu. "Let's see. We should get sandwiches and an order of the meatloaf. And milkshakes first, pie last."

I nudged his knee with mine. "I'm not sure I can eat all that, Ty."

"Don't worry, I'll finish what you don't."

Tiberius was like a young boy in a candy shop, completely and utterly excited to eat junk food—with me. I had practice in the morning and a meet at the end of the week, but I couldn't spoil his fun. A little junk wouldn't kill me, but I couldn't make any bets about the man in front of me. He might do me in.

"Let's do it! Bring it on," I said, pumping my fist into the air.

With an Oreo shake resting on the stainless-steel table in front of us, a straw on either side of the cup, we settled in and waited for the pig fest. Journey played in the background, the smell of grease wafting around us.

Ty caught my eye. "This place reminds me of a joint we used to go to at prep. It was an all-night diner we'd go to after a late game. The owners loved us and would just throw food at us. They'd say, 'Ya'll win? Then ya'll deserve to get treated right,' in that West Virginia twang. And they'd start bringing shit out. Meatloaf, turkey with gravy and all the fixin's, fries, burgers, sodas, whatever we wanted," he said with a far-off look on his face. "Took my momma once when she visited. They treated her like royalty. Never been happier for her. That's the only other time I took a girl to a diner," he said with a weak smile.

I nudged his knee with mine. "Oh, come on. I don't believe that. Nicest, sweetest, sexiest, hottest baller I know. Don't lie, you probably got a string of girls all over the place, like Jamel does. I think he told me something like '*I got a girl at home and one here*' when he rescued me," I half joked. Part of me wanted to believe I was special, but I knew I wasn't.

"Seriously, Rex." Tiberius leaned back against the red vinyl, his arms coming back to support his head and neck.

I leaned forward. "You're full of it." More half joking.

"Go ahead and ask," he taunted me.

The place wasn't that crowded, so I assumed he felt it was quiet enough for us to have the *past body count* conversation in public.

Just then, our server started tossing down plates in front of us. The aroma steaming from them was intoxicating, and I was concerned for my overall sanity. I couldn't eat like this every day, but today was an exception, so I dug in.

Lifting the chicken sandwich and taking a large bite, I couldn't help but moan. *Oh God*, it was so greasy and salty. My mom would be glaring at me and dabbing her chin at the sight of the grease traveling out of my mouth and rolling down my chin. Then she'd cluck her tongue at me and worry her lip. "Ladies don't eat junk or with their hands, Tingly Simmons," she'd say. "And they don't run and sweat either." So I took another bite of my sandwich as a mental fuck-you to her. I was going to enjoy today because there were a lot of things ladies didn't do that she did.

"This is really good," I said to Tiberius between bites and chewing. He had already inhaled a sandwich and was watching me with a curious expression.

"So, you gonna ask your questions?" A smirk—half cocky, half innocent schoolboy—flickered across his face.

"I don't think I want to," I answered honestly.

"Think you'll be surprised if ya do," he said, raising an eyebrow and giving me another one of his enigmatic looks.

"Okay, fine. What's your history? You got a girl at home? One tucked away here and another at prep?" Cocking my head to the side, I asked, "What am I? A little fun on the side?"

"Don't got a girl at home or prep. Got nobody but you here. Had one girl in my life," he admitted. "We liked each other in high school, grew up together, explored and did shit. But that was it for me. She went the wrong way when I went to prep. Been nobody since, and I'm not really sure why. I just think I never wanted to go down the same road as my dad. Now I realize what a fool I was 'cause I don't know what the fuck I'm doing."

"What?" I nearly choked on a bite of chicken. Acid raged in my stomach, burning its way back up my throat.

"Only been one. Told you back when we met. The guys are fast, but not me. In this case, you got the upper hand."

"Seriously, is that what this is about?" My voice was a raspy whisper fueled by embarrassment and anger as I waved my hand between the two of us. "A joke or something? Maybe learn a trick or two from the campus slut?" Before I could spew any more venom,

vérité

I tossed down my napkin, then stuck my hand in my pocket and grabbed a few bills to throw on the table.

"Listen, Tiberius, and listen good. I appreciate you and your friends looking out for me, taking care of shit the other night, but I'm not some girl you can toy with, learn the ropes from and make a fool of. I've already had that done, so see ya around." Then I turned and bolted.

"Shit!"

Tiberius swore softly and cursed behind me, and I imagined him trying to swing his long legs out from the table as I burst through the door and thanked the heavens I was wearing a pair of running shoes. The fried food gurgled and churned inside my belly, trying to make a reappearance, but I wouldn't allow it.

I set a brisk pace and steered myself toward the dorm, not stopping until I was deep inside the double doors of my building. Bypassing the elevators and making my way to the stairwell, I raced up one flight three steps at a time before I stopped and slid down the wall, dropping on my ass on the cold concrete. Tears came. Heavy droplets ran down my face, soaking my sleeves as I wiped them across my snotty nose.

I was such a desperate, love-hungry fool. When was I going to realize that I wasn't meant for love? It wasn't in the cards for me, especially the unconditional kind. I let my head fall into my hands, providing a cup for new tears and a curtain between the world and myself.

That's when the date occurred to me. September fifteenth. The day Pierre officially left last year, his last day on American soil as far as I knew. I'd caught a glimpse of him leaving the languages lab as I'd made my way to therapy that bright, fucking cheery fall day. The walking was supposedly good for my recuperation from the whole spleen issue. Not to mention, I had to get back to running eventually. So, every day but Sunday, I made my way to my shrink at the student health center—each day leaving and pushing myself to take a longer stroll than the day before.

Pierre had been carrying a few boxes that afternoon, his blond hair ruffling in the wind. He'd let his beard come in full, and he'd been wearing jeans and a navy dress shirt. I couldn't see his eyes, but I imagined next to his shirt, they were as blue as the Atlantic—the ocean that now separated us. Well, that and his wife. And the little-known fact that I'd ruined his career.

My pulse sped up as soon as I'd spotted him that day. I was certain he intentionally came on a Saturday, convinced he wouldn't see anyone. My entire body itched to go to him, and I scratched at my skin as though it was covered in hives of want, trying to put out the itch. Even with everything that had happened, I wanted him that day. I held tight to a stone wall, my fingers gripping the ledge until they turned white, forbidding myself from running to him. Finally, he left the quad, heading toward the parking lot, and I jogged—against doctor's orders—to my shrink.

It was that day we came up with the *P* game. I had no clue I'd still be using it a year later, or that I would reinvent it after I'd fallen for someone else.

Putrid. Telescope. Potatoes. Truffles. Paris. Touché.

Touché was right; I was such a cliché. Spoiled little rich girl from LA with mommy and daddy issues falls for the teacher, has a breakdown, and then falls for the good guy. The one who was trying out a new look, who wanted a walk on the wild side with the bad girl.

I stayed there in the stairwell long after the sweat and tears had chilled on my body, long past my butt ached from the hard floor and my muscles begged for relief. When I finally went upstairs, the apartment was quiet and still, the only noise coming from the mini fridge humming in the corner and my cell phone vibrating in my pocket.

I lay down on the futon in the common area and sat staring out the window. Stars filled the sky, twinkling with hope. Unable to take in their beauty—it wasn't meant for me—I turned my phone off and tossed it on the table. I ran my hand ran over the small incision where they took my spleen, massaging the scar tissue, before bringing it over my chest, settling on my heart.

I didn't try to massage or squeeze it back to life, just held my hand steady over it, trying to keep it in one piece.

chapter twelve

ife was back to normal by Wednesday . . . my new normal. Early practice and babysitting (aka study hour), classes, and dinner with Ginny and Bryce.

Apparently, Bryce was a new fixture at our table. I stared at his enormous arms and shoulders, at the stupid Road Runner tattoo on his bicep. I stirred my mundane salad around my plate before dipping it in dressing and shoving it in my mouth.

Actually, I didn't feel like eating, but we had a meet the next day and I needed to perform on command. My times sucked on Monday. I blamed the fried food but deep down, I knew it was the blowup with Tiberius. Stephanie thought I went out and had a wild time all weekend with the girls, so even though my time was shit, she was happy. So, yeah—I was normal. Classes, salad, and beer pong.

Of course Tiberius texted, apologized, called, and left messages, then apologized some more. I was too mad to accept any of them. He kept his distance otherwise, too nice to come by unannounced. I was aggravated with all that too. I wouldn't take his calls or respond to his texts, but somewhere deep inside I wanted him to make some dramatic gesture.

I was a fucking train wreck of a loser, wanting something I couldn't have or wouldn't happen. And my parents were calling—furiously. I had a blister on my finger from hitting DENY CALL.

Thursday passed with a similar sense of ordinariness until the meet. We came in first place, and the whole gang was raring to go out. Our school had hosted the event, and the locker room near the track was bursting with excitement. Hoots and hollers over a kegger on College Avenue and a haunted hayride reverberated in the locker room and the showers.

I showered quickly, then tossed on jeans and an off-the-shoulder navy T-shirt before heading toward the door, hoping to make a fast exit. But Nadine stopped me.

"Hey, Tingly, you coming? Come on, we're gonna have fun!" She stood there wearing a bra, a towel hooked around her waist, her hair wet. Long gone was her quiet, peaceful running demeanor; she'd been injected with peppiness and overexcitement like everyone else.

"I don't know, I'm kinda beat." I pretended to stare at the big green *H* on the wall as if it were mesmerizing.

She shook her head. "I don't want to hear it. We're gonna go to Lupe's first for some food," she said, and in a hushed voice added, "and maybe drinks." Her face brightened. "And then to the parties. You gotta at least come and eat."

"Okay," I said, plopping down on the bench to wait. There was no sense going back and eating alone in the dining hall.

Finally, Nadine appeared in a cloud of perfume, her blond hair slicked straight, painted-on jeans covering her long legs. Her big hoop earrings reflected the awful locker room track lighting, blinding me as she stepped toward me.

"Let's roll, babe," she shouted, and we headed for the back of the locker room to exit the rear of the track building.

Nadine was talking a thousand miles a minute. "You know Andrew, from the men's team? Well, he has a hookup at Lupe's for free drinks and half-priced food, so we'll go there, and then we'll hit up the party on College first and if it's lame, we'll bail. Maybe hit the frats? Or that hayride? There's gonna be booze and lots of guys to snuggle up with—"

"Tingly!" A deep voice came out of nowhere, interrupting Nadine's monologue, but I kept walking.

"Isn't that your name someone's calling?" Nadine asked. She whipped her head around, her hair brushing my cheek as it flew through the air.

Again, his voice rang through the crisp fall air. "Tingly!"

"Over there, look, Ting . . . over there!" Pointing toward the side entrance, Nadine's finger homed in on him like a missile on its target.

"Tingly! Wait," he yelled, jogging toward me.

Tiberius looked good in dark jeans and a plain white T-shirt. Dark blue high tops peeked out of his pants as he ran our way, his shirt moving with his muscles. Mesmerized, I couldn't take my eyes off his cut arms as they flexed and pumped with each stride he took.

As he neared, I focused on the ground like it was about to swallow me up. I couldn't meet his expression; it was full of hurt and anxiety. It was a look I clearly put there, and I wasn't proud of that, but what choice did I have? I needed to protect my heart.

"Hey, T. Great meet today," he said.

"Oh, thanks. You watched?" I kicked a tiny pebble with my shoe, dribbling it like a soccer ball and I was in the World Cup.

"Yeah, of course."

His matter-of-fact response surprised me, considering I'd accused him of using me only a few days before.

"Hi, I'm Nadine," my teammate said cheerfully, interrupting our tense moment.

Shit. I forgot she was there.

"Tiberius," he said, and extended his hand to shake hers.

I finally looked up and frowned at Nadine eyeing Tiberius as if she wanted to climb him like a tree and swing from his branches—or branch, as in his penis.

"Tiberius and I met in study hall," I offered. I didn't know why I kept referring to him that way. Who was I protecting? Him? Or me.

"Fun! We're going to Lupe's. You should come," she said, continuing to eye-fuck the boy with her hand on her hip, her tits stuck out farther than I thought humanly possible, and her glossy lips held in a supposedly sensual pout.

"I don't know. I don't want to intrude." Tiberius spoke with his gaze on me, seeking silent permission or forgiveness, I wasn't sure which.

Nadine's stupid girly giggle shot through the silence, making me wince. My ears actually hurt listening to her flirt, and I was reminded why I didn't do beer pong, girls' nights, or college bullshit. And why I liked presumably mature professors or strong, silent, incredibly mature basketball players.

"That cool with you, T?" he asked, breaking the silence I'd easily retreated into rather than deal with the situation unfolding in front of me.

"Sure, why not?" I tried to act nonchalant or cool, anything other than rattled.

"Great!" Nadine jumped up and down.

We turned and resumed walking toward downtown as Nadine

drew Tiberius into some superficial conversation masked as earth-shattering news. I lagged a little behind the two, drawing into myself as I watched my feet, entranced as one stepped in front of the other.

I wasn't sure how long we walked that way or what in the hell those two discussed, because it wasn't until we hit College Avenue that Tiberius dropped back with me.

"T?" he said close to my ear. He leaned toward me and the heat from his body licked through my chilled skin. His warm breath ghosted over my bare shoulder, causing goose bumps to line the skin it touched.

"Yeah?"

Splaying his hand on my lower back, he whispered, "We good? We should talk."

I tried to pick up my pace, but he kept up. He slid his hand under my shirt, coming into full contact with me, skin to skin. When his long fingers skimmed over my spine, I lost all my resolve. Thinking back to the day he ran his finger over his dead mother's picture, I knew with certainty that I'd overreacted at the diner. This man couldn't use a woman, even a filthy one like me.

"Just let it be, Ty. I understand if you can't forgive me. I was a bitch, but I don't need you to flaunt it in my face that I don't have your friendship anymore. Can't you go flirt with some other girls? Not track ones?"

We came to a stop next to the wrought-iron gates of the university, engrossed in our conversation. Nadine hurried ahead toward a good time, crossing the street and leaving us behind without a second glance.

He didn't answer. We stood there as time passed, tension and silence swirling around us, oblivious to the Hafton coeds who passed us on their busy little ways to nowhere important. I was trapped, my feet glued to the cold concrete, unable to move. I tried, but my body wouldn't let me leave Tiberius.

"Not flirting, letting you cool off," he whispered into my ear. "Want you, all of you. Not once or twice, or just for fun. Want all of you, Rex. The naughty and the nice, especially the nice, because I'm scared to death I'm gonna screw up and not be the man you need when it comes to the naughty."

Before I could respond, his mouth took possession of mine in the middle of campus. His arm wound around my waist, lifting me an inch or two so I didn't have to reach on tiptoe to meet his lips. I matched his passion in earnest as college life passed us by; we were the only two in the world at that moment.

A blaring horn brought us back to earth.

Disgruntled, Tiberius broke free, setting me down as he looked up. "Shit," he muttered.

I followed his gaze and spotted the silver SUV behind the honking. Trey steered the car over to the curb and rolled down the passenger window, revealing Jamel riding shotgun.

"Wassup?" they yelled through the window.

"I'm heading out with Tingly, you asses," Tiberius flung back at them.

"Out or in?" Jamel prodded with a smirk. Of course, they had to witness our moment.

"Lupe's . . . with her team," Tiberius said, ignoring their teasing.

"Cool, we'll come. I feel like hanging out with some skinny bitches," Jamel joked.

"Mel." It was more a threat than anything else, but coming from Tiberius, it sort of warmed me in all the right places.

"I got ya, bro," Jamel hollered back before Trey pulled the car away from the corner and into a parking spot.

I guess they're really coming.

As we crossed the street, I leaned in and said, "I'm sorry," to Tiberius.

"Don't be." He reached down and squeezed my hand. "I shoulda made my intentions more clear. I'm not looking for a quickie fuck, Rex, and neither are you. Even when you try to throw all that 'I'm a ho' garbage in my face. We all make shit mistakes."

I gulped air, swallowing pollution and exhaust fumes, but was unable to form a response. By the time we reached the door to Lupe's, Trey and Jamel were hot on our tail.

Trey grabbed the door from behind me and held it open. "Ladies first, Rex."

I shook my head. "I can't believe everyone is calling me that. And I thought I didn't like Tingly."

"Oh, come on, it's cute. Our little guy Ty and his toy, Rex," Trey teased.

I knew he was joking. Coming from Jamel, I wouldn't be so sure, but Trey was deep down a softie—like Tiberius.

"Come on, I wanna meet your team." Jamel pushed forward before stopping suddenly, turning his narrowed gaze on me. "Is that fucking prick gonna be here? Logan?"

I shook my head again. "No, he's on suspension for a fight *he got into* at a party."

"I told you we shoulda bloodied him up more," he said—not at all discreetly—to Tiberius.

"Mel, let it go, man."

We had reached a big table in the back covered in pitchers of lime-green and pink margaritas, chips and salsa, and shots of tequila, where a chorus of "Tingly!" greeted us.

"You made it! Everyone, this is Tiberius." Nadine came over and slipped under Tiberius's arm, edging his shoulder over her small frame and smiling up at him.

Geez. Is it the alcohol making her bold? Or is this her normal?

"Great time today," one of my teammates called out.

"Sit down and grab a drink," one of the guys shouted.

Grabbing a pitcher of margaritas, I announced, "This is Jamel and Trey. They're on the basketball team with Tiberius."

The track team was generally pretty nice and welcoming, and tonight was no different. My teammates slid out of their seats and scrambled, pulling more chairs around the table to make room for my friends. Considered the poor stepchildren of the athletic program, we runners were always happy to be considered athletes by the big-revenue sports players.

Nadine was still bopping up and down on her feet, her tiny little boobs jiggling with every jump. "Do you want something, Tiberius?" she asked, but his teammates interrupted.

"You want a beer, man?" Jamel asked. He slipped his arm around Tiberius and tugged him away from Nadine, steering him toward where I'd relocated.

Trey gave me a chin lift and said, "I'm gonna grab a few drinks from the bar. Ones that ain't so girly. You want anything else?"

I shook my head. "No, thanks."

Leaning close, Jamel whispered in my ear. "Don't let your friend get up on your man, girl."

Surprised, I gaped up at him. Just when I thought he didn't like me, he went all big-brother on me.

"'Kay," I whispered back.

"I'm gonna go meet some of these bitches. Behave yourself, Ty," he said through a laugh, then swaggered off toward the other side of the table.

Tiberius wrapped his arm around me and pulled me into his side. "This okay?" he asked quietly.

I nodded and took a sip of my margarita. When I peered over my glass to see Nadine looking inquisitively at the two of us, she mouthed, "Sorry. I didn't know."

"You're pretty fast, girl," Tiberius said in a low voice, breaking the awkward silence.

I smiled. It was odd how everything was okay with us. I'd basically accused him of being an epic dick, and then he came and watched my meet before joining the whole team for Mexican.

"Well, that's the point," I joked.

"Yeah, I pretty much got that," he quipped back.

A comfortable easiness seemed to settle over the two of us. I didn't get it, but I couldn't resist it either. I reached over and grabbed a chip and plunked it into some salsa. The salty flavor burst into my mouth and tasted amazing after how many calories I burned today. I ran my tongue along my lips, catching any remaining salt, and Tiberius followed its path with his eyes, not missing a single movement. His baby blues darkened, and I caught my reflection in them. I was starved . . . and not for food.

"Here, man," Trey interrupted, handing Tiberius his beer, but he didn't stay. With no further words, he sauntered down toward Jamel and what was now a huge group of girls. Not just track people, but also sorority girls from across the room and a few unaffiliated alternative types from over at the bar. They were hanging on every word that came from Jamel's mouth, and were equally as awed when Trey approached.

"Good to see Jamel is being loyal to his girl at home and the one here," I said somewhat sarcastically.

"He's no pope," Tiberius answered.

"Obviously."

"Told you when we first met, the team was fast. I'm not, but I don't judge. They're all I got, 'specially now that my mom is gone."

It was an opportunity for me to say he had me, but I didn't. I swallowed my intended proclamation with a big gulp and sipped my drink. Needing something to do, I grabbed another chip, this one loaded with guacamole, and continued to battle the urge to tell Tiberius he could count on me too.

Studying me intently, he said, "You don't have to say anything. I see your thoughts running through your mind. He's a player, and I'm not. Judging does no one any good. That's why I'm not judging you, other than by how you make me feel. Which is good," he explained, jarring my thoughts, forcing them to dig deeper into my mind. And soul.

Glancing toward the window, I noticed the sun was down, daylight now just a memory like our fight from earlier in the week. Lupe's dimmed the lights a bit and turned up the music, the restaurant slipping from happy hour into full-on party time. Some college grunge came through the speakers, and I swayed to the beat.

"These tunes are shit," Tiberius said, his hand on my hip.

I laughed. "You don't like the music?"

"Nah. This is crap. Not even a fucking beat . . . but I do like your dancing." His voice was somewhat hoarse, made scratchy by what I hoped was need. *For me.*

"I kind of like it," I teased him. "The music."

He gave me a mock glare. "Stop it, I know you're kidding. You could *not* even talk to me if you liked this shit."

"Well, what would you rather they play?"

"Taylor Swift."

I burst out laughing so hard I spilled my drink across the table, causing a commotion and everyone's attention to turn toward us.

"What you do, Tiberius?" Jamel yelled across the room.

"He wants to hear some Taylor Swift," I yelled back, practically doubled over in fits of laughter.

"Bro, I told you to date the skinny white chick, but you don't have to like that music . . . shit she likes," came hurled from the other side of the room.

Tiberius broke into a huge smile, his dimple coming out. It was such a contradiction to his daunting stature, but I loved it.

"Nah, man. She's busting balls," he hollered back. "Let's blow this joint and go somewhere else. Tingly wants to dance."

"I'm in," was shouted all around. Everyone started throwing bills on the table, then Jamel led the crowd out of Lupe's and gave instructions as to where we should go.

"I think I'm still gonna go to the party on College," Nadine said, and one of the other girls offered to go with her.

"Okay, 'bye. Have fun!" I said while hurrying off with my hand inside Tiberius's.

As many as we could fit piled into Trey's SUV; the others walked toward the address. It was an apartment right off campus. Apparently, one of the grad students who coached the team was having a party. The car was vibrating, rap tearing through the air as we drove the short distance.

It was such a different experience from the last time I rode in the SUV. I sat next to Tiberius, my thigh rubbing up against his, and I considered taking Tiberius home and not going to the party at all. But I wanted more than just the physical.

My phone vibrated in my pocket, so I pulled it out. I had two texts from Ginny and a voice mail from my parents. I deleted the voice mail without listening to it, and opened up the texts.

Ginny: How was the meet? You going out?

Ginny: Hello? You okay?

Me: Yeah, all good. Went to Lupe's with team. Now met up with Tiberius and his teammates. You?

Ginny: I was worried about you. I'm heading to party on College with Bryce. Where you going?

Me: Somewhere off campus, basketball thing.

Ginny: Oh, you'll see Chey and Stacy.

I didn't even think about our roommates and that they may be at this basketball party. I hardly ever saw them at home. They were nice and all, but hadn't invited me to any of their events. I worried they wouldn't want me there.

Me: Shit. I forgot. You think they'll be mad?

Ginny: Too bad.

Me: Who is this? And what have you done with Ginny?

Ginny: LOL. Go have fun.

Me: You too.

The car came to a stop in front of a small apartment building, the top floor all lit up. We exited the SUV like a bunch of clowns getting out of a Mini Cooper. The basketball guys unfolded their long legs and the track girls, all limbs, stretched themselves out of the vehicle.

Jamel tossed his arm around my shoulders as we walked toward the main entrance. "I'm just starting to like you, girl, but you get my boy hooked on Taylor Swift and we're done. You got me?"

Giggles rocked through my body.

Apparently, Tiberius was over the joke or Jamel having his arm on me because he simply said, "Enough."

I slipped away from Mel and walked side by side with Tiberius. I didn't get his inexperience—he was all man in his actions, protective and sensual in everything he did. But I didn't want to bring up the discrepancy between the two of us again. Plus I felt good; the margarita was taking effect. My body felt loose and pliant, and my heart pounded with excitement, which it hadn't done in a long time.

Once Trey pressed some buttons on the intercom, we were buzzed in to the building. He led the way up a few flights of stairs to the top floor. Music bled through the walls and out into the hallway, the walls shaking to the bass, and my heart now kept pace with the beat.

Trey rapped on the door with his fist, and it opened a crack. He mumbled something to the guy through the sliver before the door opened wide, revealing a large room with the furniture all moved off to the sides, a strobe light flickering purple and blue dots all around the space, and a DJ off to the side. A full bar was laid out on the kitchen counter. Amber-hued bottles lined the shelf, and a keg rested against the wall.

Trey and Jamel led the pack through the room, fist-bumping everyone in their path. Tiberius followed suit, touching his fist and yelling, "*Wassup?*" to everyone he came into contact with. Everyone knew him; for a freshman, he was obviously connected. "This is Tingly," he yelled over the music. I met so many people, I couldn't possibly remember their names.

We strolled toward the bar, where Tiberius grabbed a beer and asked, "What do you want?" His deep voice carried over the music.

"Rum and Diet Coke," I yelled back.

He whispered my order to a shorter dude manning the alcohol, and we watched as he mixed it up. "Junior manager," Tiberius explained, tilting his head toward the guy. "Keeps us out of trouble. He knows the team's gonna party, so he makes sure we stay in line."

We stood off to the side, drinking our drinks, Ty's arm linked on my waist. If I was honest, I'd never really done this whole PDA thing. High school was all about sneaking around bedrooms in Beverly Hills mansions—or boardrooms, in my case—and college started out rough. It's not like you flaunt having an affair with a professor.

The music was good. The DJ was jamming, spinning a vibe that ran through the floorboards all the way to my chest. It was pulsing deep in my rib cage, and my hips started to sway of their own volition.

Tiberius slipped the glass from my hand with ease and set it on the ledge with his empty bottle before pulling me close. His leg moved in between mine, and his pelvis ground against me.

As his head bopped with the beat, our bodies entwined and moving in time with the groove, I slid my hand around his back and into his jeans pockets. If I didn't hold on, I was going to fall. My heart rate was too fast, my head too clouded—with lust, not alcohol—and my brain was swimming with thoughts of Tiberius.

"Who is this?" I yelled over the music.

"Rick Ross," Tiberius yelled back, then he got serious. "I like this." His breath brushed my face and neck, leaving chills in its wake.

"Like it a lot, Rex."

He smelled like beer and a good kind of man sweat, and his moves were outrageous. I'd never danced like this before. It felt totally illicit, nothing like when the girls and I back in high school used to tear it up in the middle of a house party. Tiberius and I were making love with our clothes on, and I couldn't help but wonder what it would feel like when we actually did it.

I was afraid to speak, so I just pressed myself closer, my pelvis seeking contact with Tiberius.

"Don't rush it," he whispered in my ear. "This. I plan to take my time with you, Tingly. In everything I do."

His words had me wound up, my pulse soaring, faster than earlier at the meet. Why did we have to go so slow?

The song ended, and we grudgingly broke apart when Jamel appeared.

Tiberius gave him a chin lift. "What's up, bro? You good?"

I grabbed my drink from the ledge and took a swig as Jamel said, "Looking hot, Tingly. You got moves."

Another song started, a mash-up of R&B and rap. Jamel came closer and started grinding on me. "You definitely got rhythm, girl," he said, inching closer. When I didn't respond, he put a hand on my shoulder and pulled me close.

"Mel, cut it out," Tiberius said, pushing him back.

"Passing all my tests, Rex," he said with a smirk. "Pushing off that Logan prick, keeping our fight quiet, loyal to my man Tiberius, here. I'm startin' to like you," he said with conviction before moving away to grind up behind some girl with long braids and bright green hot pants.

"Is he ever gonna give me a fair chance?" I leaned up and shouted to Tiberius over the music.

"Nah, he's got a chip on his shoulder big as the Grand Canyon. But he hides an even bigger heart behind all that attitude, so let him be." He cocked an eyebrow in question. "One more song and want to get outta here?"

"Sounds good," I said, and then Tiberius was back on me, moving our two bodies in sync.

When the song ended, he grabbed my hand and started walking toward the door, giving Trey two fingers pointed toward the door like an airline attendant.

"Tingly?" a girl's voice asked. "What you doing here?"

Turning to see one of my roommates, I said, "Hey, Chey. I came for a bit with Tiberius."

Tall and solid with skin nearly as dark as her ebony eyes, she ran her gaze slowly up and down Ty's body, taking her time ogling. "I see that," she said. "I'm Cheyenne, but everyone calls me Chey." Pinning Tiberius with a challenging stare, she flaunted what her mama gave her. Which was a lot of boobs and ass and curves tucked into a tight red V-necked shirt and painted-on jeans, the type of body with something to hold on to. The kind Tiberius was used to, I supposed.

"Tiberius," he said, but offered nothing more.

"Chey's one of my roommates," I explained as she flipped her long braids behind her neck, exposing multiple piercings along her earlobe and a small tattoo––a set of dice––underneath on her right ear.

"Cool, nice to meet you. Maybe I'll see you over at T's place, but we're just getting ready to roll." And just like that, Tiberius dragged me toward the door.

"Don't be a stranger," she called after us, her raspy voice carrying through the hall.

As soon as we hit the cool nighttime air, I felt high. On life maybe,

I wasn't sure what, but high. Free.

"Tiberius, that's my roommate. You have to be nice." I slapped him playfully on the shoulder.

"Believe me, she's not gonna be nice now to you, dating a brother." He play-smacked my butt.

I stopped, and not because of the smack. "Are we dating?"

We stood in the middle of a quiet residential street, night all around us, dew starting to form, and Tiberius focused his eyes directly on me. When I tried to look away, he said, "Huh-uh, don't look at the ground, look at me."

I lifted my face.

"We been dancing around this all semester, Rex," he said softly. "I come on to you, and you push me away. Then you go and do something sweet, and I fall for you all over again. Like I said, I want you. Gonna take it slow, but yeah, I wanna date you."

"You'll probably change your mind soon," I said with a frown.

My defenses were up. He knew about Dubois, but not everything else. Tiberius was lonely and I was a likely candidate—an outcast from last year, unattached. I fit the bill. Problem was, I liked him too much. He made me too happy. And he smiled too much.

So I did the stupidest thing ever and said, "Okay, we're dating."

Beaming, Tiberius grabbed me and swung me around, pulling me onto his back for a piggyback ride. "I'm starving. Wanna come back to my place?"

"Sure." I hoped he wasn't going to start with that slow stuff again, but it was kind of nice when I really thought about it.

chapter thirteen

A week later, I was circling by the greenhouse, past the agriculture department and picking up speed, my pacer watch beeping with each stride. It wanted me to slow, but I didn't. I'd finished practice and blown off study hour because I needed an extra-long run. It was Tuesday, and I would just catch an afternoon study session after Economics. My latest download, Rick Ross, blared through my earbuds, reminding me of last week and Tiberius. Unfortunately, he'd been true to his word and was taking everything slow. A snail's pace, if you asked me.

We'd hung out over the past week and kissed and held hands, but nothing more. Each night he walked me back to my place at two or three a.m., then planted gentle kisses all over my neck and mouth, getting close enough for me to feel his growing erection, and then he stopped. And said good-bye.

The guys gave him shit. "You walking your lady home, Ty? You not old enough to have sleepovers?" Grinning like idiots, they'd taunt him as they sat around gaming and drinking until all hours of the night.

Tiberius would fling back, "Coming from ya'll, sittin' there playing video games like a buncha schoolboys."

They'd all laugh and start punching one another, eventually rolling onto the ground in a full-on brawl. And then they would get back up and play their games again.

I stretched my legs, lengthening my stride, breathing in and out of my nose as I pushed myself past the fields and downhill toward main campus. My quads were screaming but I punished them further, attempting to burn off all the nerves and sexual tension stored up in my body.

Slowing a tiny bit, I pulled an electrolyte gel out of my pocket. I planned to run the loop all over again. I couldn't speed up anything with Tiberius, but I certainly could speed up my running pace.

The guys had their first pre-season game coming up at seven o'clock. I knew Tiberius was nervous and excited, but he didn't ask me to come.

Of course, Chey made a point of letting me know she was going. I was on her shit list—permanently—which was weird. The damn girl hadn't paid me one lick of attention until now.

"Were you out with Tiberius?" she'd ask when I came home. "Were the other guys there?" It was like the Spanish Inquisition every time I walked back into the apartment.

Right now, it didn't matter because I needed to figure out if I was going to the game or not. Tiberius came to the track meet without an invite, so why couldn't I go to his first pre-season game? They were only playing another Ohio school, but still. He could have asked me to come.

Another rap song came on as I worked my way back up toward

vérité

the far end of campus. For a few minutes, my mind went blank, pulsing to the music, freed in the air, and laboring over keeping my feet going in a straight line. I was concentrating on inhaling and exhaling when I sensed someone come up next to me. I turned to the left and popped out a single earbud.

"What's up, Rex?" Lamar said, running next to me. He was wearing a pair of mesh shorts and Nike running shoes, but no shirt. Sweat beaded all over his arms and back, and it was clear he'd been at it a while. His braids were pulled back, waving from side to side as he pumped his arms, his large feet loudly slapping the pavement.

I lifted the neck of my white tank and wiped the sweat from my lip before answering. "Hey, Mar. You getting in shape?" I teased him.

"Just trying to stay trim and fast, girl." He flashed me a smile. It wasn't a flirtatious smile, simply friendly.

"You jamming to some Rick Ross?" he asked, gesturing to the scratchy, tinny sound making its way out of my lone earbud.

"Yep," I said as if I'd been caught with my fly down. I felt very exposed, and it had nothing to do with my short running shorts and skimpy tank.

"Woulda thought you'd be more of an alternative rock or teeny-bop kinda girl," he said pointedly, standing on my Achilles heel.

"A girl can like rap, can't she?"

"'Specially one of our girls."

I picked up my speed, pumping my arms. "What is it with all you boys and your tests? Christ, every day, Mel is putting me through the ringer. And now you?"

He kept pace. "Sorry, Rex. We just look out for our own. We know little Ty is a softie, and we wanna make sure you ain't just taking him for a test ride."

"Be quiet, Mar. We've been through this," I huffed out. "Did you want anything else?"

"Yeah, you coming tonight?"

"Don't know. Doesn't seem like your softie wants me to go."

"He's not gonna ask you to come, but you should."

"Why?"

"He's a great player, but he's never played at this level. Played high school and prep, but this is the big leagues. Kid's nervous, and he doesn't want to be more nervous 'bout you saying no if he asks. So just roll on over to the field house tonight. Tip's at seven." Without another word, he veered off toward the townhouses, not allowing me to say anything in return.

Watching his muscular back run away from me, I decided to slow my pace and my thoughts. As I walked the rest of the way home, my muscles cooled. Sadly, my confusion didn't.

"And now starting for Hafton, a junior guard, a marketing major, standing at six feet four, number thirteen, Trey Dawson." The loudspeaker blared through the field house, the seats practically rocking with the band and the announcer.

Ginny and I sat in the upper level, looking down at the student section and the VIP boxes for boosters. I'd suggested we might get a better view from up there, but the truth was I didn't want to be spotted. I was still in denial that I was even at the game. Not sure I would fess up to going, I kicked my feet up on the ledge and looked down toward the shiny wooden court.

The two teams took their spots for the tip, Jamel in the center, Trey and Lamar on opposite wings, an impressively tall white guy resembling the Jolly Green Giant behind Jamel, and another guy I never met before down the court.

"You know all of them?" Ginny asked, interrupting my thoughts.

"No, just the guy in the center and number thirteen, Trey, and twenty-one in the braids, Lamar."

When the ref tossed the ball up in the air, Mel lunged for it, tipping it to the white dude, who passed it to Trey, and up the court they went. They were incredibly fast, and with each pass of the ball, their muscles rippled and bulged. Hard to believe how much they ate when you watched the sheer speed of their performance.

Lamar popped one in the basket for three, and then they were back down the court to play defense against the other team wearing red and white. Before the red guys even passed center court, Trey stole the ball and was back down the court for another quick two points. He was fouled on the shot, so he lined up to shoot for the extra point while Lamar stepped back to get instructions from the coach.

"They're kinda hot," Ginny said with a grin. "Even if I don't really know the game, and well, you know I like Bryce, so don't say anything to him, but these guys got it going on."

"You're like a Catholic schoolgirl on spring break," I said to her.

Her eyes bright with happiness, she giggled, making her ponytail bounce.

"One second," I went on, "you're all soccer and books and sitting in your room. The next, you're an admirer of hot men."

This time we both laughed.

"It's kind of nice to not always be so serious," she admitted, chewing on her fingernail.

"You be whoever you want to be, Gin. I like you either way, but I'm kinda glad you're trying stuff out and getting out there. You're not messing up soccer, are you?"

"No, season's ending, and I looked good all season. No worries there."

"Then we're all good. Now, where were we? Hot guys playing basketball."

"Right," she confirmed.

I looked toward the court. We were back on defense. The opposing team got one in for two, and then our team dropped back to try to score.

Smiling, I looked at my feet on the railing; even I was getting into the spirit with a pair of navy Chucks. After all, they were the original basketball shoes.

My smile died as my shoulder blades tingled; I felt eyes on me, hot and glaring. I looked around the field house to find the entire girls' basketball team looking distinctly unhappy with me. *Shit.*

"Just ignore them." Ginny had followed my gaze and patted my arm, encouraging me to stay calm. "They'll get over it."

What the hell did she know? Did she read that in one of her books?

A whistle sounded, bringing my attention back to the game. It was a time out, and the Hafton coach was subbing some players. Tiberius ripped off his warm-up jersey and got ready to go in, but not without taking a long look at the balcony and winking at me.

Well, I guess I've been spotted.

Ginny nudged my elbow. "He's super cute."

"Shh, here he goes," I said, quieting her.

Tiberius was bringing the ball up with Lamar filling the lane, and then he tossed it up to Jamel. *Pow,* he slammed it into the basket. I stood up, cheering and clapping.

"That's called an alley-oop, if you didn't know, girl," someone said from behind me.

I turned to find Chey and Stacy directly behind me. Their shiny black braids were pulled back, and each wore a Hafton headband and a big grin on their faces. They looked like they belonged here in warm-up pants and Nike T-shirts. I glanced down at my ivory wide-necked T-shirt and skinny jeans, and felt inadequate.

Smiling at them, I said, "Well, thanks. I didn't know, but it was awesome!"

I sat back in my seat and continued to watch the game. Tiberius looked so handsome in his uniform; the jersey did his massive arms justice, and his smile radiated as he played.

"You gotta know the game if you're gonna drool all over a baller," Stacy pointed out, disrupting my drooling. She leaned forward in her seat, her lighter skin, well-chiseled body, and flat chest the complete opposite of Chey. She was the picture of confidence, practically oozing athleticism and endurance from her very pores.

I swallowed back any inadequacies and turned slightly in my seat, one eye on the game and one on my roommates. "Are you being nice or mean? I don't quite know what you want from me."

"Nice," Chey said.

"Yeah," Stacy chimed in. "We figure, if we want to get in good with the other boys, we better play nice with Ty's toy."

I turned back around, ignoring them. Why was everyone referring to me as a toy?

Ginny glared back at them, coming to my defense. "She's not a toy, ladies."

"Okay, okay, girls," Stacy said with an exaggerated eye roll. "Don't get your butt-floss panties in a twist. Ty's lady . . . is that better?"

"Oh shit! Look at that," Chey blurted.

Tiberius had run all the way down the court, dribbling the ball, and pulled up for a dunk.

"Holy shit," I whispered under my breath.

"Right on, girl. That boy can play, and he looks damn fine too," Chey said as she high-fived me. "But you gotta do something about those shoes. Chucks are for white chicks."

"Isn't that what I am?" I whispered to Ginny.

"Stop, just go with it," she said, jabbing me in the side.

The players rotated in and out of the game, and Hafton pulled off a big victory. When the game was over and the two teams shook hands and had headed for the locker room, Chey spoke up again. "You gonna go meet your man outside the locker room? 'Cause we're coming with."

"Uh, I don't know. I'm not sure if I should."

"Girl, your boy just had a damn fine game and a dunk," Chey said with a frown. "You're going to see him after the game."

"Are you sure we can?"

Stacy just grabbed my arm and said, "Come on, chickie."

"I'm heading back over to the dorms," Ginny said as she stood up. "I'm gonna go hang with Bryce."

"You sure?" I asked. I was more worried for my own safety than hers.

"Be nice, girls," she said to Chey and Stacy, then she turned to me. "Have fun, babe."

Next thing I knew I was standing outside the boys' locker room. The hallway was closed to the media during pre-season, so it was quiet enough that we could hear almost every word of the chanting and swearing coming from inside through the heavy wooden door.

"Yeah, boy, we showed their skinny asses the door."

"We gonna party tonight, brother."

"Did you see Rexie girl in the stands? Someone is gonna get laid tonight. Oh yeah, boy."

"You ready for that, Tiberius? You know the ladies love a dunk."

"Shit, that dunk was sweeeet. Boo-yah."

My cheeks burned. God, I'd never blushed so easily, but the dunk did make me kind of hot.

Stacy was obviously not affected by the locker-room talk. "See, girl, I told ya . . . you gotta get down here to see your man." She stood there, her hip cocked to the side, staring down at me from a few inches above.

Feeling out of my league, I walked over to the opposite wall and slid down it to sit on the floor. After stretching my legs out with my white-girl shoes in front of me, I leaned my head back against the brick and closed my eyes.

What am I doing?

Just then a few players started filing out of the locker room. I heard Jamel before I saw him; I couldn't look up.

"Bro, time for you to show her what fucking a brother is all about."

"Leave it, Mel," Tiberius said sharply. "Enough." He stuttered on the last word, presumably because it was when he saw me.

"Aw, fuck. Sorry, man," Jamel said to Tiberius, but he couldn't say anything more because Chey decided to interject.

"You want to show me what fucking a real brother is like?"

I rolled my eyes, even though my face was still planted in my hands. A quick peek revealed Chey gyrating her pelvis.

"Come on, Chey, let's go. Leave the poor boy be," I heard Stacy stutter, her usual self-assured conviction nowhere in sight, and I wondered what that was all about.

Then I heard someone sliding down the wall next to me, and I peered through my hands to see Tiberius's legs stretched out next to mine.

"Tingly, look at me."

I shook my head.

"Thanks for coming," he said, and placed his hand on my leg.

I spread apart two of my fingers and caught a view of his fingers splayed on my jeans. He was still hot to the touch, or maybe that was just what happened when he touched me.

"It was a good game." I spoke through my hands, my words muffled.

"Can you look at me?" he asked, moving his hand up and down my thigh.

When I looked up, my eyes were all wet, and I mentally scolded them.

"That wasn't me, Rex. You know that. That's the guys being dicks." He turned to face me, shifting his weight onto his side, running his other hand down my arm.

I nodded. "I know it's not you, but I just feel like they're all laughing because they know we haven't done anything, and it's like they have to force you to fuck me."

Tiberius flinched as if he'd been punched, then he leaned in real close. "First off, there's not gonna be any fucking when I'm finally with you. Second, I told you I'm taking it slow, savoring you. Told you that way back in the elevator. This means something, Tingly. Stop thinking about yourself like a quick fuck. It makes me sick to my stomach."

No matter how much I willed it not to happen, a tear dropped into my lap. Tiberius brought his hand to my face and swiped away a few more droplets with his thumb.

"I'm not sure you want me," I admitted, not meeting his eyes. "Maybe I'm just some phase."

verité

By this time, the hall had mostly emptied, and Tiberius grabbed my hand and pulled it to his chest. "Feel that? My heart is beating a mile a minute for you. With each beat, I want you more." Then he moved my hand to his crotch. "Feel that? That's for you." His dick was as hard as a rock, the lightweight fabric of his sweats doing little to contain it.

Then he dropped my hand. "Fuck, Tingly! You're making me act like one of them. That's not me. I don't want to have to shove my cock in your hand so you know I want you. My actions should speak for themselves. And since the day I met you, you been throwing all your little traps and bullshit in my face, all your little conquests. I'm not gonna be another one, or make you feel like you need a conquest to be worthy." He blew out a long breath. "That's the fucking truth. I want you. All of you."

"*Vérité* . . . that's the first time anyone has ever given me that," I half mumbled, half whispered to myself.

"What?"

"The truth. You're the first person to give me the truth." I looked into his eyes, sailing away in the blue, riding the waves of his emotion as I tried desperately to hold on to my life jacket—or my resolve.

"Then cherish it, and don't throw it back in my face."

"I'm trying."

"Now, did you come here to fight? Or to celebrate my first game? I got in more than I expected, but I guess it was only a pre-season game." He pulled himself to his feet, then reached out a hand to help me up.

"It was awesome--you getting in--and super cool to see, but I don't know a lot. I have to figure out all the rules," I said, a smile taking over my face. "And these shoes. Apparently, they're all wrong."

This set Tiberius off in a ripple of loud laughs. His whole body was rocking as a happy tear or two escaped his beautiful eyes. "Yeah, we're gonna have to do something about your shoes."

chapter
fourteen

Tiberius and I went out for something to eat, opting for one of the campus restaurants where we could pay with our dining cards. It was a café-type place with a salad bar and a menu full of greasy food. Reggae music was being piped in through the speakers as we grabbed a table by the window. Students whirred by the glass, texting and listening to music on their iPods, on their way to class . . . or the bars. The place smelled like fries, and I couldn't help but be reminded of eating fried food at the diner, and what a disaster that was.

Tiberius stuffed himself while I ate salad and chicken. Taking a break, we didn't tackle any more discussion of us. Or if there was an *us*.

"When I was back home, I realized how much I missed the food," he said while chowing on his burger and fries. "The type of shit I hadn't eaten in a long time. Cheap Chinese takeout and New York bagels. And fucking barbeque. Can't get that here."

"Well, you can't get all this heavy cream and whole-milk crap they serve here in LA. Out there everything is skinny, sugar-free, no calories, no-taste cardboard." I sipped on my diet soda. I'd pay for it tomorrow; the bubbles would come gurgling up my throat as my feet pounded the pavement, but I loved soda. It was an indulgence I didn't allow myself often.

"You're making friends with your roommates, I see." Tiberius raised an eyebrow and lifted his lips into a smirk.

I shrugged. "They're kinda wild, those girls. And hot for all you guy players. Pretty sure they've decided to keep their enemies closer than really be my friend," I confessed, finding it easy to share my true feelings with Tiberius.

"Well, I like runner chicks, so no worries there." He grinned again, this time over his big glass of water.

"Oh yeah? I'm also pretty sure Jamel would have your hide for saying that. He seems to have different ideas about who you should like." I stared at my finger as I traced circles around the rim of my glass.

"Good thing I don't give a shit 'bout what Mel thinks." Tiberius lifted my chin with his index finger, and our eyes met. "We've been through this. He's testing you."

"I know. Now my roommates are testing me too. I don't know basketball, and I don't wear the right shoes. Will anyone ever think I'm good enough for you?" I lowered my gaze again.

"What about your parents? Will they think I'm good enough for you? 'Cause if we're really gonna get down to it, let's get the black-white thing out there." His expression hardened, his eyes full of fury and pride.

I didn't answer. I couldn't.

"You see, I'm right. Jamel isn't really our worry; your parents are. I doubt they're gonna be down with a boy from the hood, Tingly. Let alone a black one."

I rubbed up and down my arms, feeling chilled straight to the bone, despite the fact that the café was warm with barely any air flowing from the ducts. This was more fear than anything else, because Tiberius was right. He'd hit home without even knowing.

My parents barely accepted who I was. Their last hope in life was I would find some Republican hotshot here in Ohio and come back to the uppity fold they raised me in. Well, I couldn't do that, whether I'd met Tiberius or not.

"Listen, you're probably right, but my parents aren't really part of my life. I know that probably sounds like shit to you, who just lost your mother, but it's the truth. I never fit their mold, so what I do isn't their business. Maybe I don't fit yours either because of that."

"Don't make a statement like that without really thinking about what you mean. Honestly, T, when I first saw you, I wanted to just have a friend in study hall. This isn't what I imagined," he confessed, leaning forward to rest his elbows on the table as he stared me down. "I couldn't imagine anything else now, and no one's gonna get in my way. Definitely not Jamel, the girls' team, or your own crazy thinking. You hear me?"

"Uh-huh," was all I could manage to get out. I wasn't strong enough to address this with him, so I left it at that.

Fear coiled in my belly. I didn't start this year off looking for a relationship; I'd just mended my broken heart. Could it withstand more hurt? Because no matter what Ty said, Jamel wasn't in favor of us and neither were the girls I lived with. Not to mention that Tiberius was a young, handsome guy—what the fuck did he want with me? I was damaged goods.

"Don't think too hard, T. We'll make it work. I'm sorry I said that about your parents. It was defensive and wrong, but I don't want it to ruin tonight. You coming to my game and shit, that was the fucking best."

"Okay." Another one-word answer from me. My mind was racing, crazy thoughts lapping my brain. "You sure? You know I don't want to come between you and the team."

"Yeah, let's roll." He stood and reached for my hand. "So, you liked the game?" he asked as we left the restaurant.

"Oh, definitely. You guys looked good out there, especially you." And it was true—I felt some weird pride in my heart for Tiberius. "What's that alley-oop thing?" I asked, which definitely broke the tension because he broke out into more fits of laughter. He was so tall that when he bent over with a belly laugh, I swore the ground shook.

"That's when one of the guys passes a quick high ball, and the dude who catches it high up in the air puts it up for a dunk," he answered, still smiling.

"What? What's so funny?" We were back across College Avenue now, heading back toward campus, and I stopped and turned to him.

"It's just cute, that's all. I'm glad you saw me do that. It's one of my moves, the kind of pass I was known for at prep." He threw his arm around me and started us walking again.

"Well, it's cool. Must take a lot of strength to get up there . . . for any of you" I said, somewhat teasing.

I poked him in the side, and he laughed once more. He was the sweetest, most loving guy I'd ever met, which was so strange since he was wrapped in this daunting body of strength and steel.

"What you doing now?" he asked, interrupting my thoughts.

"I don't know. I guess some studying. You?"

"Yep. Studying. Wanna grab your shit and study at my place?"

"Yeah. Yeah, I do." I didn't even need to think about it. I just did.

Trey was out. "He's got a lady friend over in Cleveland. Goes to see her a lot," Ty explained. "She came to the game, and then he took her back. He'll be back in the morning."

"Oh, I didn't see her. Is she nice?" I asked as I plopped down on one of the stools at the bar, the same one where Tiberius told me about his mother. I hoisted my backpack up to the counter and pulled out my laptop.

"She is. Her name's Cherise, but everyone calls her Cherry. Maybe you'll come to another game and meet her. She's pretty cool. Keeps Trey in line––mostly."

I couldn't help but notice whenever Tiberius got emotional over something—like my parents or Cherry—he slipped into Jersey speech. He wasn't the well-educated prep-school boy when he cared about someone or something.

"I'd like that. To come to another game."

He sat down next to me on another stool and brought his hand to my cheek, drawing me closer. "Next time you come to one of my games, tell me first so I know my girl's there." It was an order not to be messed with, not up for discussion.

Not that I had time to answer because he leaned in and kissed me. His lips captured mine, gentle at first, seeking my permission to take what he wanted. He slipped his hand under my hair and pulled me closer by the nape of my neck. My skin warmed as hot streaks of need radiated where his hand burned into my skin, and my heart galloped in my chest. There was barely enough space in my rib cage for its increased pounding.

Tiberius moaned and I parted my lips, giving him access. His tongue explored my mouth, stroking mine. I'd been gripping the side of the stool, trying to find purchase, but I let go and wrapped my hands around his neck. I drew him closer, deepening our need for each other.

He let out another long moan before breaking the kiss, still keeping a firm grip on my neck. Steadying me, he touched his forehead to mine. "You feel that? It means something."

I nodded. I felt it, but I didn't want to stop. My mouth sought his, looking for more.

"Shh," he said, quieting my actions more than my nonexistent words. "That means something. Everything else we do means something. I'm not gonna treat you like the teacher, like you don't mean shit-all to me, Rex."

"Oh."

I broke free from his grasp and saw him—really saw him for the first time. I'd had these little glimpses of Tiberius and what made him tick, but right now in this moment, it all clicked. I knew he was a gentle giant, sweet like a teddy bear when he wanted to be, but it went further.

Tiberius was the most dedicated, devoted person I knew, and I wasn't sure I deserved that. But damn if anyone was going to stop me from trying.

chapter fifteen

Tiberius walked me home after his game, our dinner, and studying, leaving me at the door with gentle kisses and big promises.

When I crawled into bed, I tried telling myself that promises were good. They were something I'd never had or believed in growing up, but had heard they existed. *Just not for me.* No matter how much I tried to convince myself that I deserved promises, I still wanted actions—because actions implied more in my emotionally barren mind.

I still was trying to understand what Tiberius meant about it meaning something when we were together. I tossed and turned in my bed, trying to reconcile how I foolishly thought it meant something with Pierre. In reality, I was nothing more than an easy piece of ass for him, and he viewed himself as a quick A+ for me.

Puttanesca. Perrier. Thriller by Michael Jackson. Tuxedos.

At first I was hot and then cold, kicking the covers off and pulling them back on, my mind playing games until dawn. As the sun slowly broke the horizon, I was finally dozing when my alarm blared through the room, signaling it was time for practice.

I could barely keep my eyes open by the end of the day when Tiberius showed up at my table in the Union holding a large coffee.

"Hey, are you a mind reader?" I asked him as he waved the steaming disposable cup in front of my nose, startling me. I inhaled deeply, breathing in every last molecule of java goodness.

"Yeah, that's me. Basketball player, mind reader," he answered with a cute smile, his dimples coming out to play. He stood over me wearing low-hanging jeans and a Nike dry-fit T-shirt that clung in all the right places.

"Seriously, how did you know I needed this?"

"See that booth over there?" He tilted his head toward the far side of the Union where green herringbone banquettes lined the wall.

"Uh-huh," I answered.

"I've been sitting there for the last thirty minutes watching you yawn," he said as he slid into the booth next to me. "Thinking about how good you look." His voice was deep and gravelly, his fresh-from-the-shower smell wafting under my nose.

"Stop," I protested, but not really meaning it.

"Why you so tired?" he asked, leaning close, whispering his question, his breath like hot lava on my skin.

I shrugged, not wanting to fess up.

He winked. "I didn't sleep so well last night either."

"Not my fault." I was pulling out all the punches, flirting on all cylinders despite my tank being on empty.

"I know, self-inflicted but worth it." He shrugged. "Go ahead, enjoy your liquid love," he said, nodding toward the cup.

I took a big sip, moaning as the hot liquid slid down my throat, warming my belly and immediately jolting my brain awake. A tiny bit dribbled down my chin, and Tiberius raised his thumb and swiped it off.

"Liquid love, you could say that again," I announced before taking another big swig. "So, what are you up to other than stalking me?" I set my coffee down in front of me, wrapping my hands around the slender cup.

"I'm done with class and was studying, but one of the guys is having a gig down in the townhouses, so I gotta go. Was hoping to find you, bring you with me." He stretched out, his legs spanning the whole width of the table, his athletic shoes sticking out the other end.

"Oh, I don't know. You sure?"

I didn't know where the hesitation was coming from. In an instant, my flirtatious self was gone, leaving a timid schoolgirl in her place. I didn't want to be just an obligation, but wanted to matter. Not to just anyone, but to him.

"I wouldn't have asked if I wasn't, Rex. Come on, let's roll," he said, standing up and grabbing my coffee.

"Don't take that! I want to finish it," I yelped.

He laughed, flashing his dimples at me. "I'm just fooling with ya."

"Good!" I declared, stomping my foot to make my point.

He nodded his head toward the door, and out we went.

We stopped by my place, where I changed into skinny jeans and a tight pale-pink tank top. After throwing on a worn leather jacket over the tank and yanking on my black motorcycle boots, I was good to go.

Our walk to the townhouses was brisk; the air was chilly now that

November had arrived. Soon there would be snow, and my workouts would be moved indoors to the gymnasium building where I would circle the track over and over again. Like my life, where I kept circling back to a dead end, a place where there were no answers or solutions, and definitely no future.

On the track, you never really went anywhere, and neither did I. My existence was one big gerbil wheel, and I wasn't sure that was enough anymore.

When we neared the townhouses, we could hear music blaring a few doors away from Ty's place. It was so loud, I was surprised the whole house wasn't shaking. As we approached, Tiberius whispered, "Stick with me, don't wander all around."

"Why?" I asked.

"Want everyone to know you're my girl."

I slapped his bicep in response, but probably hurt my palm more than him.

The place was packed wall to wall with athletes. Everywhere I looked, there were tall, broad well-muscled guys and fit, gorgeous girls. It may as well have been a *Sports Illustrated Special Edition* party. The kitchen was converted to a full-serve bar, and someone offered us a huge joint as we walked into the common room.

"Nah, thanks, man," Tiberius answered. "You want?" he asked me, raising an eyebrow.

I shook my head. I'd never gotten into smoking anything, especially with my need for lung power in running. It was sweet the way Tiberius asked me, though.

"Whattaya want to drink?" he asked me.

"Actually just water, if they have it," I yelled over the crowd.

"Okay, wait here."

I was positioned near the corner, relaxing as the tunes seeped deep into my veins. Rocking from side to side, I checked out the scene in front of me. Although everyone was loud and rowdy, they all seemed so happy. I'd never witnessed anything like it before, and sadness washed over me. Where was all the happiness in my life?

Before I could sink completely into a melancholy funk, Jamel and Lamar came crashing through the room, Lamar holding something high above his head.

"Mar! Give it," Jamel shouted.

"Dude, you're not getting this back," Lamar yelled back.

I tried to focus on what he was holding. "Oh my God," I whispered to myself, then ducked my head and covered my eyes.

"Hey." Tiberius had made his way over to me holding a bottle of beer and a bottle of water, completely oblivious to the ruckus in the middle of the room.

"Is that what I think it is?" I asked, my face still planted in my hands. I peered through one eye, spreading my fingers just a sliver so I could see him when he turned toward his teammates.

"Yeah, it is."

He handed me my water, and I brought the cool bottle to my cheek in an effort to cool my blush as I grunted in disgust.

Tiberius slanted an amused glance at me. "You girls don't run around with each other's bras?"

"Uh, no. And that's not a bra," I said with a shudder. "That's a jock strap."

"I prefer cock sling."

I couldn't help but burst out laughing. "You wear one of those?"

"Nah, not usually. I go with the compression shorts, but Mel is real protective of that area. Overly protective." He took a sip of his beer, then wrapped his arm around my back and pulled me close. The music had changed to something less pulsing, more rhythm and blues. "Enough about Jamel's junk."

He moved us as one to the beat, his leg coming in between mine, but this time it was so much more seductive. My arms stretched high to wind around his neck. With Tiberius singing softly in my ear, we danced like that for another three songs, the world falling away in one fell swoop.

"You ready to go?" The eyes he pinned on me were anything but innocent, his dimple nowhere in sight.

Taking in his change of mood, I nodded and said, "Yes," but it came out hoarse with lust.

He took my hand and guided me through the crowd toward the door.

Jamel and Lamar had settled down and were drinking in the kitchen. "Ya'll leaving?" they hollered after us. "'Bye, T-Rex."

My cheeks burned with the blush that crept back onto my cheeks. *God, these guys.*

I didn't ask if Ty was walking me home. Not wanting the night to end, barely tired anymore—unsure if it was the coffee or just being in his arms—I wanted to freeze-frame the moment. When he started walking on the path toward his townhouse, I didn't say a word, just followed. He had his arm thrown over my shoulders, and I felt like a peanut next to him.

It was a shame I didn't believe in superheroes; Tiberius could have been my own personal Superman.

"You okay with this?" Tiberius asked as we stopped in front of his place.

I nodded.

"Say it, Rex."

"Yes."

When we walked inside, I stopped in the foyer and asked,

"Where's Trey? I didn't see him at the party."

"He went back to Cleveland. Keep it on the down low. Coach'd be pissed."

We stood in the hallway, staring into each other's eyes, both of us afraid to make a move. Tiberius lifted one large hand and ran it down the side of my face, reaching back to release my ponytail and allowing my hair to fall in blond waves around my face.

Taking his time, he swept the errant pieces behind my ears before he bent low to kiss me. This time his kiss wasn't gentle. His mouth was urgent and bruising on mine, as if he'd been lost in the desert and I was his first taste of water in a long while.

He walked us back toward the wall, caging me in, never letting go of my lips. His tongue swept through my mouth as his hand traveled down my side, finding purchase on my hip. My hands wound their way around his neck as I stood on tiptoe before he picked me up and carried me into his room, still not breaking the kiss.

Once inside his bedroom, he broke away. "This okay?"

I nodded and then added a breathless, "Yes."

Turning, I walked toward the bed and crawled onto the mattress, eventually kneeling on the edge. Tiberius stood in front of me, my face finally even with his broad chest.

"Beautiful," he mumbled as he slipped off my leather jacket and slid the straps of my tank top off. Once my neck and shoulders were bare, he leaned forward and placed kisses all along them, then teased the top of my breasts with his warm breath and smooth tongue.

My senses came alive. Woodsy deodorant and musky male scent swirled in the air around me. Everything was much more vibrant— his navy shirt looked like the midnight sky, and the pale pink of my tank shimmered in the moonlight streaming through the window. My fingers tingled to touch and my skin hummed with need. My belly roared with want and hunger, but not for food.

I brought my hands to the hem of his shirt, interrupting Tiberius's trailing kisses long enough for me to fling it over his head. He followed suit and pulled my tank off, unhooking my bra to release my breasts. Finally, we were skin-to-skin, his heart beating against mine.

"Like ya, Rex," he whispered, and I smiled against his lips. "Told you it's gotta mean something."

I smiled again, this time nodding my head.

Tiberius stopped kissing me and lifted my chin, bringing us eye to eye as our hearts beat in sync.

"I like you too, Ty, but I don't get why me?"

"'Cause you're not into me for my jump shot or my jersey. 'Cause you got the best smile when you let it come out. 'Cause you're kick-ass fast in your running shoes. 'Cause you're tough and sweet, but don't even know it," he mumbled all along my cheek before he started kissing me earnestly again.

We went toppling onto the bed, his body tumbling over mine. He caught his weight on one forearm and brought his other hand to cup my cheek. Intrigued, I raised my head and licked along his flat nipple, tracing his tattoo with my tongue.

"I'm not sure that's what my school had in mind for their crest," he said with a smirk, but I didn't stop, just continued my exploration, my tongue finding a narrow ridge along his abs. I followed it down south until Tiberius yanked me back up.

"Huh-uh, Rex. You're not taking over."

I wiggled up and around until I could see his expression. The confident alpha of moments before was gone. Apparently, I'd embarrassed him.

"I'm not taking over, Ty. I just wanted to touch . . . explore you."

"Well, you don't get to bring the whole *I seduced a teacher* thing into the bedroom with me," he said, tiny specks of coal flashing through his blue eyes.

"Okay."

I wanted to reach up and press my mouth against his, but I waited for him to cave and lean in. He took my lips in a gentle kiss, and we started over. Momentum built quickly between us, and Tiberius ran his hand along my side. His palm came to cover my breast, his thumb drawing circles around my nipple. I reached around his back and smoothed my hands over the hard planes, taut with tension.

The tiny cracks in his fingers—I assumed from dribbling the ball—felt so good coursing along my sensitive skin. I moaned into his mouth, and rather than swallowing my tiny sounds, he let go of my lips and let my purring fill the air.

This time, he was the one to begin traveling south, and I let him have that move. First, he took my nipple with his mouth and sucked hard while he brought his hand up to my other one. The contradiction of his soft and smooth mouth on one breast and his rough hand on the other was driving me to the edge—fast.

"Tiberius," I whispered.

"S'okay?" he mumbled along my cleavage.

"Yeah, feels good," I said, my fingertips drawing figure eights on his back. I wanted more, but I didn't push. The hard truth was there was something to be said for how Tiberius was taking his time; I was just too impatient to admit it.

With my mounting excitement, I lost track of how long he adored my breasts, but I brought myself back to the moment, telling myself to savor whatever this was—this being what Tiberius was doing to me. My senses were already strung out when I felt him unbutton my jeans and slip them down, urging me to lift my hips so he could maneuver them the rest of the way. Kicking my boots off, my pants were gone in one fell swoop. Then, Tiberius let his tongue dip and linger along my belly button before hitting my core.

"Ah," I let out, revealing too much pleasure, yet not saying enough.

"This okay?" Tiberius asked again.

It was obvious he was afraid to push me beyond my limits. I wasn't sure if that was because of his lack of experience or something else, maybe his general nurturing nature, but I didn't have time to ponder it as he flicked his tongue along my clit. When he slowed to a teasing pace, taunting my tiny bud, causing my back to arch off the bed, it was clear he was not lacking any knowledge in knowing what to do down below—with his tongue.

"I'm gonna come. I'm gonna come," I choked out. Not knowing what he expected or wanted, I now knew without a doubt that he needed to be in charge. Wondering if I should just let go, I desperately reeled in the flood that was ready and waiting to course through my veins.

When he said, "Let go, Rex," I did on a scream. His name came tumbling off my lips into the dark night, echoing in my head, or maybe I just kept repeating it. I was so loud, they may have even heard me all the way at the party.

Tiberius made his way back up my body, planting kisses along my torso, blowing on my already distended nipples, and nuzzling my neck. I could smell myself on him, and I hoped he didn't mind.

"Wow," I breathed out, then snaked my hand down to his waistband and ducked in, grabbing his dick before he could protest. I wrapped my hand around his girth—not able to fit it all the way around—and started teasing and pumping.

"Tingly, stop, babe."

I froze. "Why?"

"'Cause you don't have to, that's why. Tonight was about you, about me taking care of you," he said before he took my hand and drew it up around his neck. Then he planted a huge kiss on me and swung me over to his side, settling my head on his chest as he asked, "Want to sleep here?"

All I did was nod before drifting off to sleep in Ty's long wingspan, my head moving with the rise and fall of his chest as the aftereffects of the most insane orgasm soothed me like a lullaby.

The next morning I woke up plastered to Tiberius's side, my arm thrown over his thick waist, my hair a rat's nest on top of my head, and my muscles more sore than after running for days.

I didn't feel like moving or fleeing. A blanket of contentment washed over my tired limbs as I took in his steady breathing, the rise and fall of his broad chest. In front of me was a dream come true, a fairy tale worthy of being in the movies, encapsulated in a weapon. His muscles were like steel, his arms coursing with veins from shooting day after day, his calves bulging from lifting high on his legs. But as I lightly ran my fingers over the smooth skin on his arm, I knew this to be only the outer packaging. Wasn't that what I'd been seeking my whole life? For someone to see me as more than a blond, blemish-free California socialite?

"Hey." Tiberius rolled over in bed, pulling me into his arms as he kissed my forehead, then moved down to my mouth.

I batted at him, protesting, "Ugh, my breath."

He paid no mind to my warning and began kissing me. He kept it closed-mouthed, our lips fusing for the briefest of moments before he pulled back and mumbled, "Morning."

"Hi." I nuzzled my head under his chin and placed a kiss on his collarbone, running my tongue along the plane from one side to the other.

"Feels good."

I looked up and pouted.

"What's wrong?" A look of panic swept over his typically relaxed features.

"I gotta go. I need to be in the weight room today. Worst day ever."

He pulled me in tighter, squishing me against him, and ran his lips along my brow. "You gotta work at being strong, T, just like everyone else."

I was smart enough to get the double meaning to what he was saying, but I didn't have the strength to get into it with him. "Yeah, yeah, I know," was all I gave back.

He gave me a quick pinch to the butt and I jumped up from the bed, squealing. I never thought I would ever squeal, and here I was doing it with a guy—in bed.

"Come on, I'll walk you to the weight room after you stop and get changed," Tiberius said matter-of-factly, leaving me no room for argument.

So I got out of bed and wrapped in the blanket to use the bathroom, and then tossed on last night's clothes to make the walk of shame.

But for the first time ever, I didn't really feel ashamed at all.

chapter sixteen

"Tingly? Tingleee? Where are you?" I heard Ginny frantically shouting throughout the apartment over the loud spray of the shower.

After turning off the water and tossing a towel around myself, I stuck my head out of the bathroom door and yelled, "What?"

It was Thursday and I had to get to my dreaded economics class. I was already going to be late as it was after taking an extra-long run, which was much needed to soothe the pulsing ache for more with Tiberius. We'd spent every night together since Monday, yet we were still moving at a snail's pace.

"Oh, sorry. I didn't know you were in the shower," she said from right outside the bathroom door.

I peeked through the crack of the door, my hair dripping all over the floor as Ginny bounced from one foot to the other. Mentally, I sighed; I didn't have time for any more drama. Then again, when did Ginny become so dramatic?

"What's wrong?" I flung the door all the way open, not caring if I was covered or not as steam flooded the hallway.

"Well, Bryce was over at the athletic complex lifting and Logan Salomon was there, going off at the mouth about how you wanted him but he turned you down. He was going on and on about not wanting Professor Dubois's sloppy seconds."

"You're kidding!"

"No. And it gets worse. A few of the basketball boys were there—"

"Shit!" I yelled, interrupting her.

"Well, it turned into a full-on brawl. Campus security was called and they hauled Bryce, Dan—he's one of the football players who got involved—the basketball guys, and Logan outta there."

Ginny finished and started to pace the length of the hallway when Chey stuck her head out of her room. "We just heard. One of the guys texted Stacy to get the assistant coach."

"How the hell did this happen? Was Tiberius there?"

Ginny gave me a helpless look and shrugged. "I don't know."

Chey burst out of her room, banging the door into the wall behind it as she glared at me. "For starters, put some clothes on your skinny butt, go down there, and help get those guys out of this."

My wet hair was now dripping over my breastbone, landing in the towel knotted across my chest. "Okay. Okay," I said and started toward my room. "Wait, are you okay, Ginny? I'm sorry I dragged you into this—"

"Be quiet," she said, holding up a hand. "You're a good person, Ting, even though you don't realize it. Bryce wasn't gonna let that shit lie. I don't know what happened between you and Logan, but either way . . . you gave me confidence when it came to Bryce, and we're both thankful. Now go help them sort out this mess."

Her phone beeped and she looked down at the screen. "It's Bryce.

They're just getting some kind of warning, but he said the basketball guys are wound tight. He thinks you need to go talk them down. They've got a game tomorrow night."

"We're going with ya, girlie," Chey chimed in as Stacy made her way out of her room, looking like hell. Her hair wasn't in her usual braids, but down and all wavy.

I turned toward Stacy. "You all right?"

"Fine. I overdid it last night at practice."

"Okay."

Chey slapped my butt. "Come on, we don't have all day."

I hurried to my room and tossed on jeans and a loose sweatshirt. It looked like I'd be missing econ today. Oh well, I'd get the notes.

By the time the three of us arrived at the security building, the guys were filing out, and I heard several of them shout my name. I didn't see Tiberius, but I did spot Jamel and Lamar. *Just my luck.* Bryce was right behind them, but Logan was nowhere to be seen.

Lamar walked swiftly toward me, grabbed my arm, and turned me to walk with him as Chey and Stacy rushed the other guys, looking for the inside scoop.

Anger twisting his features, Lamar spat out, "Tingly, that Logan dude's an asshole."

"I'm gonna fuck his ass up," Jamel said as he flanked my other side.

"Guys, come on. He was just running off at the mouth. Let it go, you got a game tomorrow."

"Shut the fuck up, Tingly, and leave this up to us," Jamel shouted, his pupils tiny pinpricks of rage.

"Where's Tiberius?" I asked.

"He's down at the financial aid department, working some shit out with his mother's death certificate. Let's go, I'm rolling down there to get him and then we're gonna deal with this shit." Jamel started walking back toward the Union where the finance department was located.

"No! Please, Jamel. Let it go," I begged him. When he ignored me, I grabbed his arm and jerked him toward me, my nails clawing at his skin as I whispered, "Don't, Jamel."

"Damn, bitch. Why're you protecting the dude?" he said through clenched teeth.

"It's not him. It's me," I said in a hushed voice. It was so quiet, I almost couldn't hear it myself.

"Come here," Jamel demanded and pulled me over to the side of the road, underneath a tree. "What's the deal?"

I was wringing my hands and my still-damp hair fell limply down my back. Swallowing the lump in my throat, I spoke softly. "You know how the day I met you, you immediately said, 'I know you . . . you're the girl that blah, blah?' Well, if you do this, I'm only gonna be known for more bad shit. Let him go. I can handle Logan, but I don't want Ty to be associated with any of this."

Jamel narrowed his eyes at me. "You know what, girl? You don't get what you got going on. Brains, booming system for a chick, personality. Stop thinking you're shit and deserve shit. Because Ty's all good, and if you want him, you better be good enough for him. I know you are, but do you?" He stopped speaking, brushed past me, and was gone before I could stop him.

With one last glance back at me, he said, "Let's go, Mar. We be giving this ass one more chance." And off the two of them went, meeting up with the rest of the crew enraptured by my roommates.

chapter seventeen

Moments later, I stood outside the finance office waiting for Tiberius.

The door flung open and his wide eyes met mine. "Rex? What're you doing here?"

I was back to wringing my hands. Not wanting to alarm him, I forced myself to unclench my fists and straighten my arms at my side. "There was a situation down at the gym. I guess Logan ran off at the mouth about me making a pass for him." That was all I managed to get out before Tiberius shouted, "Fuck!"

"The guys were down there lifting," he said as he stormed toward the elevator.

"Yeah, and Bryce, my roommate's boyfriend. They kinda all got into it, and security came."

"Do you know where the guys are? We're gonna have to pay Logan a visit," he said right before bursting out of the elevator as soon as the doors parted.

vérité

"They guys went home with a warning, but that's exactly what I don't want—you or them to pay Logan a visit." I stopped dead in my tracks and stared down the man in front of me, all six feet five inches of him.

"No. No guy's gonna disrespect you." He turned to leave again.

"Listen to me, Ty, I'm gonna tell you what I told Jamel. I can't afford to have any more attention on me like this. I'm already scorned."

"That's bullshit, T. You're not scorned. You made a mistake, and you're the only one who keeps punishing yourself over it." He leaned against the wall, tilting his head back against the plaster, and let out a long, deep breath. "No brother would ever let this go on, Rex. But I'm gonna go along with you for one more try, then I'm done. One more time, and I'm done with protecting Logan. Got me?"

I leaned on him, bracing my forehead on his chest, feeling the wild, frenetic pace of his heart and the heavy sound of his breathing. We stayed like that, quiet and serene for a few minutes, until he asked, "Don't you got class?"

"I missed it when I went to see what happened. You okay? How come you didn't tell me you had to come over here? That couldn't have been easy."

I ran my hand down his chest, sliding it over his shirt before settling on his hard abs. A shiver ran through him, electrifying my hand, lightning practically sparked through me.

"Didn't want to burden you. It's done. But this is more important. I can't let this Logan carry on, Rex." He swiped his phone out of his pocket and tapped the screen, then brought the phone to his ear. "Ya'll ready to roll?" That was all he said, no asking questions or listening to their version of the story––despite the fact he just told me he'd give Logan one more chance.

"You gonna listen to her?" he said a few seconds later, glaring at me. At their answer, his face tightened and he brushed his finger over the screen, disconnecting a call without another word.

"Looks like the team is siding with you. Unreal," he mumbled.

"I thought you agreed with me?"

"I couldn't let the guys think I gave in so easily, babe."

"Well, I practically begged Mel. Told him to remember when I first ran into him and he mentioned the professor. I don't want any more attention like that, Ty."

He tossed his arm around me. "Mel says it's the last time he's listening to you. Next time, you're not gonna stop him."

"I know," I said, and before I could say any more, Tiberius turned me toward him and took my mouth in a brutal kiss. It was claiming and passionate, right in the open daylight for anyone to see— especially for the few members of the men's track team who walked by and whistled. Our lips parted and I gasped for air.

"Well, not gonna be up for debate now who you made a pass at," he said smugly.

"Ty, seriously?" I joked, but I guessed he was right.

"Come on, I'll walk you back and buy you a liquid love. We got a walk-through before the game tomorrow."

chapter eighteen

It was a non-conference game but the season opener, so the field house was packed. I never imagined it would be this full when I rushed over there, coffee in one hand and a complimentary ticket from Chey in the other. In fact, I teased her when she said I needed a ticket.

Once again, I hadn't told Tiberius I was coming because I'd started working with that student in need of an Italian tutor, and I wasn't sure how long it would take. At least, that was what I told myself. In reality, I was afraid to let him count on me. I'd never played that role before.

Lindsay was a sickeningly sweet, shiny-haired brunette from Long Island who wanted to go on a semester abroad in Rome—with her boyfriend, of course. Her parents said she needed to learn the language before they approved the trip, so she'd been doing Rosetta Stone before enrolling in Italian Level Three this semester. It was a leap of faith on her part, but apparently her guy was "so damn hot" and she couldn't bear the thought of him being there without her.

"I *have* to pass Italian Three," she begged me. She was practically failing. Poor girl offered to pay me whatever I wanted so she could send in her deposit for Rome.

I accepted the challenge.

Earlier, we worked for two hours straight, sorting nouns and verb tenses, when I had to excuse myself. Suddenly, I found myself not wanting to miss the game.

Now I took one last guzzle of my drink and pitched the cup before entering the field house, heading to the right toward my seat. I was sandwiched between Chey and Stacy, a teammate of theirs named Tiffanie behind me.

The girl Chey called "Tiff" kept leaning forward and slapping me on the shoulder as the guys warmed up. I hadn't wanted to watch the game alone, but mostly I needed more explanations of how the game worked and the girls offered to help. In return, I had to make sure they would be the first to know where all the guys' basketball parties were. I didn't know how I was going to do that considering I was always the last to know.

The guys were hitting "layups" according to Chey before they ran back toward the locker room.

Tiffanie leaned forward, yelling into my ear with more slapping on my shoulder. "Get ready, white girl, for your panties to drop. Those brothers are gonna roll out here, sweaty and ready to go."

Chey snorted. "She knows what they look like, Tiff. She sleeps over at Ty's . . . and Trey's."

Tiffanie's eyes lit up. "No shit? Girlie! Trey's smokin'. He lights me on fire, girl! You gotta give him my digits. Talk to him about me."

My shoulder was going numb from Tiffanie and all her slapping. She wasn't a small woman; I was pretty sure she played center for the women's team.

"Sure thing," I said, afraid to mention the girl in Cleveland or anything other than my agreement. I liked Trey, but there was no way I was getting mixed up in his love life. He'd been nice enough to me all week, minding his own business when I spent the night with Tiberius.

The lights in the stadium went out and the crowd cheered. A spotlight whipped in figure eights around the field house as a rap song played with heavy bass and some yelling that sounded like "Bring 'em out!" Then the announcer came over the loudspeaker, introducing the team one by one. Tiberius was at the top of the lineup, the last one waiting to slap hands with the starting five. Chey explained this was normal for the new guy on the bench.

My heart swelled a little as the announcer's words echoed throughout the arena. "Starting at guard, a six-foot-four junior, number thirteen, Trey Dawson."

Trey made his way through the line, slapping up high-fives, and the girls all gushed and swooned around me.

"He is one fine brother. Damn, girl, you gotta introduce me to him," rang in my ears from behind me.

"Look at your man's ass," Stacy said on my left as she elbowed me. "You could bounce a quarter off that shit."

"Ladies, let's all calm down," I said, patting the air to encourage them to hush up.

Before we knew it, the team was at center court, ready for the tip-off. Hafton got the ball, and Lamar dribbled it toward the hoop. He sprang up on both feet, dunked the ball, and hung on the rim while the Jumbotron flashed a replay with the words SLAM DUNK plastered across the screen. The girls went into another series of oohs and ahs and general chatter about Lamar's body and form.

I watched as the opponent brought the ball back down the court. They were a smaller school from Georgia, and their bright-yellow uniforms left something to be desired. The other team made it all the way to the basket, where Jamel slapped the ball out of their hands into the stands.

"Ooh, he got stuffed," Chey yelled.

"What?" I asked.

"Stuffed, that's what that is."

"You mean when he slapped the ball out of his hands into the crowd?"

"Yes, Tingly. Pay attention, girl."

The first half went by fast, finishing with Trey "crossing someone up" at center court and "driving" for his second three-pointer. Hafton was up by twelve as the boys went to the tunnel toward the locker room, when Chey stood up and yelled, "Hey, Ty! Look up here!" She was jumping up and down, pointing at me, until his sight line focused on me.

Unfortunately, so did the Jumbotron. There I was, blushing, surrounded by the women's basketball team, with the camera traveling between Tiberius winking at me and me sitting there, mystified.

I sank down in my seat, hunching my shoulders to make myself smaller, and my phone pinged like crazy in my pocket. Sliding it out from my jeans, I noticed ten notifications from Facebook. I hated that app—I needed to delete it—but I pressed the icon to open it. Sure enough, ten people had just written on my wall.

"Tingly, just saw you on the Jumbotron!!"

"Who is the guy winking at you? You sure know how to pick them."

"Go, Tingly—at the game."

One of the posts was from Stephanie, my section coach.

"Hey, Tingly, just saw you starring on the big screen at the basketball

game!"

Was she here? Christ, I needed to get out of this place; the walls were starting to close in on me. Why couldn't I remain anonymous?

"Hey, girls, this was fun, but I gotta go. See you at home. Great meeting you, Tiffanie," I said as I stood and grabbed my backpack.

"Why're you leaving? Because I embarrassed you?" Chey stood up, towering over me.

"No, it's fine. Really. I just have work and an early practice," I lied, swinging my bag on my shoulder.

"Tiberius isn't gonna be happy about this," she whispered to me, the tips of her braids brushing along my cheek.

"I'll text him," I said, and then I was out of there.

I walked back to my dorm as fast as my feet could take me, and locked myself in my room. My phone buzzed with a call, and I answered in a fit of rage, not bothering to check the caller ID.

"Hello?"

"Tingly, I'm glad you answered."

Shit. Second fuckup of the day.

"What, Dad?"

"We've been trying to reach you."

"Why?" I stalked around my room, stopping to kick at the closet door to vent my frustration.

"Well, your mom and I weren't happy how things ended for you last year. And I'm dealing with it."

"What do you mean, dealing with it?" I made my way over to my bed and flopped down on my back, squeezing my eyes shut. "I thought I told you that I was fine on my own."

"Well, I know you're not in a good space out there, and I'm fixing it."

"What the hell do you mean?" I shrieked into the phone.

"You'll see, darling, and then maybe you'll consider paying us a visit?"

I hung up. Just pulled the phone away from my ear and swiped my finger across the END CALL button.

It was always *quid pro quo* with my parents. They did something for me, and then expected something in return. Although usually both things ended up in their favor—like Blane Maxwell. I'd been so in love with him, ever since we were little kids playing out back in the pool with our nannies watching from deck chairs. As we grew older and my feelings matured, it was hard to hide them. My eyelashes seemed to bat of their own volition, my hips cocked his way, and my heart rate sped up, even though I constantly pleaded for all three to stop.

Sometimes I'd flirt over a glass of lemonade or run by his house, hoping to catch a glimpse of him. He was the captain of the soccer and tennis team, and his long and muscular frame had caught the eye of all the girls in our prep school. We'd all pull up in the morning in our Range Rovers and Mercedes SUVs, unfold our bodies from the air-conditioned cabins of our luxury vehicles, and all eyes would be on Blane Maxwell. The real kicker had been, he didn't really even notice it. He was shy, quiet, a leader on the field, but not in class or student council—where his parents wanted him to show his prowess. Otherwise, how would he take over the family shipping business?

Our parents were friends, of course, society buddies who shared expensive cocktails at the club or the Beverly Hills Hotel. From time to time, they would meet at our house for an aperitif, and I would sit at the top of the stairs and eavesdrop.

"Oh, our Blane, what will we do with him?" his mom would say. "How will he find his way? He doesn't even have a lady by his side."

I wanted the position more than anything, and somehow my

parents had caught wind of this. When I was fifteen, they arranged for a big family cookout—catered, of course—where Blane and I were thrown next to each other at the end of the large picnic table set up on our deck. My dad had offered Blane a beer, calling him a man for the night, and Blane didn't even have a driver's license yet. Blane took a few sips of the pale ale while eating, and then he suggested we take a walk behind the pool house.

My heart nearly leaped out of my chest. *Behind the pool house?* That could only mean one thing. Blane Maxwell was going to make a pass at me . . . *me*! I agreed to go, and we strolled out back. I took in the rolling pink-and-purple landscape set against the Hollywood Hills, and I couldn't believe I was sharing this moment with Blane.

When we got behind the pool house, I turned and faced him with bright eyes and a pouty, seductive smile.

Blane faced me, his expression somewhat bored. "Look, I know you like me, and I know I shouldn't have agreed to this, but your dad offered your virginity to me. My dad says if I take it, he'll know I have the balls to run the family business. After all," he formed his fingers into air quotes, "'anyone willing to deflower Colt Simmons's daughter has balls enough to run the world.' And I need that company in my name," he stated matter-of-factly.

Shocked, I stood there gaping at him as a lone tear trailed down my cheek. The sun beat on my fair scalp as I stared at him, sweat pooling under my arms. I couldn't understand why Blane would agree to this, or why deflowering Colt Simmons's daughter was such a prize.

"It's because you're such a butch and flat-chested from all that running, always wearing cutoffs instead of dresses," he said, answering my unasked question.

I cocked my head to the side and stared at him. "Did I say that out loud?"

"Yeah," he said, zero emotion in his eyes. He was all business when it came to my virginity and my apparent butchiness. "If it makes you feel any better, I don't want your virginity."

It was then that I slapped him—hard—and his eyes widened with shock as my handprint marked his face, the imprint growing redder with each passing second.

"It's not you, it's me," he said, defending himself. "I'm gay, but my parents would never accept that. I need this, Tingly."

I'd never hated my stupid, stuck-up name more than when I heard it roll off his tongue. It was a family name—my mother's maiden name, in fact—and I detested what it stood for. Money, bureaucracy, political bullshit, the cornerstones of my mother's family. Now it stood for Blane's personal wishes, spoken in his whiny voice and infused with his deep-seated desires. It was like hearing nails on a chalkboard.

"I just need you to say it happened to a few girls, let it get around school. We'll pretend to date and then break up. Please, Tingly?"

I agreed to it, though, but our breakup didn't go as he'd planned. He may have made everyone believe he'd deflowered Colt Simmons's daughter, but I'd decided that Blane's father—my dad's closest business friend—was way more appealing.

My ugly trip down memory lane was interrupted by my phone ringing again. I felt around the bed for it, but it wasn't there. The ringing stopped and started again. Leaning over the side of the bed, I saw it buzzing on the floor and snatched it up. This time I made sure to check the caller ID, and saw it was Tiberius.

"Hello," I said, my voice still hoarse with pain.

"T, what's wrong? What happened to you?" His voice was laced with worry and heavy New Jersey. "Where'd you go?"

"I had some work, but I caught the first half. Sorry, I missed the rest," I said, trying to steady my tone.

"Rex? Come on. You mad about the big screen?"

"I'm just trying to lay low, Ty. Now we're everywhere."

"So? When it means something, T, that's a good thing." I could practically hear him smiling through the phone. "I thought I told you to tell me you were coming. I would've got you a ticket."

"I didn't decide till last minute. I was tutoring that girl I told you about."

"Well, you missed me. I got in during the third and fourth."

If I didn't feel like shit before, I felt it now. "Oh, Ty. I'm sorry. It's just I don't want you to be that guy. The one who picked up Professor Dubois's sloppy seconds."

"You in your room?" he asked, ignoring my remark.

"Yeah."

"Good, I'm coming up." The line went dead.

A moment later I heard a knock on the door, and ran my fingers through my ratty hair on my way to answer it.

chapter nineteen

A s soon as I opened the door a crack, Tiberius pushed his way inside and kicked it closed with his basketball shoe. I heard the lock click as he turned, and then he was on me—pushing me against the wall, hammering my mouth with his.

I let out a tiny moan, and his tongue slipped between my lips, tangling with mine. Although *slow, take-our-time Tiberius* had clearly left campus, the kiss wasn't barren of feeling. To the contrary, it was fueled with meaning. I could feel passion radiating off Tiberius, flowing from his pores.

"T, baby?" he said, breaking away from my lips. We were still pushed up against the wall in the hallway, my back flush with the drywall, his front pressed against mine.

"Yeah?"

"Good thing you weren't near me when the cameras swung our way, because I'd have done that. And I would've got thrown off the team," he said through uneven breaths.

"I don't want that." I sucked in a gulp, trying to catch my own breath as my chest heaved.

"What? Me off the team? Or me to kiss you like that?" He leaned his forehead to mine.

"You off the team, but I also don't want you saddled with my rep."

"I told ya, Rex, I ain't gonna let you hide behind that shit."

He took my hand and walked me toward my room. "Lock the door," he instructed, and I did. "You gonna ask me about my game?" He leaned against my dresser while I stood in the middle of the room under his scrutiny.

I nodded. "How'd you do?"

"Had eight points, two from a dunk. Was pretty good for the minutes I played."

"I'm sorry I missed it, Ty. Really, I am." Behind my back, I was wringing my hands and crossing my fingers like a schoolgirl who had misbehaved, hoping he wasn't mad. Then again, this was my first real relationship. Up until now, everything I'd done was child's play.

He stalked toward me, his size 14 feet eating up the carpet in three steps, and kissed the top of my head before lifting my chin and forcing me to look at him. His hands were on my shoulders, more bracing my body than holding it in place.

"Leave your running for the track, T. Leave your past where it belongs . . . in the dirt. If you're gonna run, run to me, to your future, to being happy."

He didn't say anything more. His lips came back to mine and we fell on the bed. He kicked his shoes off and crawled over me, then twisted and pulled me on top of him. His hands skimmed down my back, settling on my butt.

My bed was smaller than his, but I wasn't uncomfortable sharing the space with his large frame. I ran my hands down his sides, then sat up and straddled him. My hands came back up and roamed underneath his shirt, smoothing along his nipples, and finally lifted his shirt over his head. I looked for approval, for permission to do what I wanted to do, which was take him in my mouth. The only light in the room was the small lamp over my bed, and it cast a warm glow all over his chest and face, allowing me to see the hunger in his eyes.

Drifting down his body, I pulled off his track pants and boxer briefs. I felt him use his feet to push them off the rest of the way, and I smiled to myself. I'd been with a lot of men since I was fifteen. Blane Maxwell may not have stolen my virginity, but his dad ate great pussy. For years, I'd been testing boundaries, pushing limits, giving my parents the big "eff you," but this time was different. I wanted this to mean something, *and it did.* It wasn't only about getting off or getting caught, but about making someone I cared about feel good.

I took his length in my hand and lazily dragged my fingers up and down, paying special attention to the tip. A drop of pre-come slipped out, and I bent down to lick it before taking all of him in my mouth. He was big—it was no easy feat, but I did it. A loud moan broke from his chest, traveling through his whole body, all the way up his dick and into my mouth.

I did that. I made him do that. *Me.* This propelled me on, and I began to suck a little harder, setting an even pace up and down all of him, my tongue swirling his tip when I made it to the top. Nothing mattered but making Tiberius happy. Sure, it was passionate and I was starved for more, but I'd never felt this way before, wanting nothing more than to satisfy someone.

His hips lifted off the bed and he moaned again, this time adding, "Oh God, T," at the end. So I picked up my pace, and his tip hit the back of my throat. I resisted gagging and continued to take him, but when his hand reached down and stilled my head, I stopped to look up at him.

"T, come here. I don't want to finish like that," he whispered.

Normally, I would ignore that request and keep going, but his eyes revealed something else. He was ready to make it all worth something, and I wanted that. I wanted it all with Tiberius, so I stopped and climbed back up his long torso, where he pulled me in for a deep kiss.

"S'okay?" he asked.

I nodded.

"I want it all with you, Rex. But only because you know it means something." His chest lifted as I breathed in; we were in perfect sync.

I nodded again.

"Say it."

"I want all of you, Tiberius, because I now know it means something." My eyes blurred and I wasn't totally sure, but I think they were welling up.

Ty swiped a finger across my cheek. "What's that for?"

"It's a happy thing. You may not have slept all over town, but I have no experience with *this*," I said, flapping my hand between the two of us. "This meaning something."

All he did was reach up and grab me into a kiss before rolling me over and traveling the length of my body, leisurely dragging my pants off, and making his way back up until his mouth settled back between my legs. He took long and languid strokes up my core, settling on my hot spot, lingering softly before going into an all-out frenzy there.

I bit into the pillow in order to avoid screaming his name, but then he was gone. I went cold immediately at the absence of his hot mouth on my clit, until I turned my head to the side and saw what he was doing. He was grabbing a condom from his pants and rolling it on. He looked glorious in the light, all strong and tall and muscular. And he was smiling. This one was a little sexier than usual, no dimples.

Before the goose bumps could go away, Tiberius was back on top of me, running a hand down my side and over my breast, tweaking my nipple while he kissed me with no urgency. After all, we had all night. There was no one to catch us. We weren't sprinting; we were running a leisurely marathon. His finger traced a path down to my core, coming up wet, and he used the wetness to stroke his length over the condom before guiding himself inside me.

He wasn't unsure. He was gentle, careful, and deliberate about making it good. If he was nervous, it didn't show. His shoulders and biceps flexed as he held his weight off of me, and he started to pump in and out. Slowly at first, then faster as I lifted my hips to meet his thrusts.

He ran his tongue down my neck, biting and nipping his way back up to my mouth. "Feels damn good," he said against my lips.

"More," I whispered back, and he picked up the pace.

I wrapped my legs around his back, allowing him to deepen his thrusts. With each stroke, he hit my spot, and within minutes I was moaning and my insides were clenching his dick tight. With my eyes open, I watched my reflection in his eyes—the satisfaction of my hunger being played out before me.

"Oh shit," he said, and then he exploded inside me. My whole body shifted from the sheer force of it.

Tiberius slowed his movements, but didn't stop as we both came down. We had both stilled and were gasping, breathing heavily, when he stood and pulled off the condom, then yanked up his pants, telling me he'd be right back. Seconds later, he slipped back into bed, then proceeded to gather me in his arms, turn me on my side, and spoon me before pulling the covers over us.

"'Night, Rex," he said into my ear.

And that was exactly how I woke up the next morning . . . spooning in his arms in my tiny bed.

chapter twenty

Tiberius found me the next morning as I was guzzling a cup of coffee and cramming a PowerBar into my mouth.

"Hey." He was a glorious sight shirtless, with his track pants riding low on his hips.

"Good morning," I said between bites.

He lifted one eyebrow. "You doing all right?"

"Yeah, I was going to run and be back. I need to run, just run. Not away from you, from myself. I don't know . . . I'm overwhelmed with shit after last night," I admitted.

"You go run. I'll be waiting right here for you." With an encouraging smile, Tiberius collapsed onto the couch and snatched the remote control from the coffee table.

"I may go long," I added.

He lifted a hand to wave good-bye as he focused on the TV. "S'okay."

Well, that was easier than I thought. After tying on my shoes, I grabbed my watch from my dresser and shoved my earbuds in my ears. Then I left.

When I headed back to my room after my run, I heard laughing from outside the door as I pulled my key out and turned off my music. Ty's deep laugh radiated through the plywood, with a bunch of female giggling following right behind.

Oh shit, my dorm was turning into a brothel, and Tiberius was the entertainment.

"Hey," I called out, announcing myself as I opened the door. I didn't know what I expected to find, but considering my track record, I wasn't sure it would be pretty.

Chey was standing in the middle of the kitchenette, guzzling coffee straight from the pot while wearing nothing but a long T-shirt. Stacy was bent over in fits of laughter, her afro puffs wild and crazy, and Ginny was in the corner, crossing her legs as if she was going to pee herself in her boy shorts and a tank. Ty was leaning against the counter—still shirtless—saying, "I'm not shitting you. You do not want to get involved with him."

When he saw me, he shouted, "Hey, Rex!" like this was an everyday thing, him half-naked in my apartment and entertaining a bunch of barely dressed girls.

I waved and then turned my attention to Chey. "Do you do that every day with my coffeepot?" This set all of them off into more fits of laughter, and I knew she did.

Setting the pot back on the warmer and wiping her mouth with the back of her hand, Chey said, "No reason for the coffee to go to waste, girl."

I pretended to yack before saying, "That's disgusting."

"Babe, the girls were just telling me 'bout Tiffanie and how she kept banging you on the shoulder last night," Tiberius said. "You okay? Bruised? She's a big girl."

"I'm fine." I turned my bare shoulder toward him, saying, "See?"

He approached and leaned over, moving my tank strap aside before planting a kiss on my sweaty shoulder, right there in front of the whole crew.

"Ooh, you go, girl," Chey chanted while doing some kind of funky dance moves with her hips. Stacy chimed in and Ginny clapped.

"Not you too, Ginny?"

I moved toward the bathroom with Tiberius hot on my heels. Before I could shut the door in his face, he was inside the small bathroom, kissing me up against the sink as the counter's edge dug into my ass, and I didn't care.

He turned us and settled himself against the sink, holding me close as he asked, "Feel better after the run? Got your head straight, T?" His hand rested on the back of my neck and he dragged my head, lining up our cheeks as he breathed deeply. "Feel that? Nothing to run from. That's pure good, babe," he whispered, his lips brushing my cheek, tiny whiskers scratching my skin.

"I feel better. Never felt like this before," I admitted without our eyes meeting. "I have a bad past—"

"Told you I don't give a shit 'bout that."

"It's worse than that, Ty. You may not like a lot of it." I buried my face on his shoulder, saying some type of silent prayer that he didn't really care.

"My dad's in prison, my momma raised her bastard son, and now she's gone. Nothing is gonna change how I feel," he told the top of my head, landing a kiss there before he started undressing me.

"For someone who wanted to take it slow, you're taking it fast now," I said, breaking the moment.

"I know, 'cause I'm going to take a shower with ya," he answered.

While the water warmed up, I asked, "By the way, who were you telling Chey not to get involved with?"

"Oh, that. Not Chey, that girl Tiffanie. And Trey," he said, running his hands all over my now naked body.

"She was asking a million questions about him the other night . . . while she was slapping my shoulder," I said with a wink.

He raised an eyebrow.

"I didn't say anything about Miss Cleveland," I said, defending myself.

"I know, but that's why I warned her off. *Miss Cleveland* does not like sharing, and from what I hear, she pops out here and starts smacking girls around."

"Oh, wow. Okay. Well, I just said I didn't know anything. What's her name again? Apple? Miss Cleveland?"

"Cherry. You'll meet her, I guess, babe."

He snatched me up and deposited me in the shower. Once we were under the spray, he picked me up and I wrapped my legs around his waist. When he slid inside me, I let out a gasp at the decadent feel of Tiberius deep inside me as hot water cascaded all around us.

We were pinned against the wall, pressed against each other while Tiberius held all my weight when he said, "S'okay I'm not gloved? Want me to pull out?"

"I'm on the pill. It's been more than a year," I said without looking at him.

He brought his hand to my chin and forced eye contact. "Don't care about any of that, T."

And then Tiberius made love to me against the shower wall with one arm holding me tight and his other hand between us, touching our connection and teasing my clit. I'd never come with someone I cared about other than the night before, and this made that look like amateur night.

I had a feeling that when something meant something, it was going to be better than I expected.

chapter
twenty-one

With fall coming to a close, the temperatures dropped, and Tiberius and I grew closer. His season heated up and mine cooled down. It was mid-November and the basketball team was traveling and playing nonstop, but Tiberius still made time for me. It was a foreign concept, yet sort of sweet all the same. Pierre never made time for me unless it was for fucking, and always quickly at that. To me, the act of sex meant something on its own, and I was quickly learning how mistaken I was.

I went back to study hour with Tiberius so we could steal a stolen glance or two of each other, grabbing a few meals before or after in the Union. Usually one of his teammates would roll up to our table and join us, teasing us about each other. We weren't about any of that sickening stuff, all touchy-feely every minute, shoving our tongues down each other's throats every second, but it felt good to just be together.

The track team was moved inside for winter conditioning,

which took place painfully early in the morning, so I didn't stay with Tiberius every night. Lucky for me, he understood; he was an athlete too.

He also needed time to hang with the guys, and it had become obvious that the party scene wasn't me. So he went without me. When they weren't practicing or playing or partying, Tiberius and his teammates were always around. Somehow along the way my own roommates had infiltrated every facet of my life, and tortured the boys into hanging all the time.

We were in a little routine, but Thanksgiving was coming, and my parents kept texting and asking me to come home. I hadn't done it once before, so I wasn't sure what gave them the idea I would now. Tiberius had nowhere to go, and I knew this first holiday without his mother made his heart heavy. I just wasn't sure how to approach the subject, or if we were even at the point to share a holiday.

He'd been away the last two days at a game in New Jersey, and I was sitting at a table in the Union, twirling my hair around a pen as I tossed back my coffee and read a textbook on my iPad. At least, I was pretending to read, but really I was thinking about Thanksgiving and Tiberius.

I wanted to see him. Badly. I missed him, everything about him— his smile, the way he tossed his arm around me, when his dimple came out and when it didn't. Especially that.

Something tickled the top of my hand and I moved to swat it away, but was startled when someone grabbed my hand and held it tight. Turning, I looked up and saw the man of my daydreams.

"Hey," he said, pulling me up for a kiss. It was a soft, closed-mouth one, but not disappointing in the least.

"Hey, you. I saw your game on TV. You guys looked great, and you played the whole fourth quarter!" I knew I was grinning from ear to ear like a cheese ball. My cheeks were aching, my smile was so wide.

He ruffled the messy bun on top of my head, causing strands to come loose and fall around my face. Then he pulled me close and kissed the top of my head. "Yeah, I did." His voice was light, easygoing, and laced with hints of want and need. "You eat yet?"

"No, just been drinking coffee." I pointed toward my almost empty mug.

"Ah, the love liquid. Girl, you gotta consume something more than that. Come on, let's go out to eat. Pack up."

When his mother passed away, Tiberius inherited a small life insurance policy she'd set up for him. He also got a stipend as part of his scholarship, but I still suggested we split the tab as I packed up my backpack.

Surprising me, his mood turned dark, fast. "Uh-uh, Rex. You think I'm some freeloader who doesn't take care of my woman? Shut your mouth!"

I'd never seen this side of Tiberius. He was raging—no smile, no dimple, nothing.

Shrugging, I said lightly, "I was just trying to be fair." I hoisted my backpack on my shoulder and turned, no longer sure I wanted to go to dinner.

He whipped me around so we were facing off in the middle of the Union. "You want your parents' money? You like their handouts? Or are you making it on your own?" he asked, gritting his teeth on a tense whisper.

"You know I don't want their money," I said with an eye roll.

He knew I hated them and all they stood for; we talked a lot about them. But I still hadn't told him about my sexual escapades within their circle. I knew this was probably a mistake, but he kept saying the past was the past.

His fierce expression eased a bit. "Well, you make do with your grandma's money in the bank and your tutoring job and don't worry about me. We're making this work, and I take care of my woman. And I wanna take you out to eat." He put his arm around me and pulled me in for a hug before walking us out of there.

We went to a small Italian place where we got a booth in the back. We sat across from each other and Tiberius stretched his legs out. I was still a little unnerved about his outburst, not saying much, and he nudged my ankle with his and said, "Drop it, Rex. It's over."

"Okay." I let go of our argument and picked up a piece of bread before dunking it in garlic oil—only because Tiberius had done the same. If we both ate garlic, it wasn't a big deal.

Our food arrived soon after we ordered, and we both laughed at the heaping plates of pasta steaming in front of us. The place was crowded and all around us were couples, groups of girls, and families, all eating, smiling, talking, and having a good time. I didn't think I'd ever done anything like this with my family or my stuck-up friends from back home.

"This is great! I wish I'd grown up in a family-friendly town like this." My eyes betrayed me, getting a bit misty at the thought.

"Oh yeah?" Tiberius asked.

"It seems like everyone is just so much happier here. Genuinely happy." I twirled my spaghetti around my fork, then took a bite and chewed, closing my eyes against the tears that threatened as I moaned a little at the carb-infused goodness.

"Good?" he asked.

"Yep. Wanna try this?" Without any hesitation, he stuck his fork right into my enormous pile of spaghetti with olive oil and garlic.

"Back home, we lived in the city," he said after he swallowed, "but still had fun just hanging in the coffee shop or on the blacktop courts. Of course, kids got into trouble, went the wrong way, but I knew my mom had enough on her plate. She didn't need any more, so I stayed clean. Yeah, I tried drinking, but stayed away from the drugs and shit. A few of my old buddies ended up going down a bad path, landed in jail. And a few of us got out."

He took a long sip of his water and dug back into his own pasta with meat sauce, or *Bolognese*, as I'd teased him when he ordered. He'd countered, "I refuse to eat anything that fancy, especially when it's ground beef," and I smiled to myself at the thought before I spoke.

"You had so little, but still sounds better than our vacant lives back in La La Land. My friends and I would go to the fancy food court and eat empty calories of frozen yogurt, licorice, and diet sodas. On special occasions we'd eat at fancy sushi joints, driven there by private limos so our parents didn't have to change their plans. We'd drink stolen champagne in the limo and sake later, even though we weren't old enough."

Smiling sadly at him, I said, "Then we'd end up climbing the Hollywood sign and flashing the world, or raging in someone's media room. There were a lot of Vine and YouTube videos of us dancing, tipsy and smiling, and cruising Santa Monica with one of us sticking our head out of the limo. To anyone else, it looked like were having a blast, but in reality we were just trying to stuff a bleeding hole with gauze. Your mom worried, but our parents only cared about themselves unless we fucked up their reputation."

Tiberius listened quietly, his eyes warm pools of seawater.

I tilted my head back against the booth and took a deep breath. "If you had a son or daughter in rehab or some facility for an eating disorder, it was like a status symbol. You were so rich that you could get your kid the best care, and she or he would come out all shiny and new. As long as they didn't slum around."

I knew right away what he was thinking, that I was slumming with him, so I quickly spoke. "But that life wasn't for me. This right here—sitting and eating garlicky goodness and talking about everyday stuff—that's for me. None of that other bullshit."

He winked at me. "I don't know if you mean it, but I like it. That life sounds pointless. Christ, even if I go pro, I'm not gonna live like that. Gonna raise my kids right."

"Speaking of pro, what did the coach say about your game?" I turned the conversation, pushing my plate away.

Tiberius gave me a wide smile, his lips curling up, his eyes dancing with a blueness that rivaled a summer sky. "He said it looks like I may get a chance to start a few non-conference games."

"Oh, wow! Will any of them be at home?" I asked. I didn't go to every game, but I tried to catch most of the home ones.

He nodded.

"Cool!" And it was. I looked forward to seeing it.

"So, what's your plan for Thanksgiving?" he asked, turning the subject serious again.

"None. I went home with Ginny last year, and the year before that I spent the day waiting for Dr. Dubois to meet me, but he never showed. I guess he was with his fiancée."

"Well, we play on Saturday night, so we're all here. Trey and his lady are doing something in Cleveland at her apartment. Want to go?"

"With you?" I asked.

"I would hope so, Rex." His smile was back, and the sight of it made me melt a little.

"Um, I guess. Is Trey okay with that?"

He leaned across the table. "Yeah, he is. You're my woman. But you can't have any of your roommates tag along."

This time, I laughed. "They're gonna go crazy trying to figure out where you're all going."

"I know. I told them not to mess with Trey."

I held my hands up in the air and said, "I've been staying out of the whole mess. Ever since I caught a look at Trey's room and saw the condoms and the booze, I stay away."

At the mention of condoms, Ty raised an eyebrow.

"What?"

"I was just thinking, I don't think I'm ever gonna be able to go back to using those. You feel so good with nothing between us. Want that forever. Not just that. All of you."

His eyes were narrowed, but Tiberius was no longer smiling. He was contemplating whether he'd overstepped his bounds with me. He knew I loved to run when things got real, and he was probably wondering whether that comment was going to have me lacing up my shoes. His furrowed brow spoke volumes.

"Come on, let's think of the now," I said, standing up to go.

He threw some money on the table and we walked out. Except this time, Tiberius didn't put his arm around me.

chapter twenty-two

Tiberius tucked his "forever" comment away—somewhere deep—and I found myself disappointed. That night after he said it, he made love to me at his townhouse before he walked me back home, leaving me at my door with his usual sweet kisses. But this time there were no promises of what tomorrow would bring.

The next day I woke up and went for a run, pushing my time and pace as usual. It was freezing and my fingers felt frostbitten, my gloves no match for the brutal late fall winds. I stopped in town for a latte, warming my hands on the cup as I walked back to my dorm, but I didn't feel like going inside.

Instead I walked up to the Ag building like Tiberius and I did at the beginning of the school year, but this time I was alone with my thoughts. I could have asked Ginny to come, but she was figuring her own shit out. She also didn't have the same baggage I carried around, which was why her personality was so light—she wasn't strapped down with a million pounds of bad history.

I could talk to Chey and Stacy about it, but somehow I knew their suggestions would be a little more forward than I was used to being. Plus, they would only accuse me of being a nutty white chick. They wanted a man like Tiberius, and if I told them he'd said he wanted forever with me but I wasn't sure how to handle that, they'd admit me to a mental hospital for not jumping on it.

So I stood on the corner underneath the street sign, leaning up against the pole with my latte in hand, and did something I'd really never done before. Thought about what kind of woman I was.

Back in Los Angeles, I wasn't a forever kind of girl.

With Pierre, I thought I could be one with him. And I was dead-on-balls wrong.

With Tiberius, I didn't want to be one, but I was. Period.

The bottom line was that this situation was up to me to fix. Alone. So I decided to talk with Tiberius around Thanksgiving.

That's what I had in mind when the guys played a game at home the night before Thanksgiving. Of course, I went and cheered like a crazy girl every time they pulled up for a three or ran the court for a layup. Tiberius was getting in his fair share of minutes and contributing to the team, and the guys appreciated him for it. They were winning, so everyone was on a high, especially after winning a home game and getting off until noon on Friday after Thanksgiving.

I didn't wait outside the locker room; after the first time, I never went back there. I did wait by the back entrance for Tiberius, agreeing to go to a house party with them all. As we walked back toward campus, Chey and Stacy stepped in right behind us like heat-seeking missiles. They weren't going to miss a good time with these guys. Ginny was spending the night with Bryce before she went home for the holiday, and he stayed behind to play on Saturday too.

We hurried through the wind toward an apartment past College Avenue. As soon as we crossed the threshold, everyone began hooting and cheering for the guys. Beers were passed around and the music was turned louder. The place was full of what were considered to be "ball babies"—girls who would do anything to hang with the team. Chey and Stacy didn't fit so easily into the category because they were ball players too, but they certainly wanted to oust a few of the ball babies.

Tiberius skipped the beer, grabbed my hand, and pulled me out to dance. With his large hand spread on my hip bone, he moved us in sync; my hips and his were on the same page even when we weren't between the sheets.

"You gonna tell me what's up?" he yelled over the music into my ear, his arm flung around my back, holding me tight.

"Let's not ruin this."

"Tell me," he growled into my ear.

"You just won, and I don't want to do this here," I insisted.

Before I knew it he dragged me back toward a bedroom, opening the door and locking us inside.

"Tell me, T," he demanded, his deep voice rumbling throughout the vacant bedroom.

We were standing face-to-face, but not touching. He hovered close, but was careful to give me space. After all, I was a flight risk. If he got too close, I might bolt, and if he was too far away, he might not be able to catch me. It was a very dangerous game to be playing, and I needed to stop.

"You mentioned forever and you haven't brought it back up," I whispered, staring at the floor, hoping he couldn't hear me over the vibrating beat.

"Because I know you're gonna fucking run, that's why. I saw the look on your face. You're not ready for that word, and I'm not losing you over it. It's gonna happen," he said, then pressed me back against the door and kissed me hard.

"Maybe I am," I muttered between kisses as wetness pooled in my panties.

"Then say it, Rex." He lifted his head to see me, all of me. His eyes bored into mine, searching for the truth.

"Maybe I'm ready for forever. I don't know. I've never even considered it before, not until you. Yeah, I thought about it with Pierre, but that was nothing more than a schoolgirl's fuck-you to my parents thing. This feels real for the first time in my life, and I want that forever. Real."

Without a word, Tiberius grabbed my hand and whipped the door open. Dragging me through the party, he fist-bumped everyone who crossed his path, saying, "Yo, see you all later," in his New Jersey way, and we were out of there.

Chasing me back to my dorm, he stopped along the way to tease and taunt me with kisses and little nips at my neck. "You ready for me . . . forever?"

We tumbled through my front door, peeling off our clothes as we made it back to the bedroom before Tiberius said, "Gotta slow things."

He took his time, taking off my bra and now-soaked boy shorts before spreading me on the bed in front of him. He dragged my body to the edge of the bed and knelt in front of me, sliding his tongue along me. It was slow and teasing, but I liked it. He was working me up, and I felt each touch of the tip of his tongue. When he finally flicked against where I wanted, I arched my back off the bed, wanting more.

"Oh, Ty," I moaned, and he picked up the pace. He may not have had a lot of women before me, but Tiberius was completely in tune with my body. Maybe that's what happened when it meant something.

I came on a string of moans and whimpers, and then I was pushed up to the pillows, Tiberius looming over me. I lifted my head and caught a glimpse of him stroking himself two or three times before diving inside me. Every nerve frazzled and sparked as he entered me. I felt each stroke, every movement, and I wanted to savor each one like an ice cream on a hot day.

"Feels so good, T," he whispered across my cheek while he was deep inside me, moving leisurely. He kissed me, the remnants of my orgasm fresh on his lips. "So good," he said as he nudged his shadowed face across mine, the short hairs of his scruff catching my smooth skin.

I cried out as he started moving faster. "Tiberius, yes, more. Faster, *bébé*."

"English, Rex," he muttered.

"Faster, baby," I demanded, and he obliged.

We both held off as long as we could, taking every last ounce of pleasure before we came together. After we cleaned up, Tiberius said, "I can't move, I'm exhausted, girl. Wanna stay here tonight, and Trey'll get us in the morning?"

"'Kay. I have to send an e-mail in the morning to Lindsay about some stuff to review over the break. Can you believe she's paying me to FaceTime with her on Saturday and Sunday so she can prepare for finals? The girl's nuts." I giggled.

"For her man," he added.

"But I don't know if it's from a good place. More like she's worried about him finding someone else while he's abroad, or doesn't trust him," I mumbled as I snuggled into him. There were some advantages to my smaller bed, like being closer.

"You know that's not me?" Tiberius said out of nowhere.

"Uh-huh."

"I'm not looking at ball babies—"

I had to interrupt him with a laugh. The whole notion of ball babies was so funny to me. Then again, with my past, I shouldn't make jokes.

"Or girls in other places."

"I know, Tiberius. I know, babe," I said, then stroked my hand down his arm and let it settle across his abdomen before I fell asleep.

"Oh shit, don't do that!" Stacy's shrill voice carried through the hall.

Groggy, I opened my eyes to hear some male grumbling that I couldn't exactly make out before Chey screamed bloody murder. "Don't you fucking manhandle my roommate. Get the fuck outta here, old man!"

I started to crawl toward the end of the bed to grab some clothes and see what was happening when someone burst through my door.

"Tingly!" He stopped and surveyed the scene, his eyes widening before he spoke again. "Jesus Christ, what the fuck did you do this time? Goddamn, I flew here to try and get your life back on track, just to see you made an even bigger fucking mess of it!"

"Dad?" was all I could make out. I hadn't even felt or noticed Tiberius sit up behind me, looping his arms around me and pulling the blanket higher to cover my nakedness.

"Sir? Could you give us a minute to get decent?" Tiberius asked.

My father, Colt Simmons, standing here in the flesh and blood, was someone no one asked for a minute. He shook his head while fuming at us. "No, I certainly cannot. Get the hell out of my daughter's room. She's expecting someone else," he roared.

Who else?

Just then, I heard more commotion at the door. Stacy and Chey were swearing up a storm. Thank God, sweet Ginny was still out. She would have no clue what to do with a scene like this.

"Colt?" I heard my mom yell. "Honey, we're here!"

And then standing in my doorway were my mom and Pierre.

For Pete's sake. Peet's Coffee. Phillip Phillips.

I rubbed my eyes with the heel of my hand to make sure I wasn't seeing a mirage, but Pierre was actually there. He looked rumpled and tired, but confused by the scene in front of him.

"*Ma chérie*, what are you doing? Your father said you're waiting for me. Who is this?" he asked in his overdone French accent.

My gaze pinged like a dodgeball from one person to the next, my head whipping from one side to the other as I took in the crazy scene in front of me.

"I need you to leave right now," my father gritted out as he stared bullets at Tiberius. When Ty didn't move, my father yelled, "Now!"

"I think that would be for the best," my mom suggested in her prim-and-proper society voice, yet Tiberius still didn't move, only gave me a wary sideways glance as he waited for me to give him a clue what I wanted him to do.

I needed to say something, but my throat was as dry as the Sahara. I tried clearing it and a small squeak came through my vocal cords. "He's not going," I made out.

"The hell he's not," my dad said, whipping off his navy sport coat and rolling up the sleeves of his French blue dress shirt as if he engaged in fistfights every day. He worked in a posh office with two secretaries waiting on him hand and foot. The only fighting he did was over the phone with his massage therapist when he couldn't fit him in.

"Tigger, what is this? What did you do?" This from Pierre, who coincidentally was not rolling up his sleeves.

"Don't you dare call me that." I glared missiles at the Frenchman.

"Tingly, you're embarrassing the family name with this . . . this boy." My mother paused, her eyes growing wide before she asked, "Did he force you?"

As usual, Mom's strawberry-blonde hair was perfectly styled in a bob. Today she was wearing a pale pink St. John sweater set with matching slacks, and had silver Tory Burch ballet flats on her feet. She looked like the Pink Panther ready for the Junior League annual meeting while I sat naked in front of her, wearing nothing but a sheet, all flushed after several rounds of sex with a very large, very virile black man. As I stared at my supposedly newly married French ex-lover in front of me, a giggle bubbled up in my throat at the sheer lunacy of the situation.

Dad narrowed his eyes at me. "This is not funny, missy."

I shook my head and managed to choke out, "I know, but Tiberius isn't leaving."

"Sir," my dad reminded me.

"Sir," I added automatically, then forced myself not to roll my eyes at him before I turned my gaze on my mother. "Mom, what are you doing with Pierre?"

"Dad and I decided it was time to see you happy, and we know he devastated you when he left, so we brought him back. For you."

Then on a whisper, she added, "It didn't work out with that other girl, but Dad still sweetened the deal with a job and a house, plus he told Pierre you guys would share the trust with us if it all worked out."

"So, kick the bum out and figure the hell out when you're going to start your life with the Frenchman, Tingly," my dad said as if this were a merger and acquisition. "He's back, and we need a moving date and a wedding date."

Incredulous at their audacity, I glared at them. "The trust is all mine . . . it was never yours. So if you think giving me Pierre is going to make me feel generous with *my* trust, you're wrong. I don't want Pierre."

Tiberius stood from the bed and snagged his boxers, shoving his long legs through them before stalking over to my dad. "Get out!" His six-foot-five-inch frame loomed over my dad when he said for the second time, "Get the hell out!" He then turned to my former professor. "And you, Pierre"—it sounded like *Pear* coming from Tiberius—"go the fuck back to France. Tingly's mine."

"I'm not going anywhere, especially now that I see who my slut of a daughter is planning on sharing my money with," my dad spit back at Tiberius before turning to me. "And, Tingly, that is and will be *my* money. Your grandparents were not of sound mind when they left that to you. We are going to make you happy and work this all out." He stepped around Tiberius as though he weren't of any consequence to walk toward me and grab my shoulder harder than I expected.

Seeing me flinch, Tiberius glowered at my dad and warned, "Don't touch her!"

Through all the chaos, Pierre merely stood there, saying and doing nothing. When I turned to look at him, he was playing with his cufflink, twisting it and examining the stone in the light.

Christ, what did I ever see in that fucking excuse for a man?

Better yet, why the hell was he back? But the answer was simple: for the money. Just like my parents. Like my dad always told me: "Rich or poor, it's good to have money, darling."

With the comforter still wrapped tight around my slight frame, I stumbled like the Stay Puft Marshmallow Man toward everyone, shouting as tears spilled over my lashes, "Get out! All of you get out. Now!"

Chey and Stacy stood in the doorway as reinforcements, yelling, "You heard the chick, out!"

"Mom, Dad, I need you to leave. I have no idea why you thought bringing Pierre back would make me happy, but you need to go. It doesn't. He doesn't make me happy! You wouldn't have the slightest clue as to what would make me happy." I inhaled deeply and then yelled, "Christ! Get out. I keep saying it. Leave!"

My chest was now drenched with my tears. Tiberius tried repeatedly to put his arm around me, and I kept batting it away. My entire body was shaking under the heavy down comforter like I was naked in the middle of a snowstorm, but my cheeks were burning up as if they'd been scorched with flames.

Through all this, Pierre kept saying, "Tigger, *ma chérie*, please," fiddling with the damn cufflink the whole time.

I let my venomous gaze fall on him. "Please what, Pierre? Please fuck me? Please screw me? What the hell do you want, a get-rich-quick scheme? Maybe that was all I ever was to you before we got caught doing the nasty. Did you have your sights set on me long before I knew who you were?"

He started rubbing his forefinger over his middle finger, something I knew he did when he was nervous. *Bingo.* "You, *ma chérie*, I want you. I came for you." He stood still, now wringing his hands. He didn't even slightly resemble the cocky bastard I'd thought

I'd fallen in love with while he fucked me up against the wall.

"Stop it, Pierre. Get out and don't come back. *Au revoir.* Good-bye."

Squeezing my eyes shut, I stepped backward and tripped on the blanket. Luckily Tiberius caught my elbow and held me upright, otherwise I'd have tumbled over, which would have put a cherry on top of this fucktastic day.

Totally drained both physically and mentally, I finally whispered, "Please, everyone, leave." I squeezed my burning eyes shut, the stinging continuing to plague me after they were closed, and I began chanting, "Please, please, get out," until I finally heard them shuffling out.

"We'll leave ya'll," Chey said to me and Tiberius, who was still holding me steady with his hand. I heard her close my bedroom door before slamming the front door. With her foot, probably.

"Ty, please let go." I opened my eyes to see a storm brewing in his. Dark clouds of fury shaded his normally pale blue irises. "You should go with Trey to Cleveland. I need time to work this all out in my head. Go." I tried pushing off his chest, struggling for physical space.

"No, Rex. I'm not running. If you need space to think, I'll go back to my place and wait for you to call. When you need me, I'm gonna be sprinting back to you." He kissed my forehead and walked out my bedroom door, shutting it behind him.

chapter twenty-three

W hen Tiberius left, I collapsed on the bed, too drained to argue with him about Thanksgiving. He should go with his friend and try to enjoy the holiday, which would be his first without his mom. But he was staying to wait for me.

Wait for me to do what? I hadn't a clue.

Staring at the ceiling with my head throbbing from crying and my eyes burning from tears, I decided that I wasn't defeated physically. So I threw on long tights and wool socks, added my track jacket over a thermal T-shirt, and laced up my running shoes. I shoved my earbuds into my ears while I sucked down an electrolyte packet, then hit the open road.

I ran for miles and miles, not even keeping track on my pacer watch. In a daze, I looped the Ag building three times, made a half dozen trips around College Avenue, and finally pummeled down the hill toward the townhouses to talk to Ty. But I nearly collapsed in the road when I saw what was happening in front of Ty's door—he was standing in front of his townhouse in a testosterone-fueled standoff with my dad.

Mortified, I stumbled to a halt and turned to run back up the hill. I didn't want to witness any of this, *this* being my old excuse for a life converging with what could be my new one—if I wanted. I'd realized on my run that was what Tiberius was waiting for. Me.

"Get over here, missy," my dad bellowed, his voice pushing past my the music droning in my ears and freezing me in place.

"What, Dad?" I said through uneven breaths, my heart pounding in my chest and my legs shaking like leaves as I leaned forward, bracing myself on them as I tried to catch my breath.

"I've offered to help Mr. Jones here move schools. I could meet with the assistant dean and explain I will make a sizeable donation to the department if he assists in finding a transfer. This way, Pierre can be with you. He's going to stay here and wait for you to finish school."

"Are you crazy? Have you gone mad?" I screamed at the top of my lungs. The cold air did nothing to chill my fiery inferno of a temper. "I told you—I don't want Pierre. Should I say it in another language? Two or three languages?"

Tiberius had edged between my father and me, providing a physical buffer, I assumed. I wasn't sure who he was more worried would become physical—my father or me. I sensed another warm body standing near me and turned to see Jamel was there, his furious eyes locked on my dad.

"Tingly, I'm your father, and for once in your life, you'll listen to me." His chest puffed out as he stalked toward me, all five feet eleven inches of him full of attitude. Tiberius took a step to the left and blocked his path. Without any direction, Jamel moved to my dad's right, further blocking him.

Glaring at my father, I yelled, "You mean like when you offered my virginity to Blane Maxwell? Guess what, Dad. He's as gay as they come! He's probably spent more time staring at your ass than mine. We only lied about sleeping together. I've never listened to you, and I'm not about to start now." Tiberius left his foothold and corralled me in his arms.

"What about when you blew Blane's dad? Sucked my best friend's cock in broad daylight for everyone to see? Did you do that for me? Or was that all for your own sick enjoyment?" Spittle gathered in the corners of my dad's mouth, his pale cheeks turning ruddy. "That's poor character, Tingly. Character not deserving of the trust, if you ask me."

"It's always the trust! The trust this and the trust that! You don't even need it!" My head spun, and I felt myself starting to shiver clear through to my bones. Unsteady on my feet, I drew a long breath to steady myself. The air had started to cool, the clouds heavy with flurries, and goose bumps lined my skin. I ran my hands along my arms to stay warm.

"I don't hit old men, but you're forcing me to take a swing," Jamel barked. "Get outta here, man, and don't come back. Take that French prick too 'cause if I see him, I'm gonna bloody him." Jamel looked even taller and more daunting than usual. He was formidable as he loomed over my dad, standing up for me.

"Leave, Dad. They're right. Don't come back."

Completely exhausted, I sagged against Tiberius, my head crashing like a wrecking ball into his chest. There was nothing left. I was bones and skin; my muscles, my heart, and voice box all defeated. A war had been waged and I won, but not without casualties. Tiberius would have questions about my past, and Jamel would have more. I knew they stood up for me, and that meant something, but what would happen when my dad left? Would they toss me out too?

And where was Pierre? Funny how a few months before, I was still in denial about his affections for me. The truth was I'd transformed in his eyes from a quickie fuck to a green card and a job.

"Go," I whispered to Ty's chest.

"He's gone," he whispered back.

I looked up to see Jamel escorting my dad back up the hill where a town car waited. *Weird.* I was in such a zone when I raced down here, I didn't notice it.

"Come on, Rex." Tiberius scooped me up and carried me into the townhouse.

I clung to his broad shoulders and back like a girl being rescued from an inferno. My head shoved deep into his neck, my legs bunched into his arms, I felt us walk over the threshold and heard the door clicking shut behind us. My throat hurt from breathing heavily during my run, then screaming, and now crying again. I sobbed quietly into Ty's sweatshirt, my nose dripping onto the heavy fabric.

I didn't even have the strength to look up and see where Tiberius was setting me down, and then I felt something hard underneath my butt.

"Rex, sit still for one second," he whispered into my ear. His hand went to my shoulder, holding me steady, and I looked up to see him turn on the shower.

The bathroom immediately filled with steam, and my body relaxed in the warmth. Tiberius slowly lifted my shirt off, carefully slid my athletic bra up, and then helped me stand so he could push down my tights. I wrestled my shoes off, one foot at a time, not bothering to untie them. My socks came off with my leggings, and then I was airborne, Tiberius lifting me into the warm spray.

"Hold on to the wall for one sec," he told me.

Quickly, he shucked his clothes before slipping in next to me.

His arms came around me, holding me directly under the water so it drilled into my cold skin, sluicing down my arms and breasts. Without a word, he leaned in and kissed me, our mouths meeting under the waterfall. A moment later he backed me toward the side of the shower, pressing my spine into the tile wall as his arms caged me and he kissed me harder.

I tilted my head, loving how he slid his tongue inside my mouth and pressed his naked body against mine. With all my experience and sexual trysts, I'd never stood naked in the warm water, skin to skin, no barriers or boundaries. And now I'd showered twice with Tiberius. This time, his fingers didn't roam; he kept his hands on either side of my head, containing me. He was probably afraid I was going to bolt.

When he released my lips, they felt bruised and lonely, helpless without him directing them. Leaning his forehead into mine, he said, "Tingly, look at me."

I didn't realize how hard I was squeezing my eyes shut until he spoke. I pried my lids open, drops of water clinging to my lashes, and saw the man before me. Sometimes he looked like such a boy with his dimples and wide grin, but right now he was all man, protective and dominant.

"Means something more now," he rumbled in a low voice. "You're mine, and he—Pierre—doesn't get to mess with that. Your dad's got nerve, but not enough to win against me. Deep down, I'm a kid off the street, Rex, and I'm gonna protect you."

I giggled.

"What's so funny?" Tiberius asked as he leaned closer, caging me tighter.

"Every time you say Pierre's name it comes out sounding like *pear*, the fruit. It's funny." With an apologetic smile, I said, "I'm just wrung out, so I needed a laugh."

Saying nothing, he moved one hand off the wall and swept the back of his fingers along my cheek. I couldn't believe he was still standing there with me, naked and in the shower.

Dropping my gaze, I stared at the water swirling down the drain, terrified it represented my life. In a low voice, I asked, "Why are you still with me? I mean, you heard my father. I blew his friend—someone his age, the father of a friend—and that's just the tip of the iceberg. My name was passed around the country club locker room like a good tailor or golf pro. I come from this crazy, fucked-up world where money and all that's shiny and glittery that comes with it means everything. There's no truth, only skewed perception and lies, and you, Ty, you're so honest and good. You come from a place that's filled with so much bad, but you're not. You're better, above it all. Not me, I'm lower than low, and yet you're still here."

The water had started to run cool, and Tiberius moved to turn it off without saying a word. He snatched his towel off the rack and threw it around his waist before grabbing another from under the sink. Tenderly, he stroked the towel over my skin to dry me, his gaze on me holding nothing but love. Finally he tucked me snugly inside the worn terrycloth.

Pulling me into his arms as he leaned against the sink, the cheap mirror behind him still fogged up, he spoke. "Rex, there ain't anything low about you. You're not bad, you're lost, and after meeting your sorry excuse for a dad, now I know why."

When I brought my miserable gaze up to meet his, he breathed out, "Fuck!" then squeezed me tighter to his chest. "I always thought I got shit for a father 'cause he wasn't around and then he was behind bars, but you the one who got shit. No matter what kinda money he got, that man is shit. And I know it's your dad, but he's nothing to me."

"Me either." My voice cracked, hoarse from all the yelling and running and crying.

"And for a mom not to stick up for her kid, Christ. She's shit too, and I don't like to talk 'bout women that way." He took a deep breath and ran his fingers through my wet hair, gently separating the tangles. "Yeah, I know where I come from's bad, but we learned about respect and loyalty. Which is more than that piece of fruit from France. Aren't they supposed to be well-mannered and shit? Well, you're done with all that, Rex, because you're mine. I lo—"

A loud banging on the front door interrupted him, and we both turned that way in alarm.

"Wait here," Tiberius told me as he threw on his sweats and T-shirt from before. I slipped his sweatshirt still wet from my tears over my body and finger-combed my hair.

"Bro! She okay?" I heard coming from outside the bathroom. Jamel.

I stepped out, Ty's sweatshirt hitting me mid-thigh as I padded in my bare feet into the common area to find Tiberius and Jamel's heads close together, their expressions serious as they talked quietly.

"Thanks, Mel," I said, interrupting them.

"Hey." Tiberius moved quickly to stand in front of me. "You can tell Jamel later when we go get something to eat."

"What?" I asked from behind Tiberius.

"Get changed, and let's go be thankful or some shit like that," Jamel said from the other side of the room.

And that's exactly what we did. I went home and put on clean, dry clothes, then spent my Thanksgiving eating turkey with all the fixings at the diner with Jamel and Tiberius.

"That dad of yours is something," Jamel mumbled around a mouthful of turkey and cranberry sauce. "What's her mom like?" he asked Tiberius with a chin lift.

The three of us sat in a booth. The guys had put on jeans and collared shirts as a nod to the holiday, although both were in their basketball shoes. Not the ones they wore on the court, I'd learned a while back, but just "kicks," as they called them. I was wearing a sweater dress with tights and boots.

It was actually kind of festive, although the ambience was definitely more Christmas than Thanksgiving. The diner sparkled with twinkly Christmas lights, the jukebox was playing holiday music, and the staff wore Santa-themed nametags. Most of the tables were full with university staff who couldn't go home for whatever reason, and there was one big table of sorority girls.

"Mel, don't make me go there," he answered. "You know I respect the ladies."

"Tell me about your ma, T," Jamel asked me.

"She's a bitch. Ty's being nice, but she's a stuck-up bitch with her hair all done and her clothes never wrinkled. She comes from big money. Her daddy set my father up in business. That's why he married her . . . she was ugly." I broke out in a laugh, and Ty and Jamel joined me with their own hearty chuckles.

"She was! Her parents bought her a new nose and a better chin before she met my dad. He'd come from some money, but had this plan to expand self-serve gas stations and mini-marts out west, making them into chains and franchising. My mom's family had been in California since the gold rush. Dad was desperate for them to bankroll him."

"Shiiitttt," Jamel said, drawing out the word into at least two syllables. "Your girl's loaded."

"Anyway, they set him up and then he worried he would owe them something, so he needed a kid to secure his standing. But my mom couldn't get knocked up. They tried and tried, and she was just shriveled up and barren. No surprise for a frigid bitch. They did all this fertility crap, kept throwing money at it, and eventually something took. She never really wanted me. She knew I was part of my dad's plan, and then I never turned into what she wanted. I was just an insurance policy for my dad and a nuisance for my mom."

I hadn't noticed Tiberius put his arm around me until he pulled me close and said, "Rex, you can stop."

Jamel's eyes were bugging out of his head. "How do you have this much cash and shit it all up?"

Tiberius stiffened, but I put a hand on his arm, letting him know I was okay. I'd never been this open with anyone; it felt liberating to speak the truth. My therapist had been telling me all of last year that opening up wasn't a bad thing. She encouraged me to speak my mind, reminding me true friends wouldn't judge where I came from or past actions. I hadn't believed her, but was ready to take a stab at it now.

"There's really not much more," I said with a shrug. "When my grandparents died, my parents stopped caring about me altogether unless I could bring them another merger—like with Blane Maxwell—but they could see I wasn't going down that path. And I did everything in my power to show them I wasn't going to do what they wanted, to let them know I heard their hushed whispers and violent screaming matches at night over me. In the dark hours of the night, the truth would vibrate through the walls. They hated everything about me, especially when my grandmother left me her entire inheritance. It's in a trust, and I don't really touch it except for a little of the interest, but it burns my parents up that they didn't get their hands on that."

"That's the most fucked-up story I ever heard. I come from the ghetto like Ty, and I don't think we ever saw shit like that. People, especially the moms. Shiiiitt." Jamel leaned back in the booth and leveled a concerned gaze on me. "We got you now, T."

Tiberius squeezed my shoulder and nodded before the waitress interrupted us to ask if we wanted pie. I was relieved; any more declarations of how they had my back would have sent me over the edge. Tears already filled my eyes, and I was doing everything in my power to keep them at bay.

The guys ordered pumpkin and apple—whole pies—and amazed me by finishing them both. We laughed over funny foreign swear words, which they couldn't stop asking me about even as we walked home from the diner.

Then I went back with Tiberius, and he didn't make love to me, but held me tight all night.

Somehow, I think his abstaining said more about the depth of his feelings for me than if he'd ravaged my body.

chapter twenty-four

"On the line for an *and-one*, Tiberius Jones. He's been four for four from the line tonight," the announcer on TV said.

The team was in Michigan for a nationally broadcast game the day after Christmas, but I'd stayed back in Ohio. The regular dorms closed over break, but not the athletic housing. We were permitted to stay and train as needed.

Despite that, I was spending a few days in a small bed and breakfast, thanks to my bonus from Lindsay. She'd passed her course and was setting off to Italy after break. She'd shown up at our last session with a handful of cash, jumping up and down and smiling like a goofy girl in lust. I didn't want to accept, but she called her dad—apparently she'd fessed up to him about the tutoring—and he insisted. He sounded so nice on the phone, his velvety voice like hot cocoa on a cold night, soothing to frayed nerves, and loving when he spoke about his "only girl." He was proud of her and grateful to me for pulling her through. This was the least he could do, he insisted.

Five hundred bucks was the least he could do!

So I found a small B&B with private baths and TVs, and I checked in for the holidays. Although I'd never really celebrated a warm-and-fuzzy type of Christmas, this year I didn't want to be alone. Of course, Tiberius had asked me to come to Michigan, but I didn't want to take anything away from the team and him. So I stayed.

The house was run by a lovely couple who asked me to join them and the other couple staying there for Christmas dinner the night before, and I did––I hadn't even been reluctant. The innkeepers were retired from farming and bought the B&B to stay busy and meet people. They didn't have any kids, they explained over cocktails and dinner, so seeing young people happy and in love brought them a lot of pleasure. The other couple, newlyweds in their early twenties, had been married the week before. This was a quick little honeymoon getaway before they took a backpacking trip the coming summer.

I'd watched my hostess's eyes twinkle as she looked at her husband over a glass of champagne, and wondered if I would ever look that way. Did I look that way?

"So, do you have someone special in your life?" they'd asked over the elaborate holiday meal, and I nodded.

"Oh yeah, you do," the other young woman teased me. "I see that look in your eyes."

I guess that answered my question.

Now, I sat and watched Tiberius make his foul shot on television after getting fouled while draining a bucket, a million and one nerves sparking and flying around in my body. I jumped up and down in my room as he swished his shot, and was caught in the act by the proprietors of the B&B as I screamed at the home crowd booing on TV. Hafton was gaining a sizable lead on Michigan, and the fans were not happy. I was swearing and pacing as their booing allowed

Michigan back in the game, corralling the team's spirit, but with ten seconds left, Jamel hit a wide-open three-pointer, giving my guys the win. After doing my own victory dance, I went downstairs grinning like a kid on Christmas morning and joined the small crowd for dinner again.

When I came back up to shower and go to bed, the fireplace had been lit inside my room, the flames flickering off the white walls, casting shadows on the pale blue sateen bedspread. Bundled in a fuzzy robe, I crawled into the sheets and drifted off to sleep, my mind filled with thoughts of Tiberius. His biceps, the way they flexed when he pulled up for a shot. His smile, crazy and big, when he laughed at something silly—like my Chucks. His body and the way he danced with me, our motions becoming one. The way he chewed his pencil when he studied hard. The blue of his eyes—pale, like the bedspread—deepening when we kissed. His mouth covering mine.

And then he was there. His mouth covered mine, his breath hot on my cheek as he slid into bed next to me. "T?" he asked, his voice breaking through my dream.

Surprised, I opened one eye. Dawn was beginning to break, the fire still crackled in the corner, and Tiberius had already undressed and was lying next to me in the queen-sized bed.

"Ty? What?" I looked around the room.

"The coaches let us take the bus home late last night after the game since we won and we all missed the holidays. Some of the guys tried to connect with their families. I came here, figured one of the owners would be up early making breakfast, and lucky me . . . they were in the kitchen."

"Oh," I said, pressing my face against his chest and breathing him in.

He tilted my chin up with his pointer finger. "They knew who I was when I walked in, they heard you hooting all last night over the game. Said they peeked their heads in and you were glued to the TV," he said, his smile broad.

"I was. It was a great game."

I didn't say anything more; I just kissed Tiberius. We'd grown even closer since Thanksgiving. I'd been sharing bits and pieces of my past with him, what happened with Blane, my futile attempt to get back at my parents by sleeping with older men, and their recent last-ditch attempt to buy my affection away from him. We studied and ate together, and Chey and the guys joined us most of the time.

But he hadn't come close to muttering the words he'd started to say in the bathroom that night before Jamel interrupted. I worried it was because of my past transgressions. Perhaps sharing the truth wasn't that smart? He was here in my room, though, so that counted for something. At least, that's what I told myself.

Eager to taste him, I slipped my tongue inside his mouth as I shifted myself on top of him. His one hand came around the back of my head, tugging on my hair, holding me in place while the other found the flaps of my robe. He loosened them and slid the heavy fabric off my shoulders. When he released my mouth, he ran his lips over my shoulder and down my breastbone to my nipple, pulling me close to suck on it while squeezing the other.

Wetness pooled in the tiny thong I was wearing underneath the robe. When he moved his mouth to my other nipple, his hand crept down and pulled my underwear to the side. He sank a finger deep inside me, and I sucked in a breath.

"Ty," I said softly.

"Pretty wet," he whispered back.

I nodded, my forehead touching his. Our mouths met once again while Tiberius moved his hand to stroke himself once or twice before guiding me back over him. He lined my body up with his, and I sank down deep on him. We kissed hard, our only goal to swallow each other's moans as I rode him. His hand came to my hip for purchase and I sat up, quickening the pace. He moved his hips to meet mine, driving himself deeper, then abruptly stilled my movements.

"Fuck, slow it down, T," he whispered, always the one not to forget that this meant more, or we thought it did. Sex wasn't a placeholder for emotion for Tiberius, and he refused to allow it to be one for me.

He gathered my body close, my pebbled nipples touching his smooth ones as I rode him gently. As he lifted up to meet my thrusts, I clenched my muscles around him, biting my lower lip to avoid moaning in ecstasy. Tiberius ran his finger across my lips, and I smiled while moving my pelvis back and forth, taking every inch of him.

"Love you, Rex."

I loved that he didn't use my real name. I loved that he said that while we made love, changing my opinion of the whole act, making it symbolize our feelings and commitment. I loved that he always gave the truth to me.

A lone tear dropped from my eye on his chest and he flipped me over, bracing his weight on one arm as he showed me how much he loved me, slowly moving in and out of me. I felt every stroke of his length until we both came hard, clutching each other as the fire crackled in the background. Like us, it never really fizzled; it always sparked under the surface.

When I got up to go clean up, I whispered, "I love you, Ty," then tossed another log on the fire so it continued to burn brightly. My hope was that we would continue to burn brightly as well, and the beauty of the moment wiped away any doubts.

For now, anyway.

After checking out, Tiberius and I went back to the townhouse and ordered food with the players who'd stayed on campus. The tiny Christmas tree we'd bought before Tiberius left was still on the table, decorated in green and white tinsel for Hafton. Whether it was a symbol of what was to come or what had been, I wasn't sure, especially with the guys' taunting and teasing.

"Hey, Tingly," Lamar called out to me, "you have a good time with our guy last night? Stole him away from our post-game celebrating."

His comment made me blush, stripping away any remaining post-sex glow from my mood. A tiny trickle of regret dripped down my spine. Was I taking Tiberius away from the team? The guys were his only family now . . . was I ruining that?

Lost in my thoughts, I barely heard Tiberius yell, "Shut the fuck up, Mar. Don't be jealous!" But doubt had crept back up inside me, not allowing my brain to process his words.

The remaining days of the year passed with Tiberius practicing, me running, and eating dinner with our teammates. Chey and Stacy were back on campus after forty-eight hours with their families; it was nice to have them around again. We watched TV and hung out while the men's team used the field house—the women's team always got second pickings.

Through all the camaraderie, I forced a smile and tried to be social, but I couldn't get the damn devil off my shoulder. It gripped me with its talons, whispering in my ear that I was all wrong for Tiberius, distracting him from what was important, tainting his life with my crap when he didn't need it despite what I felt back at the

B&B.

Two days after Christmas, Ginny had texted to say she was back on campus and staying with Bryce. I couldn't help but think how much had changed since early fall. She'd been single, a young girl with a crush on a boy she'd been assigned to tutor. I'd been single, jilted and heartbroken by my professor. We'd both been focused on our sports and studies, loners when it came to our social lives.

Now we had boyfriends—also both athletes—and crazy roommates who were up in our business. Our lives kept intersecting, Bryce encouraging the football team to have my back with my very own teammate, Logan, and the basketball team becoming fixtures in our dorm suite. Our seasons were over, but we were woven even tighter into the overall athletic fabric of the school.

But I couldn't help but wonder: Was that what was best for Tiberius? I'd over-involved both teams with Logan and stolen Tiberius away from team gatherings.

By New Year's Eve, Ginny was off again to see Bryce in a bowl game, and I was at a basketball game, even though I wasn't sure I should be. I'd begun to see myself as toxic when it came to Tiberius, believing that he was the only positive in the relationship while the negativity from my baggage leached into every crevice and corner of campus.

Everything in our lives had changed, but for how long? Despite growing up in such extreme wealth, I'd never really known stability. Ginny seemed almost complacent, but I was too nervous to even feel settled.

My stomach was doing more than its usual churning, butterflies battling in my belly, as I sat in the field house waiting for the game to start on New Year's Eve. When someone tapped me on the shoulder, I almost jumped out of my seat. A shiver ran down my spine when I turned to the left and saw an enormous man sitting next to me. His cheeks were ruddy and his belly hung a bit over his pants, but you could tell that in his day, he'd been attractive.

"Tingly?" he said, his voice gruff and deep. When I nodded, he extended his hand. "Coach Smith."

Slipping my hand into his, I tried to give my firmest handshake. "Nice to meet you."

"I'm sure you're curious as to who I am and why I'm here." He spoke but kept his eyes trained on the court where the two teams were warming up, and I nodded. "I understand you're involved with Tiberius Jones."

Another nod from me. I had no idea where this was going, but I was afraid to speak or say anything that would hurt Tiberius.

"Tiberius is very talented. We expect him to be a full-time starter next year. We went to great lengths to recruit him, and we like to keep our star players happy. We also like them to be free from distractions like complicated relationships."

Tight bands constricted my chest, and I pinched my finger hard to keep from crying.

"Well, we hear things in the locker room, and I know your parents recently made a visit to campus with Dr. Dubois." He turned slightly in his seat, his kneecap brushing my thigh for a moment. "It's none of my business what happened between you and the professor, but when it affects Tiberius, it is. We've all done stuff in our pasts, and I was under the impression you had put that whole episode behind you. But that's not what I heard in the locker room. The guys got involved in a scuffle with your dad? And Dr. Dubois was there? I heard Tiberius was very upset over the whole incident."

"Sir," I said, turning my focus on his large forearm resting on the armrest. "You can rest assured that I'm done with Dr. Dubois, but with all due respect, you're not my coach, so your opinion doesn't matter. Coach Wallace believed in me enough to let me back on the squad. I don't really know you, so I'm not sure why it matters other than you think I'm going to screw something up for your team. I'm not."

Without waiting for his reaction, I got up and left. It was time to end it with Tiberius.

Even though I put on a tough face with the coach, I knew he was right. My fears had proven to be true: my family was back to screwing everything up for me. Tiberius didn't deserve that. He should have better. The best. He should get sweet and good from now on—neither of which was me or my past.

Tivoli. Toast. Tuna. Taylor Swift.

I had to stop the stupid game immediately because Taylor Swift only made me think of the night the guys were concerned I would turn Tiberius into a Taylor Swift groupie.

As if.

chapter twenty-five

M Y PHONE PINGED WITH A TEXT MESSAGE.

Tiberius: What happened? I thought you were coming to the game?

Me: Something came up.

Tiberius: You coming to the party?

Me: No. I'm not feeling great. You go, though.

Tiberius: I'm coming over.

Me: Please don't. I want to be alone.

Tiberius: WTF?

I didn't respond. Powering down my phone, I slid in between my cool sheets and cried myself to sleep. A short time later, I heard Tiberius knocking on the door and ignored him. Ginny was out and the women's team was on the road, so I was all alone on the brink of a new year.

Which was exactly what I deserved.

I felt his gaze on me before I fully woke. Prying my crusty eyes open, I saw Tiberius in the corner of the room, watching me sleep. He was leaning against the wall, one foot on the floor and the other resting on the wall behind him.

"Ty?" I asked. "How did you get in here?"

"I have my ways. What's going on, T?" He pushed off the wall and paced my room.

I swallowed. "You shouldn't be here. First, I really don't think I would like to know how you got in. And second, we need a break. It's too much, too fast."

"What?" He whipped around toward me, his face tight with tension and anger. There was no hint of his adorable dimples anywhere.

"We need a break," I repeated. "Please leave." I sat up in bed, pulled my knees up and wrapped my arms around them, trying not to rock back and forth in despair.

Tiberius narrowed his eyes on me. "That's junk, but you know, I'd never not respect your wishes so I'm trapped. And that's junk too because *you know* I'm gonna leave. I don't know what happened, but I'm gonna figure it out and fix it, Rex. I'll be back," he said. "You're not acting right, and that's such bullshit."

His basketball shoes barely made any noise as he stomped out of my room. Either that or I didn't hear it over the loud thumps of my own heart, although I did hear the slamming of the door behind him. It reverberated throughout the empty dorm suite, along with my shock at how easily he acquiesced to my request.

Obviously, he believed this was for the best. Either that or he really meant he'd be back.

The first few weeks of the New Year passed in a blur. A new semester had begun with different classes and a new schedule, but I was very careful to not share my schedule with Chey or Stacy. I knew the team was trying to find me, corner me, and gouge my eyes out or worse.

"Girl, Jamel is hot to find you," Chey told me at least once a day. "You better run faster."

No way in hell they were going to let this lie; this being pushing Tiberius away with no warning whatsoever. I varied my comings and goings, walking to class different ways each time. I was like a fugitive on the run when it came to my former life and the men's basketball team.

Funny, how the year before I hid from my own self-hatred, and now I was on the lam from people who actually cared for me.

I dragged my ass to every class, winding around back ways to the buildings. Desperate, I found coffee places farther and farther away from campus to drown myself in caffeine and my own misery. In class, I caught myself doodling, tracing emblems like Tiberius's tattoo rather than taking notes, or Googling basketball scores.

But I was also avoiding Nadine. She'd caught up to me after class the first week back. "Oh, em, gee, Tingly, I heard you ended it with that buff hunk of a guy, Tiberius. Are you okay?"

She meant well . . . or not . . . I didn't really know. She was such a typical college coed, all fun and frivolous with perky tits, and always squealing. Why couldn't she be quiet and reserved like she was when she was running? That was the Nadine I could appreciate.

"I'm doing okay." I put on a brave smile. "Just need to concentrate on school and getting out of here," I lied.

"Well, Logan said he knew it would happen, said the guy's bad news." Making her point, she whipped her head around, flipping her hair so fast it almost took me out.

I let out a little snort. "Not sure Logan is the authority on anything, but thanks for checking on me," I said with a polite smile as I edged away from her and our conversation.

"Maybe we'll all go to a party soon?" Nadine called after me brightly.

My situation was made even worse by the fact that Pierre was back. I wasn't sure how he weaseled his way back on campus or why. I'd cut off all contact with my parents after they offered Tiberius a hundred thousand dollars per year for the next five years to end things with me—in an e-mail. How they got his e-mail address, I had no clue.

This had happened sometime in the weeks between Thanksgiving and Christmas . . . wouldn't they be happy to know I did it myself? For free just because Coach Smith asked?

I'd seen Pierre a few times on campus in the Languages building. He was never really doing anything official when I saw him, mostly talking or laughing with a faculty person or an old colleague. He had something up his sleeve, and I wanted nothing to do with him or his plans. All I wanted was for him to disappear.

That wish was especially fervent today. I was sitting in a small bistro on the outskirts of campus after finishing up a tutoring lesson with Robbie, my new student. Lindsay had hooked him up with me after meeting him in her Italian class. He was a nice guy from her high school in Long Island, dark-haired and with a good build, and unfortunately was interested in way more than tutoring from me.

Nursing a latte, I closed my eyes as I tried to shrug off the day, which included Robbie's relentless advances. In Italian, of course.

The chair across from me screeched on the tile floor as it slid out. "*Ma chérie*, how are you, love?" was addressed to me in a thick French accent.

A shiver slid down my spine as I opened one eye. "Pierre, just go. Don't do this."

He sat down uninvited across from me and cupped his hand over mine, which was already holding my mug. I hated the fact that we were sitting in a café, our hands jointly wrapped around a coffee mug—something I'd only dreamed about when we were together, and now he gave it to me so easily. Back then, all he gave me was his dick and false promises. Who knew what he wanted this go-round?

"Ah, good to see you still enjoy your *café*," he mumbled, his accent more pronounced than usual. He was laying it on thicker—for my libido, I supposed.

"What do you want?" I said through gritted teeth, trying not to make a scene.

"I'm back in the area. Consulting, I think is what you Americans call it? Since your parents overlooked our relationship, and I left for the year until you were twenty-one, and I'm not American. I don't really know, but I escaped with only a slap on the wrist. That's how good I am, *bébé*. I'm sure it helped that your dad made a sizable donation to the school's agriculture department. Serves him good in his type of work."

Disgusted, I watched the way his words rolled from his lips. I used to love the way he spoke, but now I deplored his lingering Vs and the way he touched his tongue to his lips between words. He was such a pompous prick.

"You still didn't tell me what you want from me." I was getting testy, my voice raised slightly.

"You, Tigger. I want you. I left Patricia," he announced proudly, as if he'd done me a monumental favor.

I stood up, leaving my half-finished latte. "Never. Not in this lifetime, Dr. Dubois."

"But, Tigger, we could be so good together." He jumped to his feet, apparently prepared to chase after me. "With all that money, we could do anything."

"Oh, are you finally admitting that this is what this is all about?" I narrowed my eyes, finally seeing him for the absolute con artist he was as we faced off.

Pierre gave me that Gallic shrug that I used to love. "Well, in the beginning, I thought you'd get bored with me after sleeping with me a few times, then make me a quick dollar to leave you alone. But you didn't. I kept thinking you'd take an interest in one of those fraternity boys, but then you went and ruined my career."

His gaze sharpened on me. "When Patricia left . . . with all her money . . . she mentioned that I should contact your parents, maybe they would take me in or something. That gave me the idea, and imagine my surprise when they bit. They needed something from you, and I needed them. Together we figured we could get you back on track. I just didn't think I'd find a black guy in my place, *chérie*."

His candor surprised me. The man didn't miss a trick; he let it all hang out.

Edging closer, he placed his hands on my neck, leaning in to either whisper something to me or to kiss me, I wasn't sure which, but it didn't matter.

Furious, I put my hand up in the air and yelled, "Stop!" and breathed a sigh of relief as he backed away. There was no way he could touch me now after all the witnesses in the coffee shop saw me warn him off.

That was before I looked toward the door and saw Trey and Lamar crowding Pierre as he walked out, steering him forcefully toward his silver SUV parked at the curb. Had they been watching him or me? What were they going to do to him? I'd witnessed what happened to Logan when he crossed a line, so their seeing Pierre with me would probably not bode well for him. Especially if they heard his accusations about a black man taking his place.

My entire body shook from the chill that ran up my spine and out my fingers and toes. I dropped back into my seat and gathered my coffee mug closer, willing its warmth to seep through my veins. Closing my eyes, I prayed Tiberius wouldn't take it on himself to "talk" with Pierre. I didn't want Ty to get hurt—which was unlikely— or get into trouble.

Crap, that man had infiltrated every one of my free thoughts, especially when I hurried home to take a run. It was the only way I knew to shed the anxiety and stress racking my body. As I pounded the concrete, "Paid in Full" by Eric B. and Rakim boomed through my iPod, courtesy of Jamel and Trey. I'd left my iPod at Ty's one day and came back to several new playlists.

This was one of the songs Tiberius and I danced to, and I didn't know why I tortured myself listening to it, but I did. My skin burned underneath the fleece-lined leggings and Polartec jacket I wore, and it wasn't because of their insulation or warmth. My cheeks stung in the wind, probably bright pink or red. Not because they were chapped, but because of Ty and what he did to my heart.

Not my body—my heart. Tiberius saw through all the bullshit and made me feel worthy, and that alone set my soul ablaze.

It didn't help that he wouldn't let it be. He texted every day. Usually it was just *hey* or *hello* or *thinking about you*. Sometimes he mentioned that the team won.

I never texted back or admitted to watching the games, but I couldn't help myself. A few times, I sneaked into the field house and stood up by the rafters to watch the action. It was a good plan, no one saw me or knew I was there, until one night when Coach Smith cornered me again after a game. I was rushing out of the field house, running toward the exit before anyone saw me, and was shocked when the coach grabbed me and pulled me into a dark corner.

Who did this asshole think he was? Ty's boss and protector, that's who.

"It's going good, girl. Let him be," he said tersely as he gripped my forearm. "Glad you listened to me. But don't keep hanging around here. His head's clear, and he needs that."

This time, I couldn't avoid the tears falling. They poured down my face as I jerked away from him and headed back to my room, my head swimming with *T* words the entire walk back.

Touché. Tunnel of love . . . sucks. Tuna Niçoise. Tramp. Trollop.

Unfortunately these weren't the more positive words associated with the letter *T*. My little coping technique had gone over to the dark side.

Slamming my door behind me in my rush for my bed, I looked up when I didn't hear it bang shut. There was Stacy, her foot keeping the door from closing.

"You ready to come clean?" She cocked her head to one side, narrowing her eyes on me as she hooked her hand on her hip.

I shook my head and forced out a *no*, but my voice wavered from the quivering of my bottom lip.

Stacy's expression gentled as she slid onto the end of my bed. "Come on, girl. You're a mess. You broke up with a good dude. Why?"

She looked tired again, with dark circles under her eyes, but she was taking the time for me. Her concern for me broke through my defenses, but I wasn't the only one with problems. It was time for a little *quid pro quo.*

"I'll tell you if you tell me what's going on with you," I said, putting the deal on the table, and she nodded.

"Some man—no, not just a man . . . a coach—told me to back off. Said I wasn't good for Tiberius or the team. He told me I was an unnecessary distraction, and he's right."

Her eyes bulged at my revelation. "You're shitting me?" When I shook my head, she blurted, "That's not the truth, Tingly. He misses you every second. I know it; he told me. He tells the guys all the time. And look at you, you're fading away to nothing, all bony. I know you're not eating, and you been running like a Kenyan. And why? Because of this stupid coach butting in where he don't belong?"

Drawing in a deep, shuddering breath, I admitted, "Tonight I sneaked into the game, and the same coach found me. Told me Tiberius is doing well without me."

She shook her head this time. "Huh-uh, he's not. I don't know who this guy thinks he is, but he's wrong, and he can't do what he's doing."

"You have to let it be," I begged her.

Stacy nodded, but looked away from me as she did. She was

lying. *Shit.*

Turning the tables on her, I demanded, "Now, what's going on with you?"

She shifted on the bed, her gaze anywhere but on me as she said, "I was pregnant. I ended it, and I can't sleep now."

"What?" Tears gathered in my eyes all over again. This girl's problems were so much bigger than mine. "What happened? Who? Why didn't you lean on us?"

She closed her eyes, forcing out a solo tear that escaped to tumble down her cheek. "It happened right when we got back to school. Chey doesn't know. It was a stupid night, after a party. Things got carried away with a friend of mine, and we fell into bed. We didn't use protection. He'd be so mad to know I did this . . . to his baby. It wouldn't sit well, so I got no one. Chey'd freak out about it and tell him."

"Do I know him?"

Stacy lifted her glistening dark gaze to meet mine and nodded. Her nose was running, her eyes swollen and red. "Jamel." It was a whisper, almost inaudible.

My hand flew over my mouth as I gasped. "He would never let you do this alone, Stacy. He's a good guy deep down."

"I know," she said in a small, sad voice before she crawled closer, then lay down on the pillow next to me. "But he woulda made me keep the baby, and I'm here on a scholarship for ball."

She sighed as I reached out to caress her hair. "We're a messed-up bunch, Tingly. Those basketball boys have us tied in knots." Trying to smile, she added, "Except yours can be fixed, and my baby is gone," her last words said on a whimper.

I drew her into my arms and hugged her tight, sobbing along with her. Before long, we fell into an exhausted sleep, spooning like sisters in my little bed.

We were an unlikely pair, my roommate Stacy and me. I never would have dreamed that we could become good friends, drawn together by our deep, but separate, regrets.

chapter
twenty-six

Stacy had gone to sleep snuggled in my arms for the last week, ever since she'd come clean about her painful loss. Now she looked better, her eyes brighter and her spirit and body stronger.

This morning when she woke up, I took her hand in mine and insisted, "Today's the day."

Her dark eyes searched mine, looking for an out, anything that would prolong her telling Chey. Poor Chey; she knew something was up, between Stacy hiding out in my room and my being so quiet about it. It was time for her to be clued in.

"She needs to know, Stace. I know you don't want to share, but you gotta do it. Secrets are toxic, honey. Especially between friends."

When she glared at me, I felt a whisper of shame. *Like I'm one to talk.*

Forcing myself to forge ahead despite my hypocrisy, I said, "You just need to explain that you don't want her to judge, but to try to understand." With a firm squeeze to her hand, I went to go run the indoor track, leaving her to do what was needed.

The January morning was bitter so I was bundled in my big down coat, shearling boots, a hat, and gloves to make the trek to the gymnasium. Pulling up the lapels, I puffed hot air into the downy layers of my coat, trying to warm my chin. The mild weather might be the only thing I missed about Los Angeles. My blood was still thin after a couple of years of living in Ohio, and it didn't matter how many layers I wore, I could never really get warm in the winter.

As I pushed the revolving door to the gym with one gloved hand, I pulled off my dark green Hafton Under Armour beanie with the other as soon as I was inside and shoved it deep inside my pocket. I was making my way to the locker room, unbuttoning my coat so I could enjoy the warmth as it trickled through my bones, when Logan came strutting out.

Although I ducked my head to avoid his vicious stare and tried to step around him, he wasn't going to let me off that easily. Tapping my shoulder, he said, "Heard you broke up with the baller. That make you fair game again?"

Seriously? What a douche this guy was. Tried to rape me, then thinks he still has a chance.

"I was never fair game to you, Logan," I spat out, "and thank God those *ballers* were there to stop you from taking what wasn't yours to take." Pulling myself to my full height, I leaned in to make my point as his eyes grew wide. "So, just walk on by. You got lucky when I didn't report that shit, but if I were you, I wouldn't try that again with me or anyone else because *those guys* are watching. I don't have to be dating one of them for them to keep an eye on an enemy. And that's exactly what you are, you asshole."

Not giving him a chance to respond, I stomped away, ignoring his calling my name after me. After years of living among the sick

verité

pricks of Beverly Hills, I knew I was nothing more than a conquest
to Logan. Guys like him were pathetic and predictable; once he was
called out on his behavior and told the guys were watching him, he
would be constantly looking over his shoulder. That was the thing
about fake people like him—they were cowards, and didn't want
others to know the truth about them, only the facade they presented.

With a small winning smile on my face, I changed into my
running shorts and tank. Stephanie wanted the whole team at the
track at least three days a week, and there was a sign-in sheet at the
desk. After jotting my name down, I climbed the steps to the track.
It didn't take long for me to warm up, just a few laps at a rapid pace
while Katy Perry's "I Kissed a Girl" played on my iPod.

Although I was required to do thirty-five laps, I ran forty-five.
When I finally clomped down the stairs to head back to the lockers,
sweat was running down my breastbone into my cleavage, my tank
was soaked across the middle, my vocal cords were dry from heavy
breathing.

Inside the locker room, I plopped down on a bench and grabbed
a Gatorade from my bag. I was guzzling it and nearly choked when
I heard my name booming through the gym, bouncing off the tile
walls inside the cavernous locker room. "Tingly! Where the hell are
you? Tingly?"

Now what?

"You can't go in there," a girl shrieked from right outside the
locker room door.

"Tingly, you in there?" Ty shouted. "Get out here! I need to talk
to you."

I didn't answer. My head whipped in every direction, looking all
around the locker room for an alternate exit.

"There's nowhere else to run, T. Get out here!"

Great. Now Tiberius was a mind reader.

"Come on, just step away from the door, please?" the girl, probably a gym employee, pleaded with him as he continued to yell my name.

The wall vibrated from someone's fist banging into it. Or maybe a foot?

I quickly shucked off my shorts and kicked off my shoes, using my feet to push them off. Hurrying, I stripped off my wet tank, then yanked on sweatpants and a long-sleeved shirt. After throwing my coat over my arm and hiking my bag on my shoulder, I shoved my feet in my boots.

The truth was that I wanted to burst through the door and jump into the arms of the man behind the voice. But it was no longer like that between us, which was all my fault, but still. We weren't together anymore.

I tiptoed out, afraid of who or what else might be lurking on the other side of the locker room door, other than Tiberius. As soon as I peeked around it, he threw his arm around me and held his hand up, saying, "Show's over, folks." Then he rushed me out of the building, steering me toward Trey's SUV that was parked in front of the gymnasium.

Tiberius hit the button on the key fob and the locks clicked open as we approached. "You know I'd never force you to go with me, but we gotta talk, T, so get in. We're going to talk *now.*" He held the car door open, regarding me with curious eyes. "You're not running. You're getting in this car. We're getting the fuck outta here and you're going to explain what the hell Stacy is running off at the mouth about."

Knowing there was no use in arguing, I slid into the dark gray leather seat. As I reached for the seatbelt, Tiberius slammed the car door shut and ran around the front to the driver's side. He shoved the car into drive and sped off, taking us across campus and up the hill past the Ag building. As we headed off-road into the clearing behind the trees where we first really talked, he shifted into four-wheel drive. The trees were bare, the shelter no longer covered in lights, but the sun shone through the tree canopy, lighting the space.

Tiberius threw the gearshift into park and reached behind him to grab a blanket. "Wrap yourself up, Rex, because we're not going anywhere for a long while."

He cut the motor and turned to me. Banging the steering wheel with his hand, causing me to jump, he gritted out, "What the fuck?"

I sucked in a deep breath, my eyes wide. "You startled me."

"Not that, I'm sorry I scared you, but what did you say 'bout you and *who*? A coach? What coach? Don't fuck with me, *Tinglee*?"

The way he ranted on, drawing out my name at the end, cut me like a knife. I stared a hole into the dashboard in front of me as I lifted one shoulder in a weak half shrug. "I was only trying to do what was best for you."

"That's bullshit. You wanted an out. You were looking for any damn possible out, any fucking excuse to cut ties and run. You're making this shit up!"

"He said you didn't need any distractions, that my parents . . . Pierre . . . they were here and bad for you."

"Who said that?"

"That man, your coach. Coach Smith."

"Stop with the lies," he yelled, slamming the steering wheel again. "I'm my own man. Let *me* decide who or what is distracting. You're not *distracting*. Not having you in my life is . . . is a big fucking distraction!"

I'd never been on the receiving end of an angry Tiberius. His voice boomed throughout the car. A chill ran down my spine, causing my whole body to visibly shiver. Not out of fear, but panic. Panic that I'd screwed everything up, that I should have talked to Tiberius sooner, and that I'd lost him for good.

I buried my head in my hands. I'd fucked up bad. I didn't know—maybe I thought I'd end it for the season and then pick up after? But I wasn't that special. I had no idea why I thought Tiberius would wait for me.

"Tingly, look at me!" he shouted, but I merely shook my bowed head. "Look at me. Christ, you're putting me through hell. I don't have a Coach Smith!"

I lifted my head, my thoughts all jumbled, my eyes burning from tears straining to break free. My heart galloped in my chest as my hands shook, and the pit in my belly was about to rupture from stress. *What did he say?*

"You are *not* distracting," he insisted. "I'm gonna quit the team if you don't tell me what the hell really happened, and then you'll really have fucked shit up."

"You can't quit the team. Not because of me," I squeaked out. "Your coach said you were gonna be a starter next year, and they need you without any distractions. Without me." The last two words came out soft and forced because I didn't want them to be true, but they were. "Coach Smith heard about my parents and Pierre in the locker room, about their visit and the guys' involvement, and he didn't want them to be a part of it."

"Fuck!" he yelled, making my ears ring from his roar.

My hand went to massage my heart back to a normal pace. I didn't feel well at all. My breathing was as ragged as if I'd just run across the United States, and I felt like my heart was going to rip through my chest and shatter my breastbone along the way. Something wasn't sitting well in my mind, but I was too upset and frazzled to figure it out.

"I'm sorry," Tiberius said. "I'm going to calm down." He took several deep breaths before asking, "Do you love me, T?"

I nodded. "Of course I do. I did what was best for you, but I've been miserable. But you worked so hard to get here, and I don't want to be the reason anything gets messed up."

"Did you hear me?" He leaned across the center console and swiped away my tears with his thumb. "I don't have a Coach Smith."

I swallowed hard, trying to dislodge the enormous lump in my throat. "You don't?"

"No."

"A big white guy, ruddy cheeks, gray hair, pot belly, past his prime? Maybe I got the name wrong. Does that sound familiar?" I asked, my brain working overtime.

He slid his hands on either side of my face, cupping my cheeks to steady my gaze on him. "T, there's no Coach Smith, no overweight white dude on our coaching staff. He doesn't exist, so I wanna know who came to see you. What really happened?"

I tried to wriggle out of his hands, but he kept my focus on him—not with strength or pressure but the power of his gaze. His eyes pleaded with me to tell him the truth.

"I'm not lying." My denial came out so weak, even I could hear the defeat in my tone. I cleared my throat in an effort to dredge up some strength. "I was at your game, the one around New Year's, and this man sat down next to me and explained how you were a top recruit. He said the team needed you free from distractions."

Tiberius dropped his hands from my face and gathered my hands in his, never taking his focus off me. I went on to describe my conversation with Coach Smith, and his later attempt to check in on me. I tried hard not to cry, but my body trembled from emotion. Tiberius tightened his grip on my hands, only breaking away to gun the car's engine so he could turn the heat on full blast.

With his hands back on mine, he said, "First off, we may talk like a bunch of sex-starved idiots in the locker room, but we do not discuss shit like what happened with Pierre and your dad. We know better than that; anyone could hear. Second, no one on the team would say you're a distraction. Coaches like us to have one girl, not a million pieces of booty making us crazy. And finally, there is no Coach Smith. Someone set us up, Rex." He stared me down, allowing me to come to my own awful conclusion.

"My parents," I breathed out. Then the dam broke and I was a sniveling, snotty mess. "S-s-seems like the only explanation."

My head throbbed; I felt like it was going to explode, or maybe it was just me that was going to combust. I broke free from Tiberius's grip and threw open the car door, practically tossing myself onto the ground as I gasped for air. Pacing back and forth as I dragged the half-wrapped blanket behind me, I screamed, "How could they do this?"

"Babe, breathe."

Tiberius made his way out of the car and wrapped his arms around me from behind, pulling me close to calm my flailing motions and flaming temper. I let myself relax into his hard chest, stilling my body and my mind.

"They've ruined everything," I said on a sob, swiping angrily at my wet cheeks. "They've taken everything from me, but why? All I did was be born, and they actually tried for that. Like really tried, spent money to get me—their perfect pink baby. But I wasn't so perfect. They wanted to return me, fix me. I should've known they'd do anything to stop us."

Tiberius moved us backward until he was leaning against the car, and I was relying on him to hold me up. He whispered the whole way, "They're not gonna ruin us."

"I was just an investment," I shrieked. "My dad always said '*You have to put money in to get money out.*' That's what fertility treatments were to him—putting money in. It's always about that goddamn trust, you know. He's so mad that he didn't get his hands on it, but my grandparents wanted me to have it."

I was trembling with rage, my voice breaking toward the end. Between the long run inside in the dry heat and the coldness of the air now swirling around me, my body broke out into a cold sweat. I shivered while droplets slid down my back.

"And you do," he reminded me. "You have it."

"My grandparents were uppity, you know, they had their clubs and Rolls Royces and big mansions and all that. They would take me to tea, and I hated tea. But they weren't like my parents—they wouldn't care if I wore little shorts and a T-shirt rather than a frilly dress. They would talk to me, really listen to me when I told them about my Latin class or my running track at school. They even came to a few meets."

My eyes blurred at the memory, and I swiped at them as I laid my head on Tiberius's chest. Unable to meet his eyes, I said, "They saw firsthand how my parents ignored me or put down my clothes or interests. When my dad found me with Blane Maxwell's father, they took me to their house for the weekend and explained how bad they felt. They should have never given my dad so much power, but not once did they blame me for doing what I did with a grown man. In fact, they wanted my dad to press charges, but he wouldn't. *Had to save face*, he said."

Tiberius stiffened at that last part, and I looked up at him. "They told me that weekend that they made changes to their will, that the money would be all mine so I could break free and make a life for myself away from my parents. They knew what I was up against, how horrible my parents are." My words trailed off at the end until they were nothing more than a whisper. "My grandparents wanted me to be extra-ordinary in spite of all the money, the luxuries I was raised with. Because they'd had all that themselves, they understood what was important in life. And all I ever asked for was to break free," I said sadly.

I lifted my face to the sky, searching for a shooting star or some sign that someone was looking out for me. Tiberius gripped me tighter, squeezing my waist, reminding me he was my sign. My truth.

"You are breaking free," he said softly, "just doing it on your own terms. I loved my momma, but I learned a long time ago that just 'cause someone gives a sperm or some shit like that, it doesn't mean love. My dad, he's in the rearview, and I'm sorry, babe, but you got to put your parents there too."

I turned in his arms to face him. "What about us?" I asked while staring down at his sweatshirt, imagining the lines and definition of his chest beneath it.

"We're gonna be good, Rex, if you stop running." His voice turned dark as he added, "After I find this Coach Smith and fuck him up."

"Don't, Ty," I whispered.

"I am. I will."

He didn't let me answer because he kissed me. Hard. He brought his hands around my back, pulling me close, taking my mouth and swiping his tongue through my lips in one stroke. His erection pressed against me, searing through my clothes, but this wasn't about *that*. Not yet.

"I don't want you to get hurt," I whispered against his lips.

"I won't, but he will, babe," he mumbled back before deepening the kiss. He lifted the blanket, tightening it around my back, yanking me even closer to him. We continued to make out, tasting, licking, consuming, and making up for lost time.

I broke free, trying to catch my breath. "I'm sorry," I said as I leaned my forehead into his and closed my eyes.

"Shoulda come to me." He gripped my butt, drawing me closer. We were one; there was no difference in where my body stopped and his began.

My eyes screwed shut, I mumbled against his shirt, "I've messed up everything in my life. I didn't want to make a mess for you."

"Open your eyes, T," he said, and I looked up to find his blue eyes searching mine. "You didn't mess shit up in your life. Your parents did. Leaving me could've messed shit up, but it didn't because I fought for you. It's time you fought for what you want and stop trying to shock everyone around you into submission. Be the extraordinary person you are, Rex."

I ran my nose along his, giving him Eskimo kisses like a romantic fool. "Extraordinary? I thought you believed in being overly ordinary."

"There's always exceptions to the rules, and you're one of them." He ran his lips across my cheek, whispering his words along my skin until he bit my ear lobe for emphasis.

My tongue lingered along his jaw, my teeth sinking in for effect, and a moan rumbled from deep in his chest.

"Not time for slow," he demanded, taking my mouth back in a brutal kiss.

Our tongues dueled, seeking control. I ran my hands up his chest, gripping his shirt and holding on for dear life, and then I tempered my actions. Tracing his lips, I circled his mouth before entering again.

"Slow is good," I said, my words vibrating through both of us.

He nodded. "When we have all the time in the world in front of us, it is. Are you going to keep running?"

"No."

"Good. It's cold; let's get you back to my place and warm you up in the shower."

Looking up at him, I shook my head. "I don't want to go back. I want to stay here forever, in our little forest where no one can mess anything up. Where my parents can't find us, and the guys can't tease us, and my roommates can't hound us, and . . . ugh, Stacy. I forgot. She needs me to get back."

I lost my train of thought as Tiberius kissed me again passionately, pulling me tight against him. He held the blanket with one hand and slipped the other underneath to unzip my coat, then roam down my side and under my shirt. His rough hand caught on the lace of my bra, his calluses from dribbling warring with the gentle fabric, until he slipped his hand under the cup and against my naked skin.

I loved the roughness of his palm coasting along my smooth breast; the friction added a whole new sensation. I brought one leg up and hitched it around his waist, hooking it around his ass to bring my heat closer to his erection.

"Ah," I moaned down his throat as our tongues continued to dance.

"T? You good?" he asked.

"Uh-huh," I murmured. "More."

He pinched my nipple, sending ripples shooting through my belly and my core, traveling down to my toes. His finger continued to draw circles around my hard nipple, then he moved lower. His pointer finger traced down my abdomen, stopping and doing a little figure eight at my belly button before tracing the waistband of my pants. He dipped in, edging my panties away from my skin, teasing and taunting me with his slow seduction.

I was burning up in the blanket; my skin was covered in prickly heat. Using my foot on his behind, I gave myself some leverage to push myself closer, desperately trying to get some friction where I needed it.

Of course, he put his hand on my ass and stilled my movement. Holding me in place, not allowing me to grind against him, he started walking toward the nearby pavilion, his feet carrying us across the flooring as I swung my other leg up. He unwound the blanket, never letting go of me, my legs still wound around his middle and my arms over his shoulders. Placing the blanket over the wood chips, he laid us down on top of it.

If I closed my eyes, I could almost imagine the lights trimming the overhang the night we first really talked at the party. Even without them, this moment was nearly perfect. It would be made better if Tiberius were inside me, but I could tell he was in one of his "slow" moods.

He leaned over me, his frame held up on his forearm as his lips hovered a breath away from mine. "No more running, no more believing strangers?" he asked, his lips brushing mine with his words.

"No," I said. "Please kiss me."

And he did. Then he lifted my shirt, sliding it over my head before he lowered his body a bit more to shield me from the cold air and share his body heat with me. He moved his mouth lower, taking a road trip down my body, stopping to make side trips down my terrain. He ran his tongue along my clavicle, licked and sucked my nipples, and traced meaningless yet reverent patterns on my belly. He would stop every so often to blow cool breath over the heated trail he already laid, making goose bumps and ripples of want rise to the surface in equal measure. Then he would begin his travels all over again.

I nearly climbed out of my skin from the delicious frustration of it all. Tiberius was on a luxurious vacation, and I wanted a quick getaway. But I knew better than to push my luck; Tiberius would get what he wanted and at the end of the day, I'd admit that taking our time was better. It was like getting a green card to stay and work and play versus only a passport.

Finally, he arrived at the top of my pants and traced his tongue along the waistband. "Tingly," he let out on an exhale. My name sounded perfect rolling off his tongue. "You ready?"

I lifted my hips, signaling I wanted him to pull my pants off. He shimmied them down and pushed my panties to the side, allowing his tongue to leisurely course over me. He went up one fold and down the other, taking each run with infinite focus and care. I lifted my pelvis, hinting, begging—whatever it took to get him to go where I wanted. He didn't rush, though, building my sense of urgency and need, and then he softly landed on my clit. When he flicked his tongue over my most sensitive spot, I moaned out loud, disregarding the fact that we were outside where anyone could bear witness to my ecstasy. It was a loud, luxuriating moan followed by another.

"Like that?" he teased.

His words rumbled over my core, ratcheting me even higher, and I came. My body burst into a million flames in the middle of a cold field during winter in Ohio. I may as well have been at the equator.

I tugged on his sweatshirt, which he was unfortunately still wearing, and motioned for him to move back up. I slid my hands under the fleecy fabric, pulling it over his head as he made his way up. His mouth came back to mine, fusing our lips. I tasted myself on his tongue, commingled with some type of spearmint from earlier. I sucked on the tip of it, wanting to get drunk on the mixture.

vérité

I'd always been a sexual person, but it had mostly been about the forbidden aspect of it, the satisfaction of doing it with someone I shouldn't be doing it with in a place we shouldn't have been. It wasn't sensual or meaningful. This was different. Every touch, each movement was filled with passion and partnership. We were equals, lovers, friends, taking our time, not beating a stopwatch or dashing to the finish line before our parents walked in. This was the definition of the truth. *La vérité.*

"*Je t'aime,*" I whispered.

"English, T," Tiberius growled. "You could've just told me that was the worst pussy eating you ever had."

"I love you," I said, laughing. "I said '*I love you.*' For the record, the French lick or graze pussy, as in '*brouter le minou.*' And for what it's worth, that was incredible pussy licking." It was the dirtiest and most forthright I'd been with Tiberius, but it didn't feel silly or spoken only for the sake of being dirty. It was sexy and uninhibited with a person who I loved.

"Your moaning made that pretty clear," he joked back.

I couldn't help but burst out into giggles, but it didn't last for long. Tiberius used his free hand to push his pants down—*thank God* for track pants. His boxer briefs went off with them, and he was totally naked, braced over me. I reached out to stroke him, his length long and rigid in my palm. My thumb brushed over his tip and his hips jerked forward, his dick pressing into my hand. I used the moisture to coat him and stroke him a few more times before he slid his hand on top of mine, stopping my movement.

"T, stop, I want inside you," he bent and whispered in my ear. With his hand over mine, we guided him into me.

As we fit together as one, I finally understood what Tiberius had tried to convince me about the physical act of fucking feeling way better when the heart was involved. His had been involved for a long time now, and now mine was too. I hadn't believed it before when he'd said it had to mean something, but now I did.

Everything was better when it meant something.

We didn't linger much longer in the cold that day after we made love, but we did hide out in Tiberius's townhouse for a day and night before sitting down with the guys and filling them in about Coach Smith.

Tiberius was dead set on some sort of crazy revenge against the guy who'd impersonated his coach, and he wanted the whole squad on the lookout for the man. Jamel was fit to be tied over it all, and Trey punched a wall. After all, he'd had to live with Tiberius for the few weeks we were apart. Ginny and Chey had joined us for the chat, so I could fill everyone in at once. Ginny cried, and Chey decided she was "gonna kick some white ass."

We were all sitting around Jamel's condo, the music going in the background, pizza boxes and empty soda and beer bottles lining the table, when Jamel asked, "Where's Stacy? She know what happened?"

"You know what? She's been a real pain in the ass lately. Moody, weepy. I'm sick of her." Chey rolled her eyes. "Ask Tingly . . . Stacy's been sleeping in her room for a week," she added as she glared at me.

Of course, Chey knew what was up; Stacy had told her as planned. She was simply playing Jamel with this conversation. And putting the onus on me.

Jamel turned his gaze toward me, raising an eyebrow, silently asking if I knew they had slept together.

"Dude, what do you give?" Lamar asked, his hand drifting over his braids.

Tiberius put his arm around me, pulling me tight into his side. "Yeah, what gives?"

Uncomfortable at being put on the spot, I stared at the carpet and shrugged. "She's had a lot going on, I think. She doesn't need this put on her . . . all my shit."

Jamel dropped the subject until everyone was busy cleaning up, and then he sneaked up behind me while I was closing a garbage bag. "You gonna come clean? Tell me what's going on?"

"Don't, Jamel. Let it go," I said, but it was wishful thinking.

"Ya know 'bout us, right?" he said in a low voice. "We had a few nights. She want more or what? Is that it?"

He'd cornered me in the small kitchen, making me extremely uncomfortable. I was leaning against the counter when he grabbed the garbage bag and threw it down before leaning close to me. Tiberius was involved in some game on the Xbox, otherwise he would have gone into attack mode.

"I'm helping T take the garbage out," Jamel yelled before dragging me outside.

As soon as we got outside, he asked, "She want more? She pining for more of this?" He ran his hand up and down his body. "I don't do that. Got my lady back home. Here is just . . . fun and shit. Ball babies and groupies, ya know that, right?"

"Jamel, I'm not in a position to judge." I snatched the garbage bag from his hand and walked toward the Dumpster.

"It's different with Tiberius," he said from behind me. "I'm not him, but he's not into ball babies. If that's what you're worried about."

"I'm not," I said, the slamming of the Dumpster drowning the agitation in my voice. I turned and brushed past him, marching back to the townhouse, afraid I was going to cave and tell him everything.

"Then what's the big fucking deal?" he called after me. "She knows I don't really do seconds and shit, and she had me a few times."

I stopped in my tracks on the little pathway back to the door and turned to stare Jamel down. Funny how I was so scared of him the first time we met, and now I was the one with the upper hand. "She got knocked up, Jamel."

His eyes grew wide. "What'd you just say?"

"She was pregnant."

"*Was*? What do you mean *was*? How the fuck do you know it's mine?" he said through clenched teeth.

I sighed, knowing I had to tell him the rest. "She was pregnant with your baby, and now she's healing. On her own. That's what I know."

"Fuck, that bitch had no right!" he yelled. "That's my baby!" Turning, he took off running up the hill.

I should have felt guilty for sharing a secret that wasn't mine to tell, but I didn't. Stacy had gone to Tiberius and told him about Coach Smith, and we'd worked it out because of her. Jamel wouldn't care what was wrong with Stacy or if she wanted more if he didn't have feelings for her. Maybe they'd work something out.

I hoped.

The next day I woke up, got a ride to the mall, and used a little of my funds to buy a disposable phone and a new cell phone complete with a different number. My preference would have been to wait a few days to do what I had to do, but I knew if my parents didn't call off this Smith guy, Tiberius would go after him.

The guys were already making plans for a setup. They wanted me to go to a game and wait for Smith to approach, then keep him occupied until the end of the game when I could deliver him to them.

I wasn't doing that. No way was I risking Tiberius getting hurt or in trouble. The whole fiasco with Logan was enough; I didn't want the team defending me anymore.

So I called my parents using the disposable. My dad answered on the second ring using his pompous, professional greeting, probably since I'd blocked my number so it would show up on his caller ID as PRIVATE.

"Colt Simmons."

"Dad, it's me."

I paced the length of my small bedroom as Chey and Tiberius sat on my bed, nodding their heads in a steady beat of encouragement.

"Why are you calling from a strange number?"

"Listen, Dad, I changed my number again. I don't want you to try to get it or contact me or hand deliver any past lovers to my door. I've met with a lawyer. The trust is secure and in my name, and there's nothing you can do to get your hands on it, so you may as well leave me alone."

"Tingly," he growled through the small flip phone.

"I'm serious, Dad. Tell Mom too. I appreciate what you all did for me growing up—whatever that was despite all your little antics—but this last stunt was something. Words don't even describe it."

"What stunt? I don't even know what you're talking about," he shouted.

"Coach Smith and his little ploy to get me away from Tiberius."

"I don't know what you're talking about. Plus, I thought you were done with that ni—boy."

"What were you going to say, Dad? Speak up! Did you forget the polite and proper politically correct version of yourself for a second?"

My eyes welled up with tears, but despite the conflict ensuing over the phone, they were happy tears. I was taking control, and it felt good. In the past, I'd acted—ignoring calls, changing phones, and switching brokers—but had never spoken. It was time I spoke up for myself.

"Tingly, you need better than that sports player. On scholarship."

"*I'm on an athletic scholarship!*" I screamed.

Chey stood and came to put her arm around me, while Tiberius sat on the edge of the bed with his fists clenched.

"Nothing matters what you say now, Dad. This is over. Whatever you, Mom, and I were is O.V.E.R." I spelled out the last word for emphasis, and as each letter rolled off my tongue, my resolve strengthened.

"You're making a B.I.G. mistake," my dad said, mocking my spelling out words.

"No, you did when you sent the mysterious Coach Smith to see me. Didn't you think I'd find out that there *is no* Coach Smith?"

He didn't let me finish my tirade. Not Colt Simmons, he had to get the last word. "So what if I sent him? I was trying to do you a big favor. Good-bye, Tingly," he said, and hung up without another word.

I threw the damn phone into the wall and the case cracked. Hurrying over to where it fell, I stomped on it, crushing the last remnant of any relationship with my parents. Then I started laughing hysterically, bent over in full-on giggles, while Chey stood behind me, rubbing soothing circles on my back.

Tiberius stood up to gather me in my arms. "It's okay. I got her," he said, dismissing Chey, then he turned to me, his voice soft. "Rex, sit down, babe. You're going through something."

He guided me to the bed, but I couldn't just sit there.

"No, I'm not!" I shouted. "I'm fucking delirious. Let them have the last word. I'm done with them for good, and now that Smith asshole won't be lurking around anymore."

I stood up as Chey made her way out my bedroom door, pumping her fist into the air and chanting, "Woot!"

Tiberius stood up and cornered me against the dresser, pressing close to dip his forehead against mine. "Yeah, I wish you'd gone through with setting Smith up, but this was your call, babe."

"I know," I said. "Is that okay? I needed this. Needed to do it my way." It came out hushed, crashing with the heavy breathing rising from my chest.

He nodded. "Plus the guys did a number on Pierre."

"And I got you now . . . forget having the last word with my parents. *J'ai la vérité dans mes mains.*" Grabbing a handful of his shirt, I pulled him in for a kiss.

"English, Rex," he rumbled. He stopped the kiss, impatient for me to answer, his lips hovering over mine.

"It means I've got the truth in my hands," I explained. "Fuck everyone, I have you."

"Nah, fuck me!"

"Tiberius, are you getting dirty on me?" Grinning, I wrestled him to the bed and straddled his lap.

He didn't answer; he showed me. Turned out we didn't need any English after all.

chapter
twenty-seven

" Come on, Stephanie! You're a slave driver!" I shouted as I rounded the track for the umpteenth time, and she yelled, "Two more." Her voice carried in the wind as I wound my way through the lanes one more time, secretly loving the burn. Pushing my quads, I passed Nadine and kicked up dust in my wake.

It was March, and we were back to regular outdoor practices every morning before classes. The track was typically desolate at that time, other than the random university employee getting in a workout before work. The sky was shrouded in a fine layer of fog as the sun made its way high into the sky, and my cheeks pinked quickly as the temperature rose. Mostly I ran home from practice, but occasionally I was social and grabbed breakfast with the other girls. A big part of the conversation was always focused on why we'd been split from the men's team. I'd played a big role, but they didn't know that.

After I'd made up with Tiberius, and Stacy had come clean with Jamel, the prospect of keeping everything a secret about Logan festered in my gut. Finally, toward the end of February, I called a meeting with Coach Wallace and Stephanie, and explained what had happened. Jamel came with me to lend support and to corroborate my story.

In the end, it was my word against Logan's. The coach couldn't do much about it, especially since Logan had already sat out a suspension due to his imaginary fight. My report went on his record as an accusation made against him. Hopefully, that tidbit plus my threats that the guys were watching him would keep Logan in line. The one thing the coach did do was to separate our practices, forcing the men to take the warmer afternoon slot.

"One more!"

Stephanie's shouts trailed behind me as I picked up my pace for my last lap. When I finally came to a stop by the Gatorade cooler, I almost fell into a large wall.

"Hey," Tiberius said.

Thrilled to see him, I jumped up and down on my already exhausted legs. "You're back? Congrats! Elite Eight! Woo-hoo!"

The men's basketball team was in the middle of March Madness, having won enough games to narrowly make it into the final eight teams remaining the night before. I had to settle for watching on TV rather than in person because of my practices. Chey, Stacy, and I jumped and cheered all around the common area after each basket Hafton scored.

Tiberius smiled at my enthusiastic greeting before leaning down and brushing his lips over my cheek. "Got back about three o'clock this morning, but I didn't want to wake you."

I pouted at him, making sure my disappointment was evident.

"Rex, you needed to sleep and get up for practice. Don't read into it."

I pulled up on my tippy toes and kissed him on the lips. The kiss was chaste and quick, but delivered my silent apology.

"Come on, I'll walk you back," he said.

I took off in a light jog until Tiberius grabbed me by the waist and tossed me over his shoulder. "I said walk, not run, T. I'm exhausted, and no one can keep up with you."

"Ha! You're tired," I said, gloating just a little. "What did you do? Did you see what I just ran?"

His blue eyes sparkled in the sunlight as he set me back down. "Yeah, I did, which is why you should walk." He turned toward the dorms, moving at a leisurely pace, and I settled into stride next to him.

"So, are we celebrating tonight?" I asked, my mouth curving up in the corners.

"The win, yes. The other thing, no."

"Nope, we are going out for your birthday!" I taunted him. "Mel and I got the whole thing planned."

"Tingly, I told you I didn't want to do that," he said with a frown.

"Yeah, I know, but we are. We're going to the diner for dinner and then heading out to that techno dance place."

He slanted me a dubious look. "All of a sudden you're a party girl?"

"Just for tonight. We need to celebrate, Ty. And I may have ordered a cake."

He shook his head, blowing out a deep breath. Despite his reluctance to be the center of attention, he'd love it once we got started celebrating everything that was Tiberius. And there was a lot to celebrate. He was a truly good guy—no, the best. He was also slated to be the starting shooting guard next season, and was a great friend, an even better boyfriend, and the most amazing lover.

verité

Once we reached my dorm, he stopped outside and said, "I'm starving. Let's go get breakfast. What time are your classes?"

"I don't start until noon today, but what about you?"

A deep laugh rumbled from his chest. "We're excused today and tomorrow because of the tournament."

"You suck," I said, slapping his chest. "The girls are gonna be so pissed. They're never excused from anything."

"Don't tell 'em. Hurry up and go get changed so we can eat."

"I gotta shower," I said innocently, then looked up at him through my eyelashes. "Wanna join me?"

He flung the door open to my building, holding it wide with his arm. I ducked under and headed for the elevator.

"Not hungry anymore, Rex," was all he said as I pushed the button for my floor.

Eventually we made it out for sustenance as well as coffee for me, and afterward I went to class. Tiberius put on a big act again about not wanting to go out for his birthday, but looked like a little boy in a toy store when it came time to actually go. He mentioned that they never did much for birthdays when he was growing up, and I think he was secretly excited to really celebrate.

The guys all showed up and made Tiberius do a round of shots before ordering up half the menu at the diner. Chey and Tiffanie came, and Ginny brought Bryce.

Nadine had ambushed me in the locker room after she heard about the little soirée and realized she wasn't included. I'd had enough of her perkiness—both her personality and her tits—and her ridiculous backstabbing disguised as "peppy party girl." When official practices started up again, I told her as much. I was sick of being expected to accept crap treatment. My parents had demanded it for twenty-one years, and I wasn't about to let Nadine assume she could get away with the same. When she suggested Tiberius was less than the best--all according to Logan--that was the breaking point. As soon as she brought Logan up, she was dead to me.

Stacy didn't come. She and Jamel weren't speaking, and to say it was strained was an understatement. Tonight was about Tiberius, and Jamel kept the alcohol flowing and the good times coming. By the time we left the diner and made our way down the street toward the club, we were a rowdy bunch.

The club was foggy in a layer of man-made smoke and had glittery red disco balls hanging from the ceiling. As soon as we got in, Jamel and Trey hit the DJ booth, and I saw the two of them negotiating with the poor guy to take control of the list of upcoming songs. As soon as the current track ended and a familiar song came on, I knew they'd succeeded. The bass thumped all the way through the floor and up my toes into my spine as I sipped on a rum and Diet Coke.

The other guys were having fun buying Tiberius drinks with ridiculous names, and he was doing his best not to drink every single one. He had a row of various cocktails and shots in front of him— Sex on the Beach, Buttery Nipples, and Flaming Orgasms, along with plain old Jack.

When Eric B. and Rakim came bursting through the speakers, he grabbed my hand and dragged me onto the dance floor. Grinding up against me as soon as we made it to the perimeter of the hot, sweaty dancers, he sang a little in my ear as he kept us close. Holding me tight, Tiberius edged our way to the very corner of the dance floor where we'd get bumped as little as possible.

When he planted a wet, messy kiss on my face, I realized he was slightly tipsy, and I chuckled.

"What?" he said.

"You're kinda cute, you know?"

"I'm not cute. I'm sexy, babe." His chest rumbled with the words, his voice raspy and heated.

"Yes, and cute," I whispered back in his ear, standing on my tiptoes even in my wedge Nike high-tops—yeah, I got really cool basketball-girlfriend shoes. My little whisper while nipping on his ear earned me another sloppy kiss, followed by a more seductive one. Tiberius's tongue swiped through my mouth, trailing the roof before tangling with mine.

He was definitely tipsy. Mr. It-Has-To-Mean-Something and Take-It-Slow was practically dry humping me on the dance floor while fucking my mouth.

"Let's roll." His words vibrated around my mouth, and I squeezed his ass in agreement.

Tiberius gave his standard *peace out* sign up in the air as we walked toward the door. I glanced back to see Stacy at the bar, caged in by Jamel, who was whispering in her ear. She was smiling and running her nose along his cheek, so I turned back around and went home to make not-so-slow but meaningful love to Tiberius.

epilogue

One Year Later

Tiberius and I stood at the edge of Battery Park on a breezy day in July, gazing at the Statue of Liberty across the water. The World Trade Center Memorial was behind us, street vendors of every ethnicity lined the walkway to the left and the right, and shrieking kids on summer break ran everywhere. It was an ordinary day as I leaned against the railing with a disposable cup of coffee in one hand, watching the light waves crest in the water as boats made their way out to Lady Liberty. Ty was caging me in with his arms on either side of me, his pelvis pressed into my backside.

The weather was similar to the day I'd graduated in May alongside Ginny. Tiberius and a few of the guys had been there cheering us on; I'd heard them hooting and hollering as I made my way across the stage. They were my new family, and were way better than the one I'd been born into.

I hadn't heard from my parents in over a year, not since I confronted them about Coach Smith. As a precaution, I moved my trust one more time to a broker back east and changed my cell number yet again, hopefully for the last time.

I hired a lawyer to send my parents a sternly worded letter warning them against any further attempts at harassment, collusion, or attempts to impersonate a person of importance, making it clear that they would be prosecuted to the fullest extent of the law if they did. Apparently there was a clause in the trust that protected me in the event my parents attempted to harass me or challenge the structure of the trust in any way, making them subject to legal penalties. My grandparents had obviously wanted to make sure there was no way my parents could attempt an end run at changing the trust. And since my dad was overly conscious of his public image, he fell into line right away.

The wind picked up my hair, blowing it into my face as I whispered, "Love it here," over my shoulder to Tiberius, who was towering over me. If I'd thought Ohio was the best, New York was even better. *Especially now.*

"See that?" he leaned forward and murmured into my hear, but it came out "See dat?" Now that he was closer to home, his accent became more pronounced, which I found adorable. He pointed toward a spot to the left, and I nodded.

"My momma brought me there when I was a little boy. She stood right there with her arm wrapped around me and talked about the statue and how it symbolized hope, freedom, and all that was right in this country. She told me one day I'd discover the truth about what makes a man, that it's not who his father is or was, but who his heart helped him to grow up to be. At the time, I thought it was bullshit. I was an angry little kid who wanted a dad."

Pulling me closer, he said, "But she was right. Same for you, T. Your parents may have tried to mold you, change you, fuck you over, but your heart won."

I stilled as his words brushed past my ear, wishing they were tangible so I could reach out and grab them. I needed to hold on to them and keep them close to my heart—forever.

When his hand came down and squeezed my hip, a tear slipped from my eye and rolled down my cheek. I couldn't believe we were here together, especially after all we'd been through.

After my graduation, our celebration had been bittersweet. Once again, we'd been unsure if forever was in the cards for us. Tiberius had made a reservation at a swanky mahogany-paneled steak place in Cleveland, but what was meant to be a celebration felt like a good-bye party. He'd entered the NBA draft earlier in the spring, and we'd been waiting to hear if he was chosen. That night in Cleveland, everything was still up in the air.

From opposite sides of the country, we'd traveled a long way to learn the truth about unconditional love together in Ohio. In May, however, we had no clue where Ty's future might take him, if anywhere at all. He gave up his eligibility to play college ball when he threw his name into the ring for the NBA, so if he wasn't drafted, he'd need to return to school to finish his degree. And if he was selected, we had no idea who'd pick him and where he might end up. Of course, there'd been rumors and speculation, but no guarantees.

With summer classes and advance credits from prep school, he'd been only six credits shy of graduating. Since he knew his mom would have wanted him to finish, not just to have the piece of paper but a plan for afterward, he promised me he'd take the last credits via correspondence and get his college degree if drafted. Thank goodness Hafton made accommodations like that for alumni who became professional athletes.

Bringing me back to the glorious present, he whispered, "Come on," in my ear, then took my hand and walked us back up the grassy hill toward the subway. We could afford a cab, but I liked riding underground like a regular person. I wanted us to be extra-ordinary for as long as we could.

I'd taken a job with the United Nations office in New York as a translator. It was an entry-level position with decent pay and government benefits—and as far away from La La Land as possible. Everyone was smart, interesting, and most of all, interested in the real me. When my employment was locked down, I'd found a studio apartment in Park Slope in Brooklyn, and I'd spent the month of June adjusting to the change, running and breathing free all over Manhattan. Officially, I'd hung my track shoes up following my last meet, and threw my pacer watch down the back of the hill behind the Ag building. I was no longer running against time.

It had also been a long time since I played the *Perfect Timing* game, as I affectionately came to call my old *P-T* coping strategies. Life was about timing, and I believed meeting Tiberius was meant to be.

He laughed his head off every time I suggested this. "Don't give me your psycho-babble bullshit," he'd say, dismissing the important role he played in my coming to terms with the truth.

"Want to stay and eat over here or go back across the bridge?" Tiberius said, interrupting my thoughts as we made our way down to the subway station.

"I don't know. Maybe we could grab something at that new place across from the stadium?" Then I thought about that and quickly followed up with, "Oh, never mind, I'll have to share you with everyone there." I reached up to squeeze Ty's shoulder playfully, and he rolled his eyes and shook his head.

"For real." I bit back a smile. "Pretty soon you're going to be hounded everywhere, and I don't think I'm going to like it," I said half seriously, and his deep, baritone laugh echoed down the stairs to the subway tunnel. "And the ball babies," I added, poking him in the side, "and cheerleaders." I poked him again. "They're all going to want to have their way with you."

He stopped on the bottom step and lifted his T-shirt. "Never, Rex."

I shook my head, gesturing at him to put his shirt down, but smiled to myself the whole time. I couldn't believe what he'd done—he'd had the words T. REX tattooed across his waist. I didn't know what he'd been thinking, but I liked it. Especially licking my way past it.

"Put that down," I said, swatting at his billowing shirt.

Grinning, Tiberius dropped his shirt. "Come on, we'll get takeout." Grabbing my hand, he guided me toward the train back to our place in Brooklyn.

Yep, I had a roommate. Tiberius had been drafted early in the first round by the second team to find a home in New York—the Brooklyn Nets.

The draft was a crazy and exciting time for us. I'd watched on TV as they called his name and he took the stage. His face lit up for the cameras as he smiled wide, his dimples making an appearance before he schooled his excitement. The official photo from that day showed a hardass Tiberius in his black-and-white jersey and ball cap. Right before he walked offstage, he aimed a big fist bump at the camera while mouthing "Rex!"

He moved in with me right away and had been working out with the team for about a month. He loved taking me back to Jersey to eat at a few of his favorite places, and he was already set to volunteer at the local Boys and Girls Club, teaching basketball skills and running free clinics for the community.

We stood on the train, Tiberius leaning up against one of the safety poles with me tucked into his side. "I forgot, we got to make one stop on our way back," he mumbled into the top of my head, then kissed my hairline.

"Where? The stadium? I can just go home and you can meet me there."

"Nah, we have to make a pit stop over in Brooklyn Heights."

"Why?" I tilted my head to look up at him.

"I got to meet someone over there real quick. No big deal, got to pick some paperwork up." He pulled my head back against his chest.

I took a deep breath, inhaling his woodsy scent along with a small trace of sweat left over from his morning workout. He might be a good guy, but he was all man, especially in the bedroom—when it meant more than a quick romp.

"But then we can go home and eat?" I asked.

"Yeah."

After we exited the subway and were walking up toward the street, Tiberius pulled out his phone to text someone.

"Are you going to give me any clue as to what's going on?" I asked to pester him, hip checking him the whole time we walked. "What paperwork? Are you pranking me?"

"Nope," he replied with a smirk. "Come on."

He grabbed my hand and dragged me up a street to a tall, well-weathered brownstone. It was a duplex, and there was a FOR SALE sign in front of the building.

"What? Really? You're looking at houses?" I squeaked. "I thought you were happy living with me," I said, unable to control the frown that took over my face.

Tiberius gave me a patient, long-suffering glance. "Rex, it's a one-bedroom apartment. You're all over me and I'm all over you. Which, don't get me wrong, I like. But when I buy a TV that's actually a TV and not the size of a microwave, it's gonna take up the whole joint, and you're gonna be pissed. Plus, I want to put an Xbox there, and it's gonna be loud as shit. You'll have nowhere to go, and we'll fight like a bunch of sorority girls."

I turned to look at him and willed myself not to cry. I'd just thought to myself a few minutes ago how happy I was, and now this. It wasn't our first disagreement, but it was the first one to cut through my heart like a knife through butter.

"So, you're moving out," I said, doing my best not to full-on pout. "I thought you liked ordinary. What's wrong with my TV?"

"No, T. I'm not moving out. *We're* moving out."

Just then, the door on the left side of the brownstone opened and Jamel strutted out in his standard low-riding basketball shorts and bright red-and-purple slides.

"Yo!" Tiberius shouted.

"Welcome home, Rexie," Jamel hollered.

"Wait! We're living with Mel?" I squinted at Tiberius, shooting him a death glare. This was actually getting worse, not better. He knew I loved Jamel, but living with him was a whole different story.

Jamel had been picked up by the same team as Tiberius in the second round of the NBA draft. We'd held our breath until the rumors came true . . . Jamel and Tiberius were an unstoppable combo, and now they had their chance in the big league.

But that doesn't mean we have to live together!

"We bought the whole building. We got half and Jamel has the other. Mel and I are partners, fifty/fifty. It was a good investment and

I'm not about to throw away my signing bonus on rent. Plus I need a quiet place to study and finish my courses." He winked, knowing he had me when he mentioned studying. He'd promised he would finish his degree, and he was well on his way. No matter what happened with his pro career, Tiberius would have a fall-back plan and a degree in business.

I shut my eyes and braced myself for the revolving door of women I'd witness over the next few years. *None of them Stacy.* She was living in Philadelphia, working as an assistant coach for one of the universities there. We'd kept in touch since she graduated with a degree in sports management a year or so ago. Chey was in law school in New Jersey, and I thought that I'd see them regularly with my moving to New York. Now that I was practically shacked up with Jamel, I doubted I'd see them much. *At least, at my place.*

Deep down, I knew Jamel to be a solid guy. He was like an M&M, soft and smooth on the inside, a hard candy shell on the outside. But he was a green one, always horny; the guy couldn't keep it in his pants. Suffice it to say, his girl back home broke up with him when she heard he'd knocked someone up. He tried to make a go of it with Stacy, but he couldn't keep his dick out of the cookie—ball baby—jar.

"Say something," Tiberius said in my ear.

It occurred to me that I'd been standing there dumbfounded, just staring at the daunting piece of New York real estate. I gave myself a mental shake, then tried to string some words together.

"It's beautiful, huge . . . I don't know what to say. I can't believe you bought this! Your mom would've been happy that you're not throwing your money away, but this is too much for me. I mean, really—"

"Wanna see the inside?" he asked, cutting me off.

My mind raced, trying to focus on a bigger issue than having

Jamel as a roommate. "But what about the money for this? I can take some out from the trust and go in on half of it—"

Tiberius placed the tip of one long finger over my lips. "Rex, I got more money than I know what to do with, and the trust . . . I don't need it. It's yours. We can give it to our kids."

"What?"

"Our kids." It came out so matter-of-factly, rolling off his tongue easily, as if he'd never doubted we would have kids.

"This is all too much. And kids? We never really discussed that," I said, punching Tiberius in the arm. I glanced at Jamel, but he just shook his head and went back inside his half of the house, apparently not wanting to deal with our bickering.

Tiberius flung his arm around me and held me close. "Because you'd run away from me a thousand miles an hour if I mentioned it. Like now, you're going over ways to speed away in your head. I know it." Smiling down at me, he said in a low voice, "I don't mean now for kids. Later. You know I like to take things slow, and I'm not ready to share you, T."

When I just stood there, stunned, he chuckled and said, "Come on, let's go look inside, and then you can start banging on your phone and figure out when we can move in."

I scanned the street, looking for an alley, a quick escape, but Tiberius tightened his grip on me and led me toward the door.

As we stepped through the entry, I immediately fell in love. Exposed brick lined the hallway. To the left was an empty sitting room with a long wall opposite a gas-burning fireplace surrounded by an intricately carved mantel.

"That's where my TV's gonna go," Tiberius said, confirming my suspicions with a chin lift at the plain wall.

To the right was a dining room; in the back was a small alcove entry that led to a gourmet kitchen and a glassed-in sunroom in the back.

"That's your room to get away from me," Tiberius teased.

"And where I don't have to watch the girls coming and going from next door," I shot back.

He shook his head. "I think you'll be surprised. Jamel is making all kinds of changes. He's even promised to help me study on the road."

I raised my eyebrows, but didn't have time to say anything else because Tiberius pressed me up against the glass partition between the kitchen and the sunroom. His tongue teased my lips, swiping my mouth, sending a roiling wave of heat between my thighs.

When the glass was sufficiently fogged up, he winked and said, "Want to see the master bedroom?"

I squinted up at him. "There's no bed, though."

"That's okay . . . we don't need one. Hasn't stopped us before, Rex. Remember the pavilion?" He winked and grabbed my hand, dragging me toward the staircase lined with a spindled banister painted an antique white.

Upstairs, I was surprised to find a blanket spread out on the master bedroom floor along with pillows and a bottle of champagne, and a fire roaring in the corner fireplace. Twinkling lights were strung across the ceiling, reminiscent of the pavilion, and soft R&B played in the background.

Raising my eyebrows, I said, "How?"

"Jamel and a little help from a secret helper. You like?"

"It's perfect. Stunning. But how did you know you'd get me back here? Seems like you knew we were gonna do this all along."

"Rex, I know all your little escape and avoidance tactics. You were gonna suggest takeout at home no matter what."

He leaned down and kissed me, melding his lips with mine, and my body pressed against his. With an audible smack, he released my lips, and I protested with a long whimper until I saw him dropping lower, yet he didn't stop at my pulsing core like I expected. Instead, his knee hit the floor and he came up on one bended knee, his face level with my abdomen as he shoved his hand into his pocket.

My whole body began to tremble at the thought of what he was about to do. First a house, and now he was going to do . . . *this*?

"Get up, Tiberius!" I demanded as heat climbed up my cheeks and my limbs trembled from nerves.

He shook his head. "Nope, I'm going to do what I came down here to do."

"You've done enough," I insisted as I tried to pull him up. "You're enough. You, the guys, and the way you all took me in when I had no one else. This house, and being here in New York, I don't need anything more. Life is extra-ordinary enough. Don't you think?"

He took my hand, twining his fingers with mine, and he squeezed tight. "Babe, I need to do this. So let me."

Although I felt like my stomach had fallen through the floor, I gave his hand a light squeeze and promptly shut my mouth.

Tiberius gazed up at me, the emotions swimming in his eyes making them appear bluer than usual. "Tingly, will you marry me? Tie your T with mine and leave our pasts in the past, and make an extra, extra-ordinary future together?"

Despite growing up in Los Angeles, the ultimate La La Land, I'd never believed in fairy tales. But here I was, experiencing my very own happily-ever-after, and it completely overwhelmed me.

"Ouch!" he yelped.

"Sorry," I squeaked out. "I didn't mean to squeeze your hand that hard. I'm just so happy! I don't know, I never imagined this, and here you are asking me to marry you!" I slid down to the floor in front of Tiberius and cupped his cheek with my hand, then whispered, "Yes."

His dimples winked at me as he slid the small ring on my finger, an antique setting with sapphires flanking a center diamond, before laying me down on the blanket. The fire crackled, its flames casting shadows all around us while the lights sparkled above.

Tiberius didn't lie; we didn't need a bed.

All we needed was each other, and the truth.

Read more of Rachel Blaufeld in *Redemption Lane*, Book 1 in the
Crossroad Series.

REDEMPTION LANE

CHAPTER ONE

bess
Back then . . .

"Ugh, shit. God damn," I mumbled to myself as I stood up,
holding my hand to my forehead while I stumbled toward the
kitchen.

I'd woken up curled in a ball on the floor, my cheek resting in a
tiny puddle of drool on the rug immediately inside my front door.
Nipples peeking through my tiny white crop top, skinny jeans stuck
to my body, and knee-high black leather boots completed my look.

I know, not a very glamorous situation for a twenty-one-year-old
coed. But pretty much my daily ritual.

Standing, I held my palm to my forehead, running it over my

cheek as I tugged cobwebs of hair out of my mouth. Memories of the night before flooded my brain as my feet tried to remain steady on the floor.

"Ouch," I said to myself.

If I concentrated hard, I could remember being high last night, dancing on the makeshift bar until a guy lifted me off and took me somewhere else for another hit of something even better. Things were hazy after that.

Finally reaching my destination, I gently leaned my clammy forehead against the cool vibrations of the fridge/freezer combo, willing its chilled touch to drag the pain and awful thoughts away.

It didn't.

Oh well, I'd come to prefer my current state of pain to the one I'd lived in as a little girl, and later as a misguided teenager left alone to her own devices. Yes, I would take dry mouth, a wicked hangover, and incessant jonesing for my next hit over watching my mom walk out or being left with an emotionally absent father.

Any day, hands down.

Speaking of hands, my fingers drifted back to the rat's nest that was currently in my hair, my thick long waves twisted in a million different clumps only a bottle of conditioner and a tearful comb-out would solve. That was what I got for sleeping on the floor, resting my head on a burlap mat instead of a fluffy down-filled pillow in my bed.

After taking a small step backward, I opened the fridge door and grabbed the bottle of orange juice, then poured some into the dirty mug sitting next to where my bony hip was resting against the counter. I sipped it slowly, trying to avoid it sloshing in my stomach, and willed it not to come back up, which was no easy feat.

Take a tiny sip, Bess, then a big breath in through your nose and out.

I repeated this mantra until my eyes no longer watered. The natural sugar eased only the smallest pinch of pain, but just enough to make it so I could move.

When I turned a little too fast, the juice became a brutal rolling storm in my belly, threatening to come back up. Slowing my pace, I made my way to the bathroom for some useless ibuprofen and to pee.

With my butt on the ice-cold toilet seat, I looked at my watch. One o'clock in the afternoon. Okay, so it wasn't exactly morning, but it was Friday, the one day I didn't have any classes. Nothing missed, nothing lost.

I'd wiped and moved on wobbly legs to wash my hands and get the pills when I heard my phone beeping. Geez, that fucker was so loud. Where the hell was it? I leaned down, resting my hands on the vanity and thought hard, then felt it vibrate in my back pocket.

Bingo. Score one for Bess. I found my phone without running upstairs to use the Find My iPhone app on my neighbor's phone, which might have happened more times than I cared to admit.

I cupped some water in my hands and brought them up to my face, although most of it dribbled down my chin before I swallowed the tiny iridescent blue over-the-counter capsules that would bring little to no relief.

But who really wanted that?

Actual relief meant covering up the real pain that burned in the pit of my stomach, the empty ache I desperately tried to fill with boys or pills or booze. Or all of the above.

Turning and resting my butt on the sink to check out my text message, I rolled my eyes.

CAMPER: Yoga with hot DJ & blacklight. 5:30 p.m.

With stiff fingers, I typed out a response that turned into a conversation.

ME: Seriously? Happy hour instead?

CAMPER: Nope. Yoga, then margs at Texi Mexi in our sweaty yoga gear.

ME: Say pretty please.

CAMPER: Pretty please! Be ready at 5.

I didn't respond; I knew there was no talking Camper out of it. Besides, she lived one floor up, and she and her long legs and big curly head would show up at five o'clock whether I said yes or no.

Whipping around sixty-five miles an hour too fast for my current state, I faced the medicine cabinet again and pulled out the tiny first aid kit covered in pink and purple kitty stickers, opening the stupidly concealed container with caution. That box, proof of my stunted childhood, held everything that was precious and sacred to me. Carefully, I took stock of its contents: two extra-lush joints, five tabs of Molly, and a few oxy.

Shit, I was low on pharmaceuticals. I made a mental note to call my "guy" before plucking a pretty little Molly or two out of the box. I needed to dim the pain slowly seeping from my heart, and while I was at it, enhance the upcoming yoga experience a touch.

I wasn't sure how Camper did it; that girl raged as hard as I did. Didn't she?

We'd been friends since freshman year, immediately bonding when we'd found ourselves in a nearby tattoo parlor during orientation week. We were both taking the first bold move of our college lives, establishing our independence with a permanent reminder on our fresh and creamy young skin.

Despite her bubbly nature and peppy white smile that often clashed with my somber demeanor, we'd been inseparable ever since. Living the last two years in the same apartment building, taking identical courses, covering for each other, and most importantly, avoiding Friday classes so we could live it up Thursday through Sunday.

Setting my magic pills on the dresser, I stripped out of my smelly clothes from the night before. As they fluttered to the floor, I watched their descent, remembering moments of my own extremely real downward spiral.

Then I crawled naked between my cool sheets, shutting my eyes for a moment or three hours.

acknowledgments

Many projects were pushed aside to make room for this book, and without certain people, this wouldn't have happened.

A huge thank-you to my family for eating more Chinese takeout than humanly possible during this last adventure, and supporting me in all my crazy ideas. For my husband, who pretends to listen to my endless rambling—you deserve something incredible. I don't know what, but when I figure it out, I'll let you know. I love you all very much.

An extra special thank-you goes to my oldest son, who guided me in accurately writing the details of college hoops (without peeking at any other parts of the book). Thanks for having my back, J.

Thanks go out to:

Pam, my editor, for your guidance, encouragement, and iron fist when it comes to ellipses and sentences that never end. Sometimes all it takes is one encouraging comment from you to brighten my week. Leaning on you grammatically, often daily, makes this all possible.

Sarah Hansen, who also regularly talks me through my own personal angst and drama, for creating the most gorgeous cover ever. Thank you, as always.

My betas—Robin, Stacey, Virginia, and Jennifer—had this project tossed in their laps and worked fast to turn around incredible feedback and translate *shit* into French (literally). I'm pretty sure I talk to all of you more than my mom. Please don't tell her . . . and never repeat our conversations! I'll be sharing a cocktail with all of you soon, and I can't wait!

Debra Doxer, who's more than a special pen pal, you're my colleague and confidante. You gave up a weekend to find the holes in this story and set me straight. I love you dearly.

Erin Noelle, I'm not sure how or when we started talking, but thank God we did. Thank you for taking time in the middle of your own book release to encourage me. I've come to rely on our co-bitching sessions.

Nicole Snyder, who recently came into my life and helps make everything run smoothly and seamlessly. I adore you, as my daily early-morning e-mails profess. Thank you for your passion and dedication to "your authors."

Neda Amini, for taking me under your wing and helping me put together the most amazing blog tour. And for telling me I don't look old enough to have a teenage son. You know how to "woo" a girl.

Nothing in my life is complete without the sweet smile of Becca Manuel and her fan-made trailers. There's nothing like seeing your characters come alive in front of you . . . even if it's only on YouTube.

Special thanks to Emily Tippets and Stacey Tippets for making my books work and look great.

And to those who continue to believe in me . . . Terilyn Smitsky, Virginia Tesi Carey, Maryse Black, Fran and Greta of *Twin Sisters*, Michelle Kannan, Sarah Wendell, Milasy at *Rockstars of Romance*, Jennifer Wolfel, Desiree at *Love Affair with Books*, and all the women of *The Lovely Ladies and Naughty Books*. Your encouragement and advice is priceless and the pot of gold at the end of my rainbow.

For all the bloggers who work day and night to help spread the word, I can never thank you enough. I know what it means to be in your shoes . . . and you do it for the love of reading!

To my author friends who hold my hand daily—Ilsa Madden-Mills, Madeline Sheehan, Erin Noelle, Joanne Schwehm (*partner in crime*), Ashley Suzanne, Nicole Jacquelyn, Heidi McLaughlin, Jen Frederick, Susan Ward (*mom #2*), Debra Doxer, Fabiola Francisco, Christy Pastore, and Lisa N. Paul. When I yell "help," you come running, thank God!

I also have a few amazing people who cheer the loudest for me, and on a bad day that means everything. Stefani, Susan (who wants me to make a movie!), Marla, Lisa, my Charlie Hunnam girls on Twitter (Cheryl, Angela, Michelle, Office Lady, Nicole, Kelly, and Kimberly), the Electric Tunnellettes (Debra, Gretchen), and of course, last but not least . . . my mom!

Many thanks go out to YOU, the readers! I seriously adore each and every one of you. You make me want to write more, to dig deeper and be more creative. Thank you from the bottom of my heart.

If you enjoyed this book (or maybe even loved it to pieces), please leave a review where you purchased it or on Goodreads. Then send me an e-mail so I can thank you personally!

about the author

Rachel Blaufeld is a social worker/entrepreneur/blogger turned author. Fearless about sharing her opinion, Rachel captured the ear of stay-at-home and working moms on her blog, *BacknGrooveMom*, chronicling her adventures in parenting tweens and inventing a product, often at the same time. She has also blogged for *The Huffington Post*, *Modern Mom*, and *StartupNation*.

Turning her focus on her sometimes wild-and-crazy creative side, it only took Rachel two decades to do exactly what she always wanted to do—write a fiction novel. Now she spends way too many hours in local coffee shops plotting her ideas. Her tales may all come with a side of angst and naughtiness, but end lusciously.

Rachel lives around the corner from her childhood home in Pennsylvania with her family and two dogs. Her obsessions include running, coffee, icing-filled doughnuts, antiheroes, and mighty fine epilogues.

Please connect with me on:

www.rachelblaufeld.com
Facebook: www.facebook.com/rachelblaufeldtheauthor
Twitter: twitter.com/rachelblaufeld

Made in the USA
Coppell, TX
28 September 2021